Praise for

Small Town SINNERS

"Credible and tender. . . . By stressing the importance of forgiveness and honesty, Walker proves that her heart is in the right place."

—*New York Times Book Review*

"Both tender and provocative. . . . Walker creates an astutely balanced portrait."

—*Publishers Weekly*

"A nonjudgmental, nuanced, fascinating look at the teenage religious right. Walker debuts with an outstanding contemporary novel with a cast of characters who . . . are relatable for readers of all faiths."

—RT Book Reviews

"Melissa Walker writes with bravery and honesty: *Small Town Sinners* doesn't flinch from shining a stark, bright light on questions of faith."

—E. Lockhart, award-winning author of the Ruby Oliver quartet

"This one's for all the soul searchers out there, all the free thinkers hoping to answer life's bigger questions with their own voices. You will care deeply for Walker's characters."

—Matthew Quick, author of *Sorta Like a Rock Star* and *The Silver Linings Playbook*

"[Walker] writes without a shred of judgment and with plenty of heart."

—Dana Reinhardt, author of *The Things a Brother Knows* and *A Brief Chapter in My Impossible Life*

"Walker is sympathetic and respectful of her characters' faith, while putting on display the shocking, extremist scare tactics that make Hell Houses, well, hellish. I could not put this book down!"

—Donna Freitas, author of *This Gorgeous Game* and *The Possibilities of Sainthood*

Books by Melissa Walker

Small Town Sinners

Unbreak My Heart

Small Town SINNERS

MELISSA WALKER

BLOOMSBURY
NEW YORK LONDON NEW DELHI SYDNEY

First published in the United States of America in July 2011
by Bloomsbury Children's Books
Paperback edition published in January 2013
www.bloomsbury.com

The Library of Congress has cataloged the hardcover edition as follows:
Walker, Melissa (Melissa Carol).
Small town sinners / by Melissa Walker. — 1st U.S. ed.
p. cm.
Summary: High school junior Lacey finds herself questioning the evangelical Christian values she has been raised with when a new boy arrives in her small town.
ISBN 978-1-59990-527-3 (hardcover)
[1. Christian life—Fiction. 2. Conduct of life—Fiction. 3. Dating (Social customs)—Fiction. 4. Self-confidence—Fiction.] I. Title.
PZ7.W153625Sm 2011 [Fic]—dc22 2010036460

ISBN 978-1-59990-982-0 (paperback)

Book design by Danielle Delaney
Typeset by Westchester Book Composition
Printed in the U.S.A. by Thomson-Shore, Dexter, Michigan
2 4 6 8 10 9 7 5 3 1

All papers used by Bloomsbury Publishing, Inc., are natural, recyclable products made from wood grown in well-managed forests. The manufacturing processes conform to the environmental regulations of the country of origin.

Manufactured by Thomson-Shore, Dexter, MI (USA); RMA587LS122, December, 2012

For Dave,

who is always *asking questions*

(like, "Shouldn't this book have paranormal beings and action sequences in it?")

Small Town
SINNERS

Chapter One

"Take the wheel," says Starla Joy, sticking the grape lollipop she's been working on into her mouth. She doesn't even wait to see if I've followed her instructions—she just lets go and strips down, pulling off her light cotton sweater to reveal a bright red tank top dotted with white hearts.

I lunge across the front seat to make sure her old truck stays straight. A little dust kicks up as we skim the edge of the road.

"Starla Joy!" I shout. "I don't even have my license yet."

She grins at me as she takes control of the car and says, "Just two more days!"

I sit back, glad she's driving again. At least we're on a straight stretch—last time she pulled this around a curve and I nearly peed my pants. I think she did it on purpose.

Starla Joy takes the lollipop out of her mouth and holds it in one hand next to the wheel. There's a ring of bright lipstick around the stick. She's recently started wearing really strong colors. She has dark brown hair, blue eyes, and fair skin, so a ruby pout makes her look like an old Hollywood actress—from the neck up anyway. I don't think those movie stars wore tank tops and cutoffs.

"Do you think your parents will loosen up a little once you're driving?" she asks.

I stare out at the flat plains ahead of us. "I don't know," I say. "I mean, they're not that strict now."

"Ha!" she says, sticking the grape candy back into her mouth. "I love your parents, Lacey, but they're definitely strict."

I smile. "A little more freedom would be nice," I say. My mom and dad aren't draconian or anything. I mean, I have a summer job and I spend plenty of time with my friends. I've never really wanted to stay out past my curfew. Nothing much happens in my town after nine o'clock anyway.

But sometimes, when I'm in the truck with Starla Joy, driving down a dusty road and looking out at the wide-open spaces around us, I think it would be nice to have this much room to breathe all the time.

"Lacey Anne," says Starla Joy, "let's have a wild summer."

She throws her head back and laughs then, and I just smile and look out the side window, glad that I have a best friend who's as fun as Starla Joy Minter.

When we get to my house, I open the door and I can already smell Mom's brownies baking. Starla Joy and I sidle up to the kitchen counter and Mom hands Starla Joy a beater with chocolate batter still on it.

"Just don't ruin your dinner," she says. "You *will* stay over, won't you, Starla Joy?"

"I'd love to," says Starla Joy. "I'll text Momma."

Mom winks at me and goes back to the sink, where she's

peeling potatoes. Sometimes I think my parents like having my friends over for dinner just as much as I do. Starla Joy's been licking Mom's brownie batter since we were in preschool, and though I've lost my taste for it, she's still got a huge sweet tooth.

When I'm sitting in church and the light hits the stained glass just right, I think I can see God. The sunbeams stream through the clearest parts of the multicolored dove and olive branch scene above the pulpit, and there are dancing rays of heat that seem directly linked to something sacred. Starla Joy says I'm hallucinating, but my dad agrees that it's definitely the Holy Spirit. "God is all around us," he likes to say, opening his hands wide, as if he's welcoming the Lord in for one of his famously strong hugs. But I don't see God everywhere—just in those beams of sunlight, which are especially bright on this Sunday in August.

I look across the pews and see that Starla Joy's in her usual uniform of a T-shirt and jean skirt. Her sister, Tessa, sitting next to her, has on a bright yellow sundress, and her light brown hair spills over her freckled shoulders.

I catch Starla Joy's eye, and she mouths an exaggerated yawn. I shake my head at her disapprovingly. She's kidding, but her attitude sometimes gets her in trouble.

Me? I never get in trouble.

My other BFF, Dean Perkins, says that's because I scare easily. "Lacey," he'll say, "you've lost all your color from fright!" I know he's just joking because my hair is such a pale yellow that it's almost white and my skin is near translucent. Sometimes in bright light I can see blue veins through my forehead, and my mom makes me wear SPF 50 sunscreen every day, even in the winter, so I don't burn. People say I have a sensitive constitution.

Maybe that's because I've always been really close to my parents. For my sweet sixteen last week, we had a family party, complete with red velvet cupcakes and a new white Bible from Mom and Dad. As pretty as my new leather-bound Word of God is, I'd rather have a car. I picture myself in a bright blue convertible, not worrying about sunblock or the speed limit or even what people say as I race past them with the wind in my face. My very own movie moment.

I'll never be alluring in my mom's old Honda—it's not a car that makes heads turn, at least not in a good way. Still, it's something, and I know I should be grateful.

Past where Starla Joy's sitting, I see the Raymond family, all in jeans. Not many people dress up for church anymore, which drives my mom crazy. I glance down at the sleeve of her new pink velour blazer—she got it on sale at TJ Maxx, but it's an Anne Klein original. My mother always finds designer stuff when she shops at outlet stores—it's part of her picture-perfect life. And even though the pink blazer looked stuffy on the rack, Mom makes it classy with her tiny gold angel pinned to the lapel. Her black slacks are well pressed, as always, and I look up to see her flawless rose-colored lipstick mouthing the words to the Lord's Prayer.

Oops! Head down, I fold my hands in my lap and join in with Pastor Frist and the congregation. Church is almost over. Usually I don't mind lingering in the sanctuary, shaking hands and accepting the glowing smiles that come my way. I'm Lacey Anne Byer, daughter of Ted and Theresa Byer, pillars of the community. What does that expression mean anyway? I've heard it my whole life. Does it mean the whole town would collapse if we weren't upright, holding its weight? We are longtime members of the House of Enlightenment, an evangelical church that serves as the center of West River. My dad has been the children's pastor here since forever. Well, since *my* forever, meaning my whole life.

As soon as Pastor Frist finishes his sermon, I stand up and make my way down the aisle and out into the parking lot—I don't even pause to say good-bye to Starla Joy or Dean, though I do give him a wave. He nods from behind his shoulder-length curtain of hair, which looks greasier than usual.

I push open the church door and walk outside. I need to get home and go over the DMV manual one more time before my driver's test tomorrow—I expect to pass the test with flying colors, but I don't want to be overconfident. I start to sweat as I lean against my dad's white Ford Taurus and wait for my parents to bob and weave through the polite Sunday greeters. I'm sure they all want to shake hands with Dad and compliment Mom on her new pink jacket.

I told my parents that a quick exit was important to me today, though, and I think they listened. I smile as I see them come through the double glass doors of the House of Enlightenment.

Ken Wilkins is walking rapidly behind my father—trying to talk about some committee or church dinner or child-care issue, no doubt—and Dad is nodding but not slowing his pace. Ruth Wilkins ambles behind her husband. She has an unfortunate problem with facial hair, and I can see her whiskers in the sunlight from twenty feet away, though I try not to look. When

Dad and Mr. Wilkins reach our car, Dad gestures at me and says, "Well, Ken, I do hope you understand that we have to get Lacey here home to study for her driver's test."

Mr. Wilkins looks over at me. "*Sixteen*," he says, emitting a low whistle.

"Yes, sir," I say back, turning to open the car door so he'll know we *really* have to go.

"You be careful now, Lacey," says Mr. Wilkins. "Cars are dangerous, in more ways than one."

"I will, sir," I say, wondering when people will stop telling me to be careful. Don't they know I've been careful my entire life? I wouldn't even sit down in the bathtub as a toddler till Mom told me it was safe—not too hot, not too cold. That's me, careful Lacey Byer.

"We'll see you later this week, Ken," says Mom, hustling around to the passenger side of the car.

I shoot her a grateful look.

"Bye-bye now," says Dad, opening his door and ducking his head to fit his six-foot-three frame inside the Taurus.

I smile at the Wilkinses and they wave back. Mr. Wilkins looks slightly dissatisfied that he didn't get to resolve whatever issue he had, but I don't let him bother me. Tomorrow I won't be waiting by the car anymore, I won't even be in the passenger seat of Starla Joy's truck—I'll be behind the wheel.

The DMV isn't a good place to have a movie moment. There's a long line of people, and Dad has to stop and shake hands with almost everyone while I stand at the back to hold our spot. I tap my toe impatiently and look around.

I see a new person, someone I don't recognize, near the front of the line. In other towns, I guess that might be normal. But in West River, where you know everyone from the mail carrier to the pharmacist to the pet store owner—*and* their family histories—new people don't walk into your life every day. Especially not new people who look like this.

He's wearing a pink polo shirt, the kind that the football guys would definitely make fun of at lunch—I can hear Geoff Parsons's voice now, calling it "girly" and "gay"—and as he raises his dark sunglasses up onto the top of his close-cropped, golden-blond hair, I see that he has blue eyes, even from across the room. As he hands a form to the DMV lady, he grins and makes a joke that I can't hear, but it gets her laughing. He is utterly sure of himself.

I've so been looking forward to this day—I mean, how many times in a girl's life does she take her driver's test? Well, if you're Starla Joy you take it three times, but I'm planning on just taking it once, God willing. Now, though, I can think of nothing but this guy. Who is he? Where did he come from? How does he put the DMV lady—who is truly one of the most grouchy people in town—at ease?

He looks like he walked out of a movie. He makes me think that maybe I don't need a convertible to turn heads.

"Lacey, your form." Dad touches my arm and I snap to attention. The line moved quickly, and I'm up next. I hand over my license application to the waiting clerk. She stamps it and tells me my road-test evaluator will be right out. Dad and I sit down in the waiting area, with its brown-gray walls and buzzing yellow lights, and I concentrate on *not* looking at the golden boy. He can't just breeze into West River with a Hollywood smile, wearing a pink polo shirt and charming the DMV lady. People are going to talk.

"So?" asks Dean later that afternoon when I get to the clearing in the woods where we've been meeting since third grade. Even though it's eighty-five degrees out, he's wearing a flannel shirt with jeans.

Starla Joy is sitting next to Dean on our fallen log, stringing dandelions together into a bright yellow circle the color of the sundress her sister wore in church yesterday.

I hold up the item they've been waiting to see. "I am an officially licensed driver!"

"Praise the Lord," says Starla Joy, barely looking. "Now I won't be the only one who has to drive Dean's ass everywhere."

Dean thumps her leg hard.

"Ouch!" she shouts, breaking into a laugh and rubbing her shin. "I was just kidding."

"Don't say 'ass,' Starla Joy," I chastise.

"Okay, Mrs. Byer," she says, and I guess I do sound like my mother.

"Let me see the picture," says Dean, holding his hand out for my license.

I give it to him and he studies it for a moment, a long piece of hair falling over his face. His fingernails are painted black today—he started doing that last year, though sometimes he mixes in Wite-Out and makes them gray.

"You look kind of . . . ," Dean starts.

Starla Joy snatches the license from his hand and doesn't hesitate to fill in the blank.

"Intense," she says. "Wow, Lacey, I've never seen this kind of concentration in your eyes."

"Does that mean I'm usually unfocused?" I ask, not quite sure if I'm offended.

"No," says Starla Joy. "You're just usually . . ." She pauses, like she doesn't want to insult me. And I know that if she were talking to anyone else, she'd barrel on ahead and not worry what they thought. That's her way. But with me she's careful. Everyone is.

"You're usually softer," Starla Joy continues. "And you're not even looking at the camera—you're paying attention to something behind it."

"Let me see that," I say, reaching out for my newest and dearest possession.

In the picture, my long blond hair falls limply over each shoulder, despite my efforts this morning to use a little mousse at the roots and blow it dry to create volume. Why do magazine beauty tips never work for me? I wore a bright blue tank top because I thought it would look nice in the photo, but that made no difference since my dad made me put a white cardigan on over it. And Starla Joy's right. My hazel eyes *are* looking over the camera and they're burning. They're focused on the guy I saw at the DMV.

"So when's the first Hell House meeting?" I ask, looking down at my dusty, blue flip-flops and hoping to stop the photo analysis.

"As if you haven't had it circled on your calendar for months!" says Dean. "August 12. You know that."

"Back to this picture," says Starla Joy, not falling for my change-of-subject attempt. "What caught your attention so much that you looked away?"

"I don't even remember," I lie. "But anyway, isn't it like a law that you can't have a good driver's license photo?"

"I plan for mine to be smoking hot," says Dean, tucking the ends of his hair behind his left ear.

I smile at him, glad he can be this way around us still—mock conceited and teasing like he used to be all the time, back before he started wearing flannel in the summer.

Dean pulls a small bag of carrots out of his front pocket and starts munching. Last year he gained like forty pounds and his mom put him on Weight Watchers. He doesn't talk about it much, but at least he's open enough to eat his healthy snacks around us.

Starla Joy ignores Dean's carrots and reaches into her own bag for Doritos.

"Torturer!" shouts Dean.

"They're both orange," she says, grinning at him.

"Starla Joy," I say. "You know that isn't fair."

Dean and Starla Joy have always fought like siblings; I play the middle.

"I'm allowed to have a snack too," says Starla Joy.

I give her a look.

"What?" she asks. "Am I supposed to starve while he's over there chomping away?"

Dean turns his back on us and stares out into the woods. I can't quite tell if he's mad or just pretending to be. I see the sunlight streaming through the trees behind him. This clearing looks the same as it always has. It's a central point between all of our houses and the church; a secluded, shady place where we used to build forts and play hide-and-seek. Now we mainly sit and talk, but it still has this magical energy to it, like God is here, or at least one of His angels.

"Can we divvy?" I ask, using the word we used when we were little and we'd share all of our Halloween candy.

Dean turns around slowly, eyeing Starla Joy.

"Okay," she says. "I'd like a carrot stick."

They both hand me their snack bags and I give each of them the same amount of Doritos and carrot sticks.

"You don't want any?" asks Dean.

"Nah," I say. The truth is that I'm kind of hungry, but there's not much in these bags and I'd rather my friends stop snipping at each other than have, like, four Doritos and two carrot sticks.

Starla Joy smiles. "Portion control," she says to Dean.

"Yeah, I know all about it, smart-ass," he replies.

I raise my eyebrows at him.

"Smarty-pants," he says. "Is that better?"

"Yes," I say. "Much."

Starla Joy chuckles. "You're such a mom, Lacey," she says.

I smile, but I don't like it when she says that. I don't want to be like a mom. They never get the spotlight.

Chapter Two

Dean was right—August 12 is circled on my calendar in red. On this Wednesday, the full two-dozen members of Youth Leaders, our high school group at church, are seated in the sanctuary, voices buzzing about Hell House. Some people will volunteer today for behind-the-scenes jobs, like set design and lighting, but I'm planning to hold out for what I really want—a lead role in the show.

I'm only going to be a junior and I should wait until next year to get a meaty role, but I want one now. I'm ready . . . I think.

Last year I watched Julia Millhouse play a pregnant teenager. When the lights went up in the nursery, where they staged her scene, she said her lines with so much emotion that people in the audience started to cry. I'd see them come through the lobby after the show and hear them talking about her performance. I want that spotlight. I want to be able to affect people that way too.

I've grown up with Hell House all my life, but Dean's cousins in the next county over think it's something weird that religious nuts do. It's not. It's a way to show people the right path. After all the scenes of sin, Satan threatens the audience. My dad always plays the devil—he thinks it's funny to be the children's pastor *and* the Antichrist. And Pastor Frist's Jesus bathes Hell in white light at the very end, leading the audience into Heaven (also known as the church library, all done up in white sheets and cotton clouds), where they get decision cards. Most people fill out the cards and agree to at least explore a Christian life. It's a magical weekend and an incredible outreach, especially for young people who don't have a path to Christ like I've grown up with. Mom always reminds me how lucky I am to have that.

I'm sitting with Starla Joy and her sister, Tessa, who's finger-combing her wavy brown hair as we wait to hear about this year's production. Tessa played an EMT last year in the drunk driving scene, and she got to say, "I'm sorry, Mrs. Kerner, your daughter is dead." Everyone thinks she'll get a big part this year since she's pretty much the senior girl with the most rank here. Even in church—especially in church—there's a social hierarchy.

Dean's late, as usual, and when he finally comes in I have to remind him to pull off his hoodie while he's in the sanctuary. His hair is all over the place and I help him pat it down and tuck it behind his ears so he looks semirespectable. He has a Fiber One bar in the front pocket of his sweatshirt and he's sneaking bites.

"What?" he asks when I look at him sideways. "Like you've never snuck in a snack, Miss Pop-Tarts."

He's right, I did used to eat strawberry frosted Pop-Tarts during church . . . when I was five years old.

My father and Pastor Frist get up to start the meeting, and I look around the pews anxiously. I should be focusing right now, but I can't seem to clear my mind. I'm annoyed by how much I've been thinking about the guy from the DMV, and now he's in my head during the most important church meeting of the year.

"This year, we're using a new script that a bunch of pastors have worked together to create," says Pastor Frist. "And Pastor Joe Tannen wants a report on our outreach so he can learn more about Hell House's influence."

Everyone gasps excitedly, and I'm immediately paying attention. I can't believe Dad kept this information from me, but he does love a surprise. Pastor Tannen has a congregation in Oklahoma, and even though he's like eighty years old, he's always been a huge figure in the evangelical world. It's amazing that he wants to know more about Hell Houses. They're kind of like haunted houses, which is why we do ours over Halloween weekend. Tour guides dressed as demons take the audience through the church, room by room, to view scenes of sin: a drunk driving crash, a suicide, domestic abuse, and an abortion. My dream role—the one Julia played last year—is Abortion Girl.

"All right, all right," says Dad, waving his hands to quell the energetic whispers. "We're primed for this too. And it means there's going to be some intense material this year—even more than in years past."

I look over at Dean, who's resting his chin in his hand. I elbow him and he sits up straight. I don't know why he's not more excited—this script is going to be amazing.

"The first scene—or should I say *sin*—is Gay Marriage,"

says Dad. "I'm sure we all know about people who've chosen this path. Some are even famous celebrities."

A low "boo" rises up from the crowd, mostly led by Geoff Parsons—the kid who hasn't stopped calling Starla Joy "butter-fingers" since she dropped a key fly ball during a church softball game in eighth grade—but Pastor Frist quiets it quickly.

"Now, now. Hate the sin, not the sinner," he says, and his broad smile makes the skin around his eyes crinkle fiercely. "This scene will be a very powerful opening for our best Hell House yet."

That gets a cheer.

"The sacred institution of marriage between a man and a woman is further disgraced by the unholy union of a man and a man," continues Pastor Frist, "and Satan wouldn't have it any other way, would he, guys?"

Sometimes Pastor Frist smiles to punctuate a rhetorical question, and his big white teeth look like they're living entities. Like they could jump right out of his mouth and beam at you up close, in 4-D. It's always freaked me out a little.

Another low "boo" rumbles, and my dad takes the mic. "This scene will be done carefully," he says. "We'll have a married couple playing the role of husband and husband, because there will have to be physical contact here."

There's a ripple through the crowd as we imagine two men kissing. I'm relieved it'll be a husband-and-wife couple performing. It's only right.

"I think Mrs. Wilkins could play a guy," whispers Dean, and Starla Joy cracks up. I hit Dean on the leg—Mrs. Wilkins can't help her whiskers. Tessa rolls her eyes at us like she's so mature and goes back to inspecting her split ends.

The Hell House prep meeting always goes like this—I've sat in on a few just to be with my dad. He and Pastor Frist go back and forth, introducing each scene and its underlying message, why Jesus calls on us to cover certain topics this year. But today, in this meeting, I'm on the edge of my seat. I actually get to audition this year—I get to be considered for a lead role, and whoever plays Abortion Girl becomes a part of town history.

"Now, we haven't worked out all the scenes yet," says Pastor Frist. "We'll have another meeting soon. But we did want to tell you about Pastor Tannen's involvement, what the opening scene would be like, and we also wanted to show you an incredible new addition to the prop closet."

Pastor Frist gestures to Dad, who reaches under the pulpit and pulls out a gun. And I mean a *gun.* It looks like something a drug dealer would have—black and solid, scary looking.

"That isn't real, right?" whispers Starla Joy.

I blink. I'm not sure.

Dad holds it flat in his hand, moving his palm up and down to demonstrate that it's heavy, not like the plastic guns we normally use as props. "This baby is from Utah," he says. "It has the weight of a real gun and it sounds completely authentic when fired."

Then he turns to the back of the church, points right at the dove shape in the giant window, and pulls the trigger. A huge *bang!* echoes through the sanctuary. Every single person jumps, Tessa screams, and Maryanne Duane, who carried around a note last year that got her out of gym class every day at school, starts crying.

"You can't say it's not dramatic," whispers Dean. I see him smiling. Well, if it takes a real-looking gun to get him into Hell House this year, then I'm glad we have one. I've never shot a real gun, but I know most of the guys in town have been to the rifle range. Even Starla Joy's mother has a handgun that she carries around with her since their dad left. People say she sleeps with it under her pillow, but I've never asked Starla Joy about that.

Dad turns around, grinning. "I'm sorry, Maryanne," he says. "These are just blanks—I promise. But I think your tears prove that this little lady is effective." He eyes the gun admiringly and places it back under the pulpit.

Suddenly, I hear a voice above the mutters. It's coming from the back of the sanctuary.

"Pastor Byer," says the low voice, and though it's soft, it echoes with a quiet confidence. I turn to see the golden boy from the DMV slowly walking down the center aisle. He's wearing khaki shorts and a sunny yellow polo shirt, and he hasn't taken off his sunglasses, even though he's inside. I wonder if he always wears them. He's closer to the front now, almost to my row, and he lowers his voice to continue.

"Excuse me, but isn't that a little . . . ," he pauses, glancing over at our row. His eyes move in my direction, but I can't tell if he's looking at me—the lenses are too dark. "Extreme?"

A hush has fallen over absolutely everyone. You could hear the Holy Ghost breathe it's so quiet.

Then my dad's familiar voice answers, and it's tinged with the fervor he gets when he feels really passionate about something.

"Son," says my dad, staring back at the preppy newcomer with determined eyes. "You gotta shake 'em to wake 'em."

The new guy's lips turn up in a half smile, and he nods his head, finally lifting up his sunglasses. He joins our row, sitting down next to Dean. "Yes, sir," he says.

Chapter Three

When I get home that night, all I want to do is talk to Starla Joy and Dean about what happened today at church. My parents whisked me away after the Hell House meeting, so aside from a few "OMW!" texts (for "Oh my word!"), the discussion about the new guy hasn't started yet. I didn't even get to say hello to him after the meeting, which wasn't very neighborly.

I'm sure Dean and Starla Joy are messaging up a storm, but our only computer is in the living room, and Dad's using it while Mom makes dinner.

I sit down on a stool in the kitchen and take a pretzel stick from the jar on the counter. Mom looks up.

"I won't ruin my dinner," I say. "I'm just really hungry."

"Good," says Mom, smiling at me, "because I made a lot."

She pauses for a moment like she's thinking about something. "Honey, do you think Dean will get involved with the craft auction again this year?" she asks.

"Probably," I say, shrugging and crunching on my pretzel.

"It's going to be great," she says. "Leslie Davis and I just started planning it. Laura Bergen can bead some more of her gorgeous earrings and I'll see if Dean can build some of his miniature houses. People just love those for Christmas decorations."

I nod. Mom can get very excited about charity auctions.

"I'll ask him about it at dinner tomorrow," she says, smiling at the thought.

Dean's coming over to help my dad with a project he's working on in the garage. Dad likes tiny little scale models of towns, and I just don't see what's cool about them. Dean does, though. He and my dad have been building this one together for months.

Mom turns back to the stove, and I watch her stir the sauce for spaghetti. She starts humming—the sign of a good mood—and I see my opening.

"Mom," I say, "if you're not going out tonight, maybe I can take the car and pick up Starla Joy and Dean so we can get ice cream or something after dinner." It's not a lie—we will get ice cream. And we'll talk about the new guy! I'm almost giddy with anticipation, but I'm trying to act normal. It doesn't help.

"I don't think so, honey," says Mom, her hands covered in blue flowered mitts as she pours the water from the pot of spaghetti over the strainer in the sink.

"Maybe tomorrow night, kiddo," says Dad, when I turn to the living room with plaintive eyes to get his take on this obviously unfair negging of my completely reasonable request. "We need to go over some rules for the car now that you'll be taking it out on your own."

I frown but I don't say anything. I've never been able to push the issue when it comes to my parents. I'm their only child, and I guess they just want to watch out for me. But I feel a tightness in my chest, like there's something constricting it, and I have to take a deep breath to get the air flowing again.

"Dinner's ready!" says my mother brightly, ignoring my sigh and taking off her purple polka-dotted apron. She starts shredding some fresh Parmesan as a final touch.

When Mom sits down, we all bow our heads automatically. Every night Dad says the same prayer, but he tweaks it a little so that I'm grateful for something specific in my day. He's been doing that since as far back as I can remember. Tonight Dad says, "Lord, thank you for bringing this food to our table so we may enjoy time as a family and the sustenance of you, our God. Thank you for this year of Lacey's official Hell House debut, which she will use to turn hearts your way. In Jesus's name we pray. Amen."

"Amen," we echo.

I decide to go for a walk after dinner. My parents may still control the car, but it feels good to just say, "Going for a walk," and then head out the door without waiting for permission. Baby steps.

I take my iPod and put it on shuffle so it can set my mood for me. It cycles to an old Abandon song. I turn left and walk down the street, taking in all the different mailboxes—the Carters have a painting of cardinals on theirs, the Gregorys went for solid black with a simple red flag, and the Shipmans' is shaped like a boat. Ha-ha.

Suddenly I hear a loud car coming down the road behind me. Our street is a known cut-through in town, so people drive too fast sometimes. One of Mom's pet projects is trying to get speed bumps put in, but she hasn't been successful. Maybe because the mayor uses this route to get home from city hall.

I step onto the Shipmans' lawn and look over my shoulder at the approaching car. It's loud. Really loud. Like someone took off the muffler. It's also red. I half expect it to be some vintage hot rod like Starla Joy's father used to work on in their driveway when he was still around, but when it speeds past me I see that it's an ancient eighties BMW with rust on the trunk. And I see a flash of the person in the driver's seat. It's him.

My heart speeds up. *Please see me and stop, please see me and stop.* But the rusty red BMW just speeds past, and I'm left to continue my normal, everyday neighborhood walk. See, this is the difference between real life and the movies—in a movie, he would have stopped. Or at least waved or something. He probably didn't even see me. I'm transparent.

I've never had a boyfriend. Last year my dad gave me a True Love Waits ring as a symbol of how I've promised to remain a virgin until I get married. It's silver and shiny, with a cross in the middle and two hearts on the sides, but I feel like it's unnecessary. I don't need a ring to remind me to stay pure—I haven't even kissed a guy, let alone gotten close to anything beyond that. Maybe because I've known everyone who lives here my whole life, and they've known me—and I've always been a good girl. I don't think the boys in this town see me that way at all.

Starla Joy has kissed people. Two, in fact, but both of us know we won't go any further until we're married. I don't want some throwaway boyfriend; I'm waiting for something that lasts, like in that movie *The Notebook*, which Starla Joy and I have watched together about thirty times. Even though Dean makes fun of me for believing in fairy tales, I want a love like that one day, one that spans decades and withstands hardships and even disease. It's just hard to see the guys you've been with since kindergarten as anything more than paste eaters sometimes. The thought of something different is . . . exciting. He doesn't know who I am or what I'm like or how I'm supposed to be. I could be brand new. If he'd just talk to me.

I'm heading back to my house after half an hour of meandering around the road I've walked all my life when the loud sound of a missing muffler rises over the strains of Taylor Swift's best love song. And I turn to face the car.

He aims right for me as he slows down, leaning the hood a little to the left so I'll be dead center in his headlights. I'm too astonished to be scared. *Something is happening.*

The car stops a foot in front of the curb and his blond-with-sunglasses-on-top head pops out of the driver's side window. "I'm Ty," he says, smiling a smile that lights up the street. "Wanna go for a drive?"

Chapter Four

I stare back at him blankly. I have never even met this guy. Well, I guess I saw him at the DMV, and then he sat near me in church . . . and he did just tell me his name and technically that could be considered "meeting," but really? I would *never* get in that loud red BMW.

But why not? Maybe that's why nothing happens to me—good or bad. I don't take risks.

I'm actually considering getting in the car, but he breaks first.

"Okay, fine, you won't get in, I'll get out," he says, turning off his engine.

He steps out of the car and into the night. When he slams his door shut, I jump, wondering if anyone heard.

"Are you really leaving the car in the street like that?" I ask, staring at the way it's diagonally angled at the Shipmans' lawn.

"Who's gonna care?" he asks, smiling confidently.

Everyone.

He gestures to the curb. "Sit with me?" he asks.

My heart is pounding and I feel the need to stabilize my balance a little, so I don't say no. I actually sit down next to him.

"Your dad's a pastor at the House of Enlightenment," he says, nodding like he already knows this for sure.

"Yeah," I say. "I'm Lacey Byer."

He nods. Then it's quiet again, and he doesn't ask another question, just stares at the dark pavement by our feet. My head is down too, but I can see him out of the corner of my eye, and I have the urge to get a better look at his face, which is just inches away. I slowly raise my glance, but as I do, his head pops up.

"Where are you from?" I hear myself ask. The words just tumble out of my mouth; I want to distract him from the fact that I was looking at him just now.

He stares at me with these blue eyes, squinting a little, like he's trying to figure something out without speaking. I start to blush because he hasn't answered my question, and I realize I'm looking at him like he's an alien or something, like I expect him to say he's from Mars or the Planet of the Apes.

"I lived just on the other side of the state," he says. "A few hours east of here in a small town. Have you been out that way?"

He's staring at me again, and as I shake my head no—I've never been anywhere—I start to think about what I look like, how he's seeing me. My hair is pulled back in a loose ponytail, and a few strands are falling in my eyes, which I can tell are wide with surprise at this moment, here with new-in-town Ty. I'm wearing my favorite blue tank top, and I have on a jean skirt that goes down to my knees. I wish it were shorter, like the ones Starla Joy wears. My bony arms are by my sides and my legs are pulled into my chest protectively. I must look like a scared little bird.

But I don't want to be fragile right now. Ty probably spends his summers swimming at country clubs where girls watch the sun glint off his golden hair as beads of water drip down his tan skin. I feel myself flush, but luckily it's ninety degrees out so that's not out of the ordinary. I straighten my spine, trying to seem older, more confident. More like a girl that Ty would want to sit out on the curb with after dinner.

He reaches his hand toward my face, and I jump up, standing so fast I nearly topple over. *Nice work, you silly, frightened starling.* There goes my cool-and-confident vibe. I put my hands in the back pockets of my jean skirt.

Ty laughs softly. "Your hair was . . . ," he starts.

"I know," I say quickly. "It's always in my face." And I wish I'd stayed still so he could have brushed it back. That would have been nice. But now I'm standing here awkwardly and there's this silence again.

"I'm sorry if I startled you with the car," says Ty. "I just wanted to, um, meet you, I guess."

I hear a dog barking in the distance—probably Mrs. Pearson's beagle—and I have the urge to bolt.

"I have to go," I say.

"Okay," he says, standing up to brush off his jeans. "I'll see you in church then, Lacey."

"Okay," I say. And then, because I want to make something more happen, I add, "You know, Hell House auditions are next week."

Ty just stares at me through the shadow of night. I can hear the crickets chirping on the carefully kept lawns of my neighborhood. Usually it's comforting, but right now it sounds empty.

"So how does Hell House work, anyway?" Ty asks, mercifully breaking the silence. "Does each sin get progressively more sinful?"

He's looking at me in a way that makes me wonder if he's messing with me.

"A sin's a sin," I say.

"I've heard about Hell Houses," says Ty. "I've read about what kind of scenes they include." He smiles, and then asks, "Do you think murder and using drugs are the same level of offense in God's eyes?"

"Well, they're both sins," I say. "And I'd avoid either at any cost to have hope of getting into heaven."

I try to stand up straight while I assert my opinion, and I hold my head up like I've seen Tessa do when she talks to boys, challenging and flirtatious.

But my attempt to be someone I'm not, to be someone braver and bolder, isn't working. He stares at me as though I'm a strange creature, like I just said something in a foreign language and he can't quite translate it. My confidence falters.

"Well, I should go," I say again, backing away from him slowly. I don't know why I'm so nervous, but I feel like if I turn around, I might break into a run.

He reaches out for my arm and touches it, gently, but not like he thinks I'm fragile. I realize that he's been saying things to me seriously, and not speaking to me delicately like everyone else does. He doesn't know me, doesn't know that I'm shy and quiet.

"That one's yours, right?" He points to my house.

"Yeah," I say, wondering how he knew.

"Cool," he says. "Well, good night, Lacey Anne Byer."

He waves a small wave.

"Good night," I say, turning to walk back to my driveway and breathing a sigh of relief that no one drove by while his BMW was all askew like that. I don't know how I got so caught up that I forgot to worry about the neighbors. They'd definitely tell my father that I was sitting on a curb with the new guy who wears sunglasses in church. That would not go over well.

As I drift off to sleep that night, just before I leave the waking world for slumber, a thought pops into my head: *How did he know my middle name?*

Chapter Five

Though I think I hear the rumble of an unmuffled BMW outside my house a couple of times in the next few days, I don't actually see Ty or his red vintage machine for almost a week after that night on the curb. It's almost like I dreamed it.

When Dean came over to work with my dad in the garage, I almost told him about talking to Ty, but I didn't get a chance. He and Dad were together almost the whole time, laughing and talking about spatial relations in miniature models or something I don't understand and don't care to find out about. It's nice to see them together—his own dad isn't really the buddy-buddy type.

Mom made grilled chicken like I'd suggested, and she brewed tea and put out gingersnaps for dessert—another nod to Dean's diet, I guessed, because we normally have ice cream. We stayed around the dinner table long after the dishes were cleared, talking about Hell House and what kind of outreach we're hoping for.

"I'd love for Dean to have some kind of role this year," Dad told me after Dean left. "We'll work on him—it'd give him a confidence boost."

"Thanks, Daddy," I said, kissing him on the cheek and feeling happy to have parents who watch out for my friends like that.

It's late on Saturday afternoon, and Starla Joy and Dean are sitting in the back corner table at Joey's Barbecue, downing sweet tea refills. Since getting my license, I've picked up a few extra summer shifts as a hostess/waitress here so I can save for my own car—I've already got about four hundred dollars in babysitting, birthday, and Christmas money.

Starla Joy drove me to work today in the old truck she and Tessa share, because my mom needed the Honda for church errands.

I'm handling the slow in-between-lunch-and-dinner shift and trying not to make eye contact with the taxidermy on the walls. There's one squirrel that's particularly disturbing because its mouth is open, wide and fierce, like it died trying to bite whoever killed it. To soften the décor, I suggested putting little bud vases with daisies in them on each table, next to the ketchup and barbecue sauce. I think it's a nice touch. As I walk back and forth between my friends' table and the few customers we have, today feels like every other day at work this summer.

Until Ty walks in.

I hear the bells over the door jingle and I turn automatically, ready to smile and seat whomever it might be. He looks like he stepped out of one of those old high school movies in his soft green polo shirt. I kind of love that he's always wearing those. He raises his dark sunglasses over his head as he catches my eye. Starla Joy and Dean, as well as Mr. and Mrs. Wilson at table four—the only other customers this afternoon—go silent.

"Hi, Lacey Anne," says Ty, nodding my way. "I'll take that spot by the window."

I look over at Starla Joy and Dean and watch their jaws drop. They have a ton of theories about Ty. Starla Joy keeps calling him MTV Boy because she thinks he looks like a reality show star, but Dean just thinks he's a normal guy from somewhere else who hasn't yet learned that no guys really wear pastel shirts in West River. I didn't tell them I met him for real already. I'm not sure why, but it feels like a secret. I've been nodding noncommittally as they put forth various ideas, feeling slightly guilty that they don't know I've already had an actual conversation with the subject of their unrelenting speculation.

"Sure," I say brightly, grabbing a laminated menu and leading him far away from Starla Joy and Dean. "Table six it is."

I sit him down next to the Wilsons, who smile politely before they start to whisper to each other as Ty passes by. Everyone knows he's new in town.

I hustle back to the drinks station and pour a glass of water, avoiding Dean's and Starla Joy's eyes. When I return to table six, I take my ordering pad and a pen out of my ruffled blue apron, which suddenly feels childish.

"Do you have anything for vegetarians?" asks Ty, and I stifle a smile.

"It's called Joey's Barbecue," I say. "What do you expect? Fried beans or something?"

"So you're saying you have nothing for a non-meat eater?" Ty asks.

"Well . . . ," I say, thinking about it. "The beans are cooked in fatback and the potatoes have bits of bacon in them . . . but I guess the hush puppies might be plant-eater friendly."

"Hush puppies?" he asks.

"They're like fried bits of cornmeal and onion," I say. "You eat 'em with butter or ketchup or whatever. You've never tried them?"

A shadow crosses Ty's brow, but just for a moment. Then he smiles at me.

"Okay," he says. "I'll have a pulled pork sandwich and a side of hush puppies."

"So you're not a vegetarian?" I ask.

"Not today."

And then I don't know what to say, but luckily I have a job to get back to.

I walk over to the kitchen and clip his ticket to the hanging line of orders. Since it's such a slow afternoon, I have to shout for Mel, the cook, who's probably outside on his cell phone talking to his new online girlfriend. Then I notice Starla Joy waving rapidly, motioning for me to come over.

I stride her way, trying to look nonchalant.

"What?" I whisper through clenched teeth.

"He *knows* you," says Dean, leaning over the table until it tips off balance a little and Starla Joy's sweet tea almost spills all over the blue plastic tablecloth.

"Careful, Dean," I say. "I don't want to clean up a mess today—my shift is almost over."

Starla Joy ignores me.

"When did you meet him?" she asks.

"It's a small town," I say quietly. "Besides, he probably just saw my name tag."

"Nice try, but he said Lacey *Anne*, and that just says Lacey," says Starla Joy. She points at my plastic name tag. "When were you going to tell us?"

Why did I have to pick such a super-observant best friend?

"Later!" I hiss. I hear Mel shout "Order up!" and I rush to get the sandwich. When I walk it over to Ty, he's staring out the window intently. I want to say something when I put down his food, but he looks like he's deep in thought so I just place the plate gently on the table and turn around.

"Lacey," he whispers, and I turn back. But his face is still looking away from me, so I must be a crazy person who just imagined him whispering—*how weird of me!* I turn around again, but then I feel his hand on my arm. And I start to tingle.

"What time are you done working?" he asks. I look over my shoulder at Starla Joy and Dean, who are unabashedly staring at me, mouths agape . . . again.

"Ten minutes," I say, glancing at the clock above the door, though I know exactly what time it is.

"Can we take a walk?" he asks, smiling a smile that could make a leading lady go weak in the knees.

And I know that Dean and Starla Joy have been waiting for me to get off work all day so we can catch some psychological thriller that Dean's been wanting to see for forever, but we always do the same things and I really, really, really want to talk to Ty again, so I just say, "Yes."

Then I walk into the back to change out of my apron.

* * *

Turns out it's near impossible to ditch your two best friends for a new person on a day when they've been waiting for you for hours. Especially when those two best friends are insanely curious about said new person.

Ty doesn't seem to mind meeting Dean and Starla Joy though. I kind of thought he wanted to walk just with me, but when they insist on coming along, he nods amicably. He's even open to the idea of going to the movies. And he puts up with an intense line of questioning as we head back toward the center of town.

"What town did you say you came from?" asks Starla Joy, after Ty gives her the same vague answer he gave me.

"A tiny town," he says, looking down at the road. "You wouldn't know it."

Starla Joy gives me an exasperated glance, like, *What's with this guy?*

"And you moved here with your family?" asks Dean, struggling a little to keep up with Ty's long strides. Actually, we're all struggling a little but Dean tends to sweat easily so he's showing it the most.

"Yeah," Ty says. "My aunt. She's the new church librarian."

He raises his head and looks at me.

"Oh," I say, surprised I hadn't made the connection. Vivian Moss has been working at the church for just two weeks. She's really young—I guess I thought she was here on her own. "Miss Moss is really sweet."

"She can be," says Ty, giving that half smile again.

"And where are your parents again?" asks Starla Joy. This is the kind of question she feels justified in asking, if only because her own father isn't around anymore.

"They're not here," says Ty. He says it pleasantly, not defensively, but I can tell that he doesn't want to go into further detail.

"Well, it's nice that your aunt is working at the church," I say, before Starla Joy can drill Ty more. "I think my dad had a hand in hiring her—I remember him telling us about her at dinner. Didn't she have family in West River once or something?"

"Yes," says Ty, his pace slowing a bit as we reach the railroad tracks on the edge of the town center.

"So what brought her back?" asks Dean.

But Ty doesn't answer. He looks left, then bends down to feel the tracks. He pauses there, in silence, for almost a full minute.

"What's he doing?" whispers Starla Joy.

"Feeling for a train vibration," hisses Dean.

"But he can see there's clearly nothing coming," Starla Joy says quietly.

I stare at the back of Ty's head, where a piece of soft blond hair curls over the collar of his cotton polo. I study the outline of his back muscles, and I feel a trickle of sweat run down my arm.

"Six minutes," Ty says, looking down at his watch. Then he stands up and crosses the tracks.

I glance at Dean, who just shrugs, and we all follow Ty, stopping on the corner to buy matinee tickets at the movie theater.

"I'm kind of hungry," I say. I never eat at Joey's on my shift anymore—I got sick of barbecue a week into working there.

"Duh," says Starla Joy. "Popcorn."

"I need something more substantial," I say.

"Popcorn has a lot of fiber," says Dean.

"RJ's," I say insistently. We head into RJ's Pizza Shoppe, which is next to the theater, and I order a plain cheese slice.

I carry it outside, folding it in half and eating it quickly so we won't be late for the movie.

"Hurry!" says Starla Joy. She's a total sucker for previews.

"Go on," I say. "Get your fibrous popcorn."

Starla Joy and Dean head into the lobby, but I notice that Ty is still standing outside, staring in the direction of the railroad tracks. He glances at his watch, and just then I hear the whistle of an approaching train.

"Six minutes," he says with a wide grin.

We watch the train rush by us, and the wind that the passing freight cars churn up makes my hair blow all around my face. I look at Ty and smile. He's still staring at the cars as they chug past.

I fold the grease-stained paper plate that held my pizza slice and drop it in a trash can next to the tracks. I remember there was this boy at my elementary school who used to love to watch trains. All of his projects were train related and he had a huge electric railroad set in his backyard.

Ty turns to face me. And then I get a flash of that boy's face.

"Tyson," I think to myself. And Ty's eyes widen in surprise, maybe delight. I must have said that thought out loud. He smiles encouragingly.

"Tyson Davis," I say more confidently, meeting his grin with my own. This is Tyson Davis, the boy who left just after first grade. He's the only member of our tiny class that ever moved away. For a while it felt like there was a hole in our ranks, but I guess after a few years we all just forgot. I step back for a second and take him in, seeing him from head to toe with new—but familiar—eyes. Six to sixteen is a long way to grow.

Ty laughs and pulls me in for a hug. "I thought you'd never guess," he says, as my head presses in to his chest and he squeezes me like an old friend. "It's Ty now," he adds, sounding more serious as we break our embrace.

A thousand thoughts run through my mind: *Why did he come back? Where are his parents? Why didn't he say something earlier, especially with all the questions we asked?* It's like he needed me to know who he was without having to tell me.

And then I feel a rush of happiness. I'm glad it's him. It makes sense, the way I felt when I first saw Ty. He isn't a mysterious stranger, he's Tyson, a boy I've known my whole life. Even my parents knew his family. I want to ask him my million questions, but he grabs my hand and says, "We'll miss the movie," and he pulls me toward the theater.

But I hold back, still grasping his fingers.

"Don't you want to talk?" I ask.

"Sure," he says, smiling brightly. "After."

And that's all I need to feel warm inside, knowing that there'll be an after. As we walk through the glass door, he puts his arm around me, like he's been doing it for years.

"Want a drink?" he asks.

I nod, feeling closer to him now that I've figured out who he really is. And also because of his arm.

I'm about to tell Starla Joy and Dean—and by default the whole lobby—that this is the long-lost Tyson Davis. As I open my mouth, though, I think better of it. I want to keep what I know to myself for now, just for the length of the movie. It's a secret that will sit in the dark with me for a couple of hours before it makes its way into my circle.

Ty buys me a drink with his own money, and I see Starla Joy notice that and raise her eyebrows before she turns and heads into the theater with Dean. When Ty and I get to their row, the lights are starting to dim for previews, and we take the two seats on the aisle next to my friends.

"This is supposed to be like *Goodfellas* meets *The Bourne Identity* meets *Silence of the Lambs*," whispers Dean, more excited than I've seen him in weeks. He would stay in his room alternating old movies with new video games all day if his mom would let him.

"Mafia who are international agents involved with a serial killer?" asks Ty.

Dean nods happily.

We sit down and Ty's shoulder touches mine. It feels exhilarating. I lean back in my seat, glad that for now—even just these two hours in the dark—I'm the only one who knows that sweet little Tyson Davis is back.

Chapter Six

When we get out of the theater, it's dusk. The sun doesn't set until pretty late this time of year, and this hour is my favorite—when the fireflies come out across the meadows. I can see a few tiny glow spots hovering over the train tracks as Starla Joy, Dean, Ty, and I start to walk back toward the restaurant where we parked.

As I step over the rails, I think about Ty's timing of the train, the moment when I figured out who he is. I look up at him and catch him staring at me with a smile on his lips.

"Should we tell them?" he asks.

Starla Joy whips around, always eager for any kind of information. "Tell who what?" she asks, and I start laughing as Dean turns and walks backward to face us and get in on the gossip.

"Do you guys remember that boy Tyson Davis?" I ask.

"Sure," says Starla Joy.

"Yeah," says Dean, sticking his hands in his hoodie pockets, despite the fact that it's sweltering out. He kicks up some dust with the backs of his heels as he walks. "He left after first grade and never came back. Did he Facebook you or something?"

"No," I say, smiling slyly. "But I went to the movies with him recently and I think you guys would like him now, too."

"Huh?" says Starla Joy, staring at the sky like she's trying to figure this out. "You went to the movies with Tyson Davis and we didn't know about it? When could that possibly have happened?" She barrels on while Ty and I look down to hide our laughter. "I know you spent Wednesday at the church, and on Thursday you had the late shift at Joey's, and Friday we did, like, nothing at our spot in the woods before you went fishing with your dad, and I've been with you all day today, so . . ."

I look over at Dean, and I can tell he's caught on. His eyes are crinkled knowingly and there's a tight smile on his lips, but I can see from his expression that he wants to keep Starla Joy on the line a little longer.

"Lacey and I do lots of things that you don't know about, Starla Joy," says Dean, turning around in front of us so no one can see his face. He's probably laughing inside.

"Y'all do not!" says Starla Joy, stomping her foot. "I know just about every hour you and Lacey spend together and what you're doing." She turns to me. "There's no way you've gone to the movies with a guy we used to—"

Then she goes silent and looks over at Ty. "Ty . . . son?" she asks, a lightbulb look in her eyes.

"Hey, hey, Sarah Joyce Minter," Ty says, using the name every teacher calls Starla Joy each year, until she corrects them with her preferred moniker.

We all stop walking and he gives her a hug, which makes

me prickle a tiny bit against my will. Guys usually like Starla Joy more than they like me. And maybe Ty will too. But I shake that thought away as Ty grabs Dean's outstretched hand and gives him a manly half hug, pat-on-the-back style.

"Hey, man," says Dean. "How are you?"

"I'm good," says Ty. "It's nice to be back."

"Wait a second," says Starla Joy, still confused. "When did you . . . ? How did you . . . ?" She stammers out a few questions before I rush in to save her.

"I just figured it out before the movie," I say.

"The trains," says Dean, nodding knowingly as we start walking again. "Tyson Davis was always obsessed."

"Still am," says Ty. "But it's Ty now."

"Okay, Ty," says Starla Joy. "So why the secret identity game?"

He looks toward the parking lot at Joey's, now coming into view. "I just want to ease back into things," he says. "Kinda feel out where I belong, now that we're all older. Find out who my friends are slowly."

That makes sense, I think, as I nod my head and look up at him.

He catches my eye and smiles as we reach the cars. "Can I drive you home, Lacey Anne?" he asks.

I look at Starla Joy, who's twirling her dark hair around her finger and pointedly *not* looking at me. Then I glance at Dean, who gives me a nod.

"Sure," I say, not knowing why I need my friends' approval, but grateful for Dean's gesture.

"Okay, *bye,*" says Starla Joy, louder than she needs to. I wonder if she's annoyed or just making fun of me, but in this moment I don't really care.

Dean waves and they load into Starla Joy's truck, driving

away just as Ty opens the passenger side door of his old BMW for me to get in. *He's chivalrous,* I think.

The ride home is only about four minutes long, but somehow the first minute—when we're not talking—feels like an eternity.

Then Ty says, "So what part are you going for?"

"Huh?" I'm relieved that he's talking, but what is he talking about?

"In Hell House," he says. "What part?"

"Oh," I say. And I just let it out, like it's no big deal. "I want to play Abortion Girl."

Then there's a pause, and he looks at me like I'm crazy. And I feel crazy. Because I've never voiced that wish; I've never told anyone that I dream of that role. It's the cornerstone of the whole show—the lead, really—and I want it.

"Abortion Girl . . . ," whispers Ty, like he's just figured out what I mean.

"I know, I'm silly," I say, starting my backpedaling ramble. "It usually goes to a senior and I'm just a junior this year and there are lots of other girls who'd probably be better for it and—"

Ty stops me. "No, I just was trying to remember that scene," he says. "I've never actually been to Hell House."

Of course! He left before he was old enough to go to one.

"Your other town didn't have a Hell House?" I ask.

"No," says Ty, laughing a little. "It's kind of a unique thing."

"Really?" I ask. I mean, I know we're the only church in the county that hosts one, and kids do come from miles around to go, but I just figured most places had their own version. My aunt's church two towns over has a Hell House, but I think they call it Judgment House or something, which sounds too soft to me. I like the shock factor of the word "hell"—it appeals to kids who aren't on the right path, but they always get drawn in by the outreach and they end up signing a card to pledge their life to Jesus by the end of the show. It's effective.

"Yes, really," says Ty. "I'm not sure how I feel about it either."

"What do you mean?" I ask.

Ty looks at me for a moment, but then he waves his hand dismissively. "Never mind," he says. "Anyway, tell me why you want to play Abortion Girl."

"Oh, well, teen pregnancy is an issue in this town," I say. "I don't know if you remember. I mean, we were young so it wasn't like girls in first grade had trouble with that, but you know, in high school people are older and . . ."

My voice trails off, and I realize that not only am I stating very obvious facts ("in high school people are older"—*duh*!) but I'm also talking about pregnancy with a boy. And pregnancy means sex and if I make it sound like everyone at our high school has sex—which they don't—OMW! What am I saying? *Backtrack, backtrack.*

"You know, it's important to show girls that the wrong choices can lead to really painful consequences," I finish.

"And guys too," says Ty.

"Right," I say. I look at him, wondering if he's making fun of me. But he's just smiling sweetly.

As we pull up near my house, Ty doesn't go into my driveway. Instead, he stops along the curb. I didn't ask him to do that, but I'm glad he did. The trees in the yard block my parents' view, and I'm not ready to explain to them why I got dropped off in a boy's BMW, even if that boy is someone my parents knew when he was younger.

"So, besides movies, what's there to do in West River these days?" Ty asks, leaning back in his seat and turning to face me.

I unbuckle my seat belt and angle myself toward him. "There's ice cream downtown and a really nice bookstore," I say.

"Thrilling," he says, with an air of sarcasm that offends me a little. This is our home, and even though maybe I'm supposed to be all jaded about it like some kids are, I actually love it.

"Well, I'm sure things are *much* more exciting where you've been living," I say snarkily, reaching for the door handle.

"No, Lacey," Ty says, touching my arm to keep me from going. I feel a tingle work its way up to my shoulder. "I didn't mean it that way. Believe me, I was bored out of my mind most of the time."

I smile back and let out a sigh. "Sorry," I say. "I'm overly sensitive because some people always talk about getting out of here and traveling and stuff."

"And you don't think about that kind of thing?" Tyson asks.

"A little," I say. "I don't really want to go to State, like my parents did. They tell me how they want me to be a teacher, because I like English so much. But I'd like to do something like be a lawyer maybe, or even a judge."

"Really?" asks Ty, like he's curious about me, like he wants to know more.

"Yeah," I say. "I mean, I like thinking things over a lot, considering different sides of problems and figuring out what's right."

"That's cool," says Ty. "You could totally be a judge."

I smile at him and swat his arm. "You don't know whether I could or not," I say. "You just re-met me."

"I remember you," he says. "You always had big ideas and a

really nice laugh. And you were always making sure everyone got along."

I see his face turn a little red, and mine does too as I let out a nervous giggle. I can't believe I told Ty that, about my wanting to maybe go into law. I haven't really talked about it with anyone.

"I should go," I say, watching the front porch light come on through the trees in our yard. My parents are expecting me home, and they know what time the movie ended.

"Oh, sure," says Ty. He gives me a small wave. I open the door, close it with a gentle click, and hurry up my driveway, bouncing happily. I'm so glad Tyson Davis is back.

The next night at dinner, Mom's wearing a new pair of earrings. They're small crystal hearts, and they sparkle in the light as she sets down Dad's plate of baked chicken and green beans.

Earlier, I went into the garage to ask Dad about Ty's return. I fingered Dad's fishing rod as he sorted the new lures he'd just bought. He prides himself on his immaculately neat tackle box.

"That's an amazing flash spinner," I said, holding up a shiny lure and letting it twirl in my fingers and catch the light.

"Isn't it?" said Dad, looking up with a smile. "I expect to hook some beauties on that one."

"Yeah," I said, putting it back down in its spot.

"So," I said. "Did you notice the new guy who was at the Hell House meeting?"

"I did indeed," said Dad. "In fact, just this afternoon I learned that our new congregation member is the young Tyson Davis. He's staying in town with his aunt, Vivian Moss."

"I know," I said.

Dad looked at me with a question in his eyes, and I felt nervous for a moment.

"I served him a sandwich at Joey's yesterday," I said, leaving out the part about the movies.

"It seems he's been away from the church for a while," said Dad. "I expect you can help him come back into the fold."

I nodded casually, letting a smile creep across my face.

Then Dad returned to sorting his fishing lures, and I went back in the house without asking any follow-up questions. Having my dad practically tell me to hang out with Ty was a plus. And I didn't want to seem too interested.

As Mom brings her own plate over to the table and finally sits down with us for dinner, Dad reaches out for my hand, bowing his head for prayer. I close my eyes.

"Lord, thank you for bringing this food to our table so we may enjoy time as a family and the sustenance of you, our God. Thank you for Theresa's beautiful earrings, and thank you for their sale price." I laugh a little. Dad squeezes my hand affectionately—he likes to try to make me laugh during prayer some nights, and I can tell he's in a good mood. "Thank you for Lacey's curious nature. In Jesus's name we pray. Amen."

Chapter Seven

"The home and family are major targets for the Kingdom of Hell," says Pastor Frist.

The second Hell House meeting is finally here. Dad is being maddeningly silent about how the production is going to be staged this year, but we'll all find out today. I'm in a row with Dean and Starla Joy and Tessa. Ty's not here—the other night I got the feeling that Hell House isn't really his thing, but I'm going to try to convince him to get involved.

As Pastor Frist describes the domestic abuse scene, I can feel a few eyes sweep over Starla Joy and Tessa. Everyone knows their dad hit their mom when they were little, and that's most of the reason why he's been gone for three years and no one talks about it. I squeeze Starla Joy's hand and she sits there, still, not reacting. I see Tessa lean in toward her sister protectively. They fight sometimes, but Tessa has always looked after Starla Joy, especially when things with their parents were really bad, just before their dad left.

Thankfully, Pastor Frist doesn't linger on that topic. He explains that the scene will involve spousal abuse, and then hands the mic back to Dad, who moves on to talk about the drunk driving scene.

"The false highs and constant lows of alcohol are never more sobering than when you realize that you are a killer," says Dad, using his ominous voice, the one he employs when he plays Satan in the show. He explains that the scene will be a combination of an out-of-control party and a drunk driving accident that results in an innocent bystander's death. I zone out a little—this is pretty standard.

But when Pastor Frist starts talking about the abortion scene, I listen extra carefully. I want the part so badly. The emotional range it takes to play a girl who has ended her baby's life is immense—and the scene is beautiful. Last year, the Youth Leaders decorated the walls with pink tissue paper and had speakers set up to play audio of a heartbeat, so when people walked into the room, it was like being inside a womb. Julia, who played Abortion Girl last year, sat in the middle of the room, where she met her murdered baby at various ages—those roles go to younger kids who say things like, "Why did you kill me, Mommy?" It's an intense moment, and like I said, most of the audience usually leaves that room weeping. Abortion Girl is the best part in the show.

"This year's abortion stage will not be a womb," says Pastor Frist. People start to chatter a little, like they might object—that scene is so moving it shouldn't be messed with—but then Dad tells us that the setting will be a hospital gurney where an abortion has just been performed.

"Wow," whispers Tessa, who has perked up and is listening intently.

It sounds so powerful. *I'm going to do it,* I think. I'm definitely auditioning.

The next day, in the living room, I go over the lines for Abortion Girl. I know that on Saturday it won't be a secret that I want this part. But I feel like if I tell my friends I'm going for it, they'll try to talk me out of it. Not because they don't believe in me or anything like that, just because, well, it's a senior girl part. But still, I can't help wanting it. And if I'm going to be able to break out of my quiet shell in the audition, I have to practice.

"I made a mistake . . . I want my baby back!"

I say this line over and over again, trying to get into the emotion of it, trying to imagine that I'm lying on a hospital bed covered in blood. I'm saying it quietly so Dad won't hear—Mom's at church for an auction planning committee meeting—but when the emotion overtakes me, I let out a scream that punctuates the line.

Dad flies out of the bedroom in two seconds.

"Lacey?"

My face turns red.

"Oh, sorry," I say. "I was, um, practicing for Saturday."

"Trying out your scream?" he asks, his worried face softening into a smile.

"Something like that." I can feel that I'm sweating—I really worked myself up—and Dad sits down next to me on the couch and puts his hand on my forehead.

"You're not going overboard, are you?" he asks. "Hell House can be intense for everyone involved, and you've never been eligible for a lead role before."

That's true. Since Dad's a big part of the church, I've been able to have small parts—like as a kid who gets killed by the drunk driver one year, and a weeping little sister at the suicide victim's funeral another time. But this is my shot. I decide to tell Dad what I'm planning.

"I'm rehearsing for Abortion Girl," I say, half expecting him to laugh at me. I stare up at my father and watch him break into a grin. But it's not a mocking one, it's encouraging. Proud, even.

"That would be a great role for you, Lace," says Dad. "You'd be excellent."

"Excellent at what?" asks Mom, coming in the front door with an armful of papers. She heads straight for the metal filing cabinet in the corner by Dad's desk.

"Lacey's going to try out for Abortion Girl," Dad says.

Mom turns her head over her shoulder.

"That's some mature content, Ted." It bothers me when she talks to Dad and not me *about* me. I take a deep breath to relieve the feeling of tightness that's gathering in my chest.

"I've seen the show a hundred times," I say. "I know what the role is. Besides, I'm the one who sees girls at school go through the real thing—I like the idea of putting myself in their shoes. It'll make me a more loving and empathetic person."

"But to put yourself in the mind-set of that situation . . . ," says Mom, opening the file drawer and carefully tucking away her papers one by one. "That's a big deal, Lacey. It might affect you in ways you won't understand."

My mom thinks I am eight years old. She wishes I'd stay quiet and shy and boring forever. This much is clear.

"I think she'd be great," says Dad, ignoring Mom's objections.

"Really?" I ask, turning back to my father and deciding not to listen to Mom. "I mean, I know it normally goes to a senior."

"It goes to the girl who's best for the part," says Dad. "If that happens to be a senior, so be it, but I don't see why a junior girl couldn't do it just as well—if she gives a good audition."

I smile. "Thanks, Dad."

"So let's hear it," he says.

"What?" I ask.

"Your lines. If you can't do them in front of me here, you're gonna have a hard time at the audition on Saturday."

I look down at my script.

"Shall I play the Demon Tour Guide?" asks Dad.

"Sure," I say. I like the idea of rehearsing with my dad—and he has a great demon voice.

"So, let's see here . . . ," says Dad. He leans over my pages and we run the lines, devil and daughter together.

At my audition, I actually weep. I'm not talking a few tears, I'm not talking a couple of sniffles—I'm talking full-on sob session. Somehow I just got carried away with the character of this girl who makes a big mistake. Well, two really. Because she had sex out of wedlock and then she had an abortion. It's a double-sin scene. Maybe that's why it affected me so much.

When I walk out into the church lobby, Starla Joy's eyes widen.

"Lacey!" she says. "What in the world—"

"You did it, didn't you?" Ty stands up from the lobby bench and strides over to me, interrupting Starla Joy. "You tried out for Abortion Girl."

I nod, and Starla Joy hands me a tissue from the front table. I blow my nose and Ty puts his arm around me for a quick squeeze.

I wait for Starla Joy to say something snarky, but she doesn't. She just smiles and says, "I didn't think you had it in you."

"What?" I ask.

"The courage to go for what you want," she says. Her eyes flit to Ty and I wonder if she's talking about more than just the Abortion Girl part. I blush and look down, hoping Ty didn't notice.

She's right, of course. In the past I haven't gone for what I want. I've been safe and good and all those things that were expected of me. But I prepared for this—it's like I was ready to reach a little higher this year—and when I got into the audition room, something shifted. I went for it.

We all sit on the lobby benches. Dean isn't here—he signed up to work on the stage crew and be an extra wherever he's needed, but he's not auditioning for a bigger role. I tried to get him to go for Cyberporn Boy, who looks at lewd sites online, or even Satan's Helper so he could work with my dad in the Hell scene, but he said he gets stage fright and can't have a big role. I know he's making that up—he played Joseph in last year's Christmas pageant—and I almost kept pushing him to audition, but Starla Joy said to just let him brood. Sometimes he needs alone time.

A few minutes later, Tessa walks out of the audition room and throws her arms up in the air. "I nailed it," she says. "Abortion Girl is mine."

Then she pushes open the double doors and says, "Come on, Starla Joy. Momma's making spaghetti."

Starla Joy gives me a sympathetic glance and a quick wave before she follows her sister out to the parking lot. When I look up at Ty, I see his eyes are focused on Tessa's retreating shape.

Sometimes I understand why Starla Joy gets mad at her sister. She tends to just claim things, like a guy or a part in a play. As if there's no chance that someone else might be competition. I think she's a little conceited.

I try to shrug off that feeling because it seems unkind, but I have trouble letting it go. I want this part. When will it be *my* time to stand out?

I exhale slowly to let go of my annoyance. Then I turn to Ty.

"So, what are you doing now?" I ask him. It's a small sentence, but it still feels like I'm putting myself out there for rejection if he's busy. Which is silly, I know, but . . .

He's looking past me, at the bulletin board that holds announcements about Bible study groups and bake sales. Ty didn't audition for Hell House, though I tried to get him to probably harder than I did with Dean. He just kept saying it's not his thing, but I'm hoping I can bring him back to church a little bit this year. I mean, my dad asked me to, after all. I'm also hoping we can finally hang out alone and maybe I can have a boyfriend by the time school starts. I know that's not a very modest or noble goal, but I do think it would be nice. I stare at his amazingly angled cheekbones and have to will myself not to reach up and touch his face.

"Well, I came here to help Aunt Vivian move some new books into the library, but I'm all done. So I thought I'd spend the afternoon with you," he says. "Where should we go?"

I breathe a sigh of relief. He likes me! He wants to spend time with me. But I immediately get nervous again because after all of my big talk about how West River is a really great town, I'm blanking. Dean and Starla Joy and I would just go get snacks and sit in our spot on the woods, or maybe go to a movie if it's a week when a new one opens. Sometimes we walk around downtown—which is really just one block—but does that really count as going somewhere? I glance around the room, hoping a poster or something will help me out.

"I have an idea," says Ty, saving me. "There's a spot I remember, from when I lived here before."

"Okay," I say, thankful that he chimed in. "Let me just tell my dad."

I practically skip over to Dad's office, where I find Mrs. Tuttle, the secretary. "Hi!" I say brightly, a big smile plastered on my face. "I know Dad's busy with auditions, so can you just tell him I'm going to hang out with friends and I'll be home by curfew. Okay, thanks. Bye!"

I don't wait for the flustered Mrs. Tuttle to answer—I know she'll assume I'm going to be with Dean and Starla Joy—and though my dad did say he'd like me to befriend Ty, I don't think he imagined me spending time alone with him.

"I'm ready," I say to Ty when I get back to the lobby, a little breathless.

"Follow me," he says, crooking his arm so I can link mine through it as we walk outside to the parking lot and his waiting rusty BMW.

Chapter Eight

Once we get off the main road in town and start onto a back street through the fields, I know just where we're going.

"The picnic spot," I say, pleased with myself for remembering. In elementary school, our main field trip involved Ulster Park—which is a playground, really—and a picnic on top of the hill above the swing set and monkey bars and a rickety slide. I haven't been here in forever, but we used to come to this spot like three times a year with our teachers, maybe just to give them a break from the super-hot classrooms.

"Is it still there?" asks Ty. His question is answered as we turn into the dusty parking lot and see the swing set and the grassy hill right in front of us.

"I guess it is," I say.

"Don't tell me you never come here anymore," says Ty, turning off the engine.

"It's been a while," I answer, opening up my door and stepping out into the still air. I toss my cardigan—which is very necessary for the air-conditioned church, but not so much for the hot air out here—into the backseat.

"Shade?" asks Ty, unlocking the trunk and pulling out a faded blue sleeping bag that looks like it's seen better days.

I must look a little scared because he says, "I just thought we could sit on this—it's old but clean."

"Oh, sure," I say. I wonder when I became a girl who leaves the town limits to lie out on a sleeping bag with a boy she hardly knows. But then I chastise myself for that thought. I *know* him—he's Tyson Davis! And besides, my dad practically asked me to talk to him about church and stuff. So technically this is all in God's plan.

Ty spreads the sleeping bag at the high point on the hill, and we sit down and take turns sipping from his earth-friendly stainless steel bottle of water. I pull my hair off my neck and twist it into a self-holding bun because I'm starting to sweat, despite the shade.

I look down at the playground and see that weeds have grown halfway up the monkey bars and the swing chains look rusted from underuse. I guess no one comes here now that they built a new playground near the center of town. Looking at it now, remembering how much fun we used to have holding hands as we flew down the extra-wide slide, makes me feel a little melancholy.

"So are you upset?" asks Ty, picking up a blade of grass and twisting it between his thumb and forefinger.

"Upset?" I ask, wondering if Ty can read the nostalgic thoughts on my face.

"About Tessa competing with you for Abortion Girl," he says, turning to look at me.

"Oh," I say, realizing my exhaling-the-annoyance moment must have been kind of obvious. But the truth is, I'd forgotten that part of the day already. I'm so caught up in being here, on this sleeping bag, with Ty.

"I guess I was," I say honestly. "But not because of Tessa. Just because I thought I might get it."

"You still might," says Ty.

"You think?" I ask, staring at him and wondering what he sees when he looks back at me.

"Yeah," he says.

"Why?" I ask.

"Because you're so passionate," he says.

I look down and feel myself blushing.

"I'm not really," I say.

"No, you are," says Ty. "About Hell House, about the church, about getting this role, about everything."

"You really think so?" I ask.

"Of course," says Ty, laughing at my hesitation.

"Other people think I'm quiet," I say. "They call me shy." *Shy.* It sounded like such a bad word when people said it about me when I was younger. "Oh, she's shy," like it meant I had a mental deficiency or something. But now that I'm in high school, shy is safe and respectable in people's eyes. I've become Lacey Byer, the good girl, who's always acted appropriately. And who's never had a movie moment.

"I see how much you want that role, Lacey," he says, and I look up at him then. "You've got a fire in you."

"I do?" I ask. I've always felt like there was something strong inside me, but no one's ever noticed it on the outside before.

"Yes," he says. "That's why I thought you might be angry at Tessa."

"No," I say. "She's a senior, and I can try out for Abortion Girl next year."

And as I say it, I think that's true. It's only fair for Tessa to have the part if she wants it.

"You're so good, Lacey," says Ty. "I don't know how you do it."

"It's the Christian in me," I say, shrugging my shoulders and smiling at him. "We're supposed to be good."

"Humph." Ty makes a grunting noise, like he doubts what I've said.

"What?" I ask.

"Nothing," he says, tossing the blade of grass he'd been rolling between his fingers.

I stay quiet, thinking that this is what my dad must have been talking about, that Ty has strayed away from the church somehow. I'm excited. I think I can bring him back. Hell House is the best tool we have for kids our age—it's interesting and fun and scary and controversial. Two years ago there was this kid Jack Suggs who everyone said was on drugs, but after he went through Hell House, he turned things around. He went into some rehab program and even got into college last year.

I'm about to say something to encourage Ty to go on, but then he says, "I don't know. It's just that I'm not sure what I believe anymore." And I give him time to talk, because I've learned this from my father. People need space to say things that are serious, things that are hard.

"It's not that I don't believe in God," he continues, bending his legs and resting his elbows against his knees as he looks down at the ground between his feet. "It's just that I don't always agree with Him . . . or at least with what I've been taught about Him."

"Mmm-hmm," I say encouragingly. I stare at the side of his legs, which are covered in golden hairs, and I wonder what they would feel like to touch.

"Like, do you really think that all people who commit sins are bad?" asks Ty, whipping his head up to face me. I look away from his legs and meet his eyes, but I don't even have a chance to respond before he goes on. "Because, I mean, sins are *everywhere*, Lacey. And if telling a white lie is as bad as feeling jealousy, which is as bad as lusting after someone, which is as bad as abortion, which is as bad as murder, then I just don't know what to think."

That was a mouthful, and I'm still parsing out what Ty said when he stretches out on the sleeping bag and puts his hands behind his head. I look down at him and he looks so sweet and confused that I have an urge to reach out to him. But I don't. I just lie back beside him—carefully leaving a foot or so between us—and stare up at the sky.

We spend the next few hours talking about these things—the big questions of what sin means and what good Christians can do in the face of it. I even tell him about how my dad sometimes brings up his own failings and uses them as lessons for the children's group, like the time he talked about cheating on a test in high school. He went back later and confessed to his teacher, who let him take another version of the exam.

"That's like a pseudo sin," says Ty, laughing. "Seriously, that's the worst your father's ever done?"

"I guess so," I say. I've never thought about it that way. I've always thought of my dad as pretty much perfect.

Ty has three Power Bars in his car, so even when dinnertime comes and we get hungry we don't drive back into town. We stay out on the hill, like it's our new spot.

By the time the fireflies start glowing, Ty and I are listing our own mini sins. I tell him about how I lied to my parents at age ten, when Dean rented an R-rated movie we were dying to see, and he mentions his first peek at a triple-X site online, which makes me blush.

"Maybe I should have pushed *you* to try out for Cyberporn Boy instead of Dean," I say.

"Lacey Anne, every guy at school could play Porno Boy with no problem," he says. And I want to object but maybe he's right.

"Hell House is an ideal," I say. "It's like a guideline. Of course some of the scenes are more serious than others. Like Abortion."

"What's the scene like anyway?" asks Ty.

I describe it to him the way my dad described it to me when I asked for more details after the Hell House meeting—the girl on the table, bleeding a lot, the doctor pulling a fake fetus out of her body (it's hidden under the sheet), and all the screaming.

Ty's eyes bug out when I'm done.

"What?" I ask.

"You know that's not what it's really like, right?" he asks.

"What what's really like?" I ask.

"An abortion," he says. "I mean, not like I know firsthand, but I'm pretty sure it's quick and clean and safe ninety-nine percent of the time." He raises an eyebrow. "And I'm positive that it doesn't involve major blood or anything really violent. Most women walk out the same day."

"How do you know so much about abortion?" I ask.

"I don't know," says Ty. "The Discovery Channel?"

"Well, it's more like we're dramatizing something for theatrical reasons," I say, though I guess I hadn't ever really thought about what an actual abortion might be like. I don't want to seem stupid to Ty.

"Anyway, Abortion is one of the more serious scenes, like Suicide and Domestic Abuse—those are the heavy ones."

"So you're admitting those are worse than Cyberporn?" Ty asks.

"Yes," I say. "Those are worse."

Ty smiles at me in a self-satisfied way, like he won a point or something.

"But all are bad!" I say. "I mean, that doesn't give you free rein to go home and log onto BigBoobsandButts.com tonight."

"How did you know about my favorite site?" Ty asks, standing in fake indignation and offering me a hand.

I let him pull me up and we both laugh. I can't believe I just used the words "boob" and "butt" in front of a guy, even if it was in a website name. But it feels okay, it feels easy.

"It's after eight o'clock," says Ty. "I should get home."

"Me too," I say quietly.

Ty looks at me and smiles. Then he puts his hand on my cheek.

"Thanks, Lacey Anne," he says, his face leaning closer. "I really feel like I can talk to you. I knew it would be that way."

He stares right at me and I can hardly breathe as I see the flecks of green in his blue eyes.

I'm about to lean into the kiss that I feel hovering between us. I want this to happen. I want to let go.

Then Ty lets his hand fall and says, "You're just too good for me."

After a silent ride home, in which I try to figure out all the ways in which I could have been kissed but wasn't, Ty drops me off on the curb with a wave. I hug myself and rub my bare arms, daydreaming about what might have happened, how perfect my first kiss could have been. How perfect it might be with Ty.

I stroll up the driveway and into the house about ten minutes before nine, which is my summer curfew (and a full two hours before Starla Joy's). Dean doesn't even have one. Usually Mom and Dad are in bed reading by now, but when I walk into the living room I hear Dad say, "Lacey, come sit down. We need to talk," while Mom shifts uncomfortably in her seat.

I sit in the big chair next to the sofa and fold my hands in my lap, the way Mom likes me to. "Is everything okay?" I ask.

Dad looks pensive; the lines in his forehead seem darker and deeper tonight.

I suddenly wonder if I'm in trouble. That's never happened before. I can't really be in trouble because I'm home on time and I told Mrs. Tuttle that I was with friends, and that's not a lie—I was—and I realize that my palms are starting to sweat. I'm almost glad that Ty didn't kiss me today, because maybe I'd look different after being kissed. But as it is, I haven't done anything wrong. Not that being kissed would be wrong, really, but maybe my parents would think—

"You were out with Tyson—I mean Ty—Davis?" says Mom, interrupting my thoughts. And even though it's a statement, I hear a question mark at the end, like she's not sure. I also detect a nervous hum in her voice.

That's when I realize they're both truly upset.

"Yes," I say, smiling reassuringly. "Ty is a really nice guy. Starla Joy and Dean and I all went to the movies with him last week, and today we went to Ulster Park and talked."

I figure bringing up my lifelong friends will be a plus and will assure them that I'm not going out with Ty in a romantic sense, and the way I said that could mean that all four of us went to the park today. But I didn't really lie. Not officially.

"Well," says Dad, scratching the side of his head vigorously, "that's certainly nice of you all, seeing as how he's new in town—"

Then Mom chimes in again. "It's just that, well, he's a little . . ." She hesitates.

"A little what?" I ask, genuinely curious.

This hasn't happened before. My parents have never been uncomfortable about my friendships. They're really open and loving, even with people like Geoff Parsons. And Ty is a part of the church community, after all.

"He's been away for a while," says Mom, looking at Dad and not me.

"Away?" I ask.

"What your mother means is that Ty has . . . ," starts Dad. "Well, we've heard from his aunt that he's had some . . . *experiences* while he's been gone."

Huh?

"What do you mean, experiences?" I ask.

"Well, honey, it's—" Dad starts.

"It's nothing," interrupts Mom. Her left hand goes to one of her new earrings, twisting it around in her nervous way. "Never mind."

They are acting so weird. I'd press them, but I don't really want them to press me back and find out I was alone with Ty today, even if we were talking about God and Christianity. Because we also talked about porn. I feel my face heat up just thinking about it.

"Okay," I say, wanting desperately to go upstairs to the pile of books by my bed. I'm in the middle of a really great one about a girl who can see other people's dreams. "So is it okay if I go to my room?"

"Yes," says Mom, and she heads into the kitchen for a final wipe down of the counters, even though she's probably already done that three times since dinner.

"So what did you guys grab to eat?" asks Dad, ruffling my hair as I stand up to head down the hallway. "Is Dean still on Weight Watchers?"

I laugh, and I almost tell my dad about the picnic spot, and Ty and the Power Bars, but I hesitate. I don't think he'd approve.

"No," I say. "We grabbed normal food at Wendy's."

My stomach clenches up when I lie, but I'm starting to think Dad won't understand why I was out with Ty—even though he told me to help Ty come back to God, which is what I was doing.

Dad smiles and leans in, out of Mom's earshot. "Sneak me home a Frosty next time," he says.

"I will, Dad," I say. "I promise."

Chapter Nine

The next day, Starla Joy, Dean, and I sit a while in our spot in the woods and then we get snacks at Sulley's Drugstore counter, where they have french fries and fountain soda—the place hasn't changed since my parents used to come here. Later, we meet up with Tessa. She doesn't usually hang out with us, but today she says her friends are acting stupid and she wants to be with her little sister. Starla Joy plays it cool, but I can tell she's happy.

We used to spend a lot of time with Tessa—she's only seventeen, a year older than we are, after all. She always knew what music we should hear, how to get the perfect mermaid braids into my thin hair, and which makeup colors looked best with each of our skin tones. According to Tessa, I'm a winter, and Starla Joy is a fall. She told Dean he's a spring, and he even took her advice about trying a blue nail color once, but then he went back to his regular black.

In the past couple of years, though, Tessa's grown more

distant. She's been dating Jeremy Jackson for the last year and a half, and the two of them together are like a country love song—small-town high school romance personified. He plays basketball and he even dunked in a game once; she's not a cheerleader because she's almost too cool for that, but she's friends with all the girls who are. Tessa and Jeremy even make eyes at each other in church, though I try not to be too obvious when I watch them. Today's reunion is nice.

Tessa's wearing a silk floral scarf tied around her neck, like you might see in a magazine. Starla Joy experiments with bright lipstick and I dream of turning heads one day, but Tessa? She's already there. She's in a whole different social sphere, mainly because she's insanely beautiful. She could be a J.Crew model.

The four of us just walk around town, doing nothing much. We consider going to the movies, but we've seen everything that's playing. So we get ice cream and line up on a bench on the main street in town. Tessa swings her legs underneath her and asks me how it feels to have my license.

"I wouldn't know," I say. "So far my parents only let me take the car to go back and forth to work."

"They'll loosen up on the rules soon," says Tessa. "You're responsible."

"Maybe," I say. "They got so weird the other day when I was hanging out with Ty."

I drop it into the conversation casually, but I hope Tessa will notice.

She does.

"Ooh! So what's he like?" she asks. Her long, wavy brown hair touches the tops of my legs as she leans over Starla Joy to be close to me.

"He's cool," says Dean, breaking in. "He's awesome at *World of Warcraft*."

"You've been hanging out with him too?" asks Starla Joy.

"A couple of times," says Dean.

"Blah, blah, blah," says Tessa. "I want to know what *Lacey* likes about him . . ."

"He's really sweet," I say. "Just like he used to be."

"But now he's hot too," says Starla Joy, and the three of us crack up.

"Is this afternoon turning into a chick flick?" asks Dean, and his speech is slurred because he's licking his Rocky Road ice cream rapidly so it won't drip down the cone. "Should I turn on my PSP to drown out the gigglefest?"

"Spare me, Dean," says Tessa. "You know that if there was a new girl in town you'd be all over it."

Dean smiles. "Yeah," he says. "What I wouldn't give for a new girl who'd appreciate the many layers of my personality."

"Or who'd just put up with your video game playing," says Starla Joy.

"That'd be good too," says Dean, reaching for his back pocket. Usually he keeps his PSP there but today he promised to leave it at home because Starla Joy and I are increasingly annoyed with the way he looks down at it all the time while we're trying to talk to him.

"Darn it!" he says.

I shake my head at him.

"This interior-only life isn't healthy," Starla Joy tells him.

Dean rolls his eyes, but he *is* more himself today.

"I'm sitting on a bench eating ice cream and talking about Ty, aren't I?" asks Dean, fluttering his lashes to make fun of us.

Tessa throws her head back and laughs, and for just a minute it's like we're on a stage and the spotlight is focused intensely on her—the way her hair shines, the way her eyes sparkle, the tilt of her chin and smooth curve of her neck. Her laugh twinkles in the air, and I see a few people walking by turn to look.

"Dean, you know we love you," says Tessa. He stares back at her like she's the sun, and I wonder if that crush he used to have on her ever went away. She reaches over and ruffles his hair.

"So tell us more about hanging out with Ty," says Tessa, refocusing on me.

I look down at my flip-flops, pleased to be the center of her attention. But I don't want to tell everyone about the things we discussed—a lot of it seems personal.

So I tell them how Ty told me he thought I was passionate about life.

"Wait—he actually called you *passionate?*" asks Starla Joy. "As in, he used that word?"

"Yes," I say. "I remember because it made me blush."

"Oh my gosh, he wants to make out with you!" says Starla Joy.

My mouth drops open and Tessa says, "Sarah Joyce Minter!"

"Well, he must," she says.

"Um, excuse me," says Dean. "I hate to break this to you ladies, but guys want to make out with girls. It's normal."

"But they don't talk about it outright like that," says Starla Joy. "Oh, Lacey, that's *exciting.*"

"Starla Joy!" I say.

"Will everyone stop saying my name in that shocked voice?" she asks.

"I don't think he meant it that way," I say. But I can't really explain the context since he was talking about how I wanted Tessa's role in Hell House.

Tessa smiles. "I'm sure he's a nice guy," she says. "But even so, be careful, Lacey." I wish people would stop saying that to me. Tessa isn't careful. Careful is boring.

When I get home just before dinner, Mom's taking tuna casserole out of the oven and Dad's on the computer in the corner of the living room working on Sunday's sermon. I flop down in a chair near him with my book, and I'm almost to the end of chapter eleven when I hear the rumble of an unmuffled engine in the driveway.

Dad's eyes swing to the front window as the beams of Ty's headlights sweep through our living room. I hear his car door slam after the engine cuts off, and I look over at Dad. He nods. "Go see who it is," he says.

But I know who it is.

"Hey," says Ty, when I open the front door just as he's about to ring the bell. "You left your sweater in my car."

I must have forgotten it when he drove me home the other night. I hadn't even missed it. But I'm glad he's here. Only I'm annoyed at his timing, because I can feel both Mom and Dad staring at the door. I swing it open wider so Ty can see them eyeing us.

"Thanks," I say, taking the blue cardigan from him.

"Sure," says Ty softly. Then he looks past me and waves at Mom and Dad. "Hi, Mr. and Mrs. Byer!" he says loudly.

"Hello, Tyson . . . Ty," says Dad, with warmth in his voice as he corrects himself. He walks over to us, not inviting Ty in but meeting him at the door. "How are you adjusting to life back here?"

"It's nice, sir," Ty says. "Especially since I get to see old friends like Lacey Anne."

My mother coughs in the background.

"Yes. Well, that's fine," says my dad.

Fine? They're talking like they're from some old sitcom. My parents are never this stiff. I look back at my mom and she's doing that earring-twisting thing again.

"Well, I'd better go," Ty says, more to my parents than to me. "My aunt's making dinner."

I know he must want to escape this awkwardness, and I feel bad.

"Good night," Mom says, a little too quickly.

"Say hello to Vivian for us," Dad says as he heads back into the living room.

"I will," Ty says. "Thanks."

I know if it were someone else—if it were Dean or Starla Joy or any other Youth Leaders member showing up on our doorstep—they would have asked them to stay for dinner. What do they have against him?

I give Ty a shrug, and I smile in hopes of conveying that I'm sorry he walked into this predinner, parent-filled zone when maybe he planned to return my sweater and have an excuse to kiss me.

Ty grins, though, so I know he understands, and then he walks back to his car and drives away.

"That certainly is a loud vehicle," says Mom. "What kind is it anyway?"

"It's a BMW," I say. "They're really safe." I don't know if that's true but I have to try to win points for Ty where I can.

"So you left your sweater in his car?" Dad asks, raising an eyebrow.

"Yeah, I guess," I say. My face turns red, although there's no reason for it to. It's hot out, so I obviously didn't take off my sweater in his car, I just brought it along with me. But I wish I could control my blushing. "Dean says I should staple my sweater to my waist because I'm always leaving it places."

Great. Now I've gone and rambled in defense of shedding clothes in Ty's car, which isn't even what happened. Are my parents really insinuating that anything remotely untoward took place? 'Cause it didn't. And they should know I'm not like that.

"Okay," says Mom, sighing and returning to the kitchen with an efficient gait. "Dinner's ready."

When we sit down and my parents take my hands for prayer, I feel that tightness again, the kind that makes it hard to breathe, and I start to think that the way my parents are acting—the way they seem wary of Ty—is causing it. They're not giving him a chance, maybe just because he moved away, which seems really narrow minded.

"Lord, thank you for bringing this food to our table so we may enjoy time as a family and the sustenance of you, our God. Thank you for the beautiful woman who cooked the meal," my father says, and I can almost feel him smiling at Mom. "Thank you for the sun today, and for the safe return of Lacey's sweater. Help her to be more careful in the future. In Jesus's name we pray. Amen."

And instead of saying "Amen," I want to scoff at my father's annoying sweater mention. But I don't need *that* between me and God, so I just say "Amen" and get on with dinner.

Chapter Ten

For the rest of the week, I work three double shifts at the barbecue. School starts on Monday, so Mom has been making me do all these last-minute summer chores, like getting my room cleaned up and organized and helping her with her to-do list for the last church supper of the summer.

I do everything she asks in a zombie state because there are two things that take up 90 percent of my brain right now: number one, Ty, and number two, Hell House. The cast list gets posted Sunday.

When the day finally arrives, I wait outside the church for my dad to open the doors early, so I can see the list before the other Youth Leaders. I begged Dad all week to tell me how auditions went, but he's frustratingly disciplined about things like that, and he wouldn't say a word.

Still, I'm not surprised when I see the name "Tessa Minter" next to "Abortion Girl." She knew she had it. The bright side is that my name is in parentheses after hers, which means I'm the understudy, and I'll have a good shot at it next year.

I make myself smile big as I see some other people crowding around the list. After all, they don't know I really wanted the part, and there's no need for them to.

I got the role of "Party Girl Passenger" in the drunk driving scene. I end up dead, which will include fun blood packets that splatter and dramatic lines like, "Whoa—stop!" and "Look out!" so it'll still be cool.

Besides, I'll have my movie moments another way. Ty's in church today.

"So . . . Party Girl Passenger," says Starla Joy as she sits down next to me and my mom in the front row. She knows not to mention Ty in front of my parents—I told her how they're weird about him.

"Congratulations, Demon Tour Guide," I say. It's impressive that Starla Joy got that role—she's the only girl who landed one of the six demon parts.

"Starla Joy, are you joining us in the front pew today?" asks my mother.

"If I may," Starla Joy says in her polite-with-adults voice. "I have no idea where Dean is, and Tessa's at home sick so Momma stayed with her. I just called and told Tessa the good news about Abortion Girl."

"She'll do a wonderful job," says Mom, patting my hand sympathetically. Which annoys me.

"She will be great," I say. Then I look up at my mother. "I'm not bitter, Mom. I promise."

Mom smiles. "It's not the right part for you this year, Lacey," she says. "You're not ready."

I pull my hand out from under hers. *She's still treating me like I'm a kid, like I can't handle anything, even a church performance.*

Mom doesn't flinch when I move away, she just continues chatting and smiling.

"Starla Joy, that lipstick looks so pretty on you," she says, talking over me.

"Why, thank you, Mrs. Byer," says Starla Joy. "And your broach is just beautiful."

I sit quietly between them as they go back and forth. My mom and Starla Joy have always bonded over superficial things. And even though I can't pull off Starla Joy's bright red lips, I *am* wearing lip gloss today so I should get some credit. I'm glad when Pastor Frist starts his sermon.

This Sunday, I pay less attention to the streaming sunlight from the stained-glass windows and more attention to the feeling I have, like someone is looking at me from the back of the sanctuary. I finally turn and glance behind me, and Ty's sparkling eyes make my heart jump. He smiles at me. I feel a blush rising as I turn back to Pastor Frist, and I hope Mom and Starla Joy don't notice.

After the service, there are homemade cookies and cups of red punch in the lobby where people gather to mingle. I didn't see Ty on my way out—he must have left early—and I'm disappointed for a few minutes as I make small talk and try to hold people's gazes even as I want to scan the crowd for his curly blond hair.

Eventually, I see Ty come into the lobby from outside. I try to catch his eye, but he heads straight for my dad and starts talking to him. Maybe he's asking about me, about us dating. Dad would like a guy asking for permission to date his daughter. Maybe Ty will win him over. I pretend to stare at the blue-and-red lettering on the homemade potluck dinner poster behind my father's head for a minute or two, but when they don't turn my way, I decide to approach them. That's when I discover they're not talking about me.

". . . just drove him home, but he's definitely upset," Ty says.

"And you're sure it was the Parsons boy?" asks Dad.

"Yes, sir," Ty says. "I know punishment isn't the church's role, but I just think that with him getting such a big part in Hell House . . . well, it isn't quite fair after something like this."

"Something like what?" I ask, not worried about eavesdropping when this sounds so serious.

Dad looks at me with sad eyes. "Lacey Anne, don't worry," he says. "If you want to miss the Youth Leaders meeting today to go see Dean, I'll make your excuses."

"Miss the YL meeting?" I ask. "Why would I do that? And what's going on with Dean?"

I look over at Ty.

"I found him in the art room," he says. "Lots of the props he'd built had been painted with 666, the symbol of the devil."

What?

"What?" I ask, but my voice falters because I'm freaked out. "Why? Who was it?" I look at my father. "Dad, what's going on?"

"Now, Lacey, don't you worry," says Dad, putting a hand on my back. "You just go see your friend and make sure he's okay."

Ty puts his arm around me, and I'm too upset to even care that we're right in front of my father. "Let's go," he says, and I nod. Dad doesn't stop us as we push a path through the post-worship social hour. On the way out I see Starla Joy talking to Mrs. Wilkins, and I catch her eye. One look at my face and she knows to make her excuses.

She hurries over to us.

"What is it?" she asks.

"It's Dean," I say.

"We'll explain outside," Ty says.

Starla Joy follows without a single question.

By the time we get to Dean's—a two-minute drive—Starla Joy is as caught up as I am. Ty isn't being very forthcoming, though.

"I want you to know what *Dean* wants you to know," he keeps saying when we ask him who did this. I don't tell him that I heard him mention Geoff Parsons, but I can't help feeling confused and a little hurt. Since when does Ty know more about Dean's life than Starla Joy and I do?

When we pull into Dean's driveway, Starla Joy opens her door and jumps out before the BMW's fully stopped. Her ballet flats kick up gravel in the driveway as she runs up the porch steps and doesn't knock—just walks in. Ty and I are right behind her.

Dean's mom has her arms folded across her chest when we enter.

"Hi, ma'am," I say. Starla Joy must have barreled past her on the way to Dean's room.

"Lacey, Ty," says Mrs. Perkins. She smiles softly, but it's one of those smiles that's filled with tears. "Mr. Perkins is still at church, but I came home. Would you like a snack?"

I can smell something baking—chocolate cake?—and I look around the living room. There's a stack of *National Geographic* magazines on the coffee table next to some issues of *Real Simple*. A mug of tea, still steaming, sits on a porcelain coaster atop the kitchen counter in the distance. Sunlight streams through the windows. It's comforting to see everything at the Perkins house in its place, even today. This is what my mother must mean when she straightens up our house manically and calls it "cathartic cleaning."

"No thanks," I say.

Mrs. Perkins nods and motions up the stairs. "Dean's okay," she says. "He'll be glad to see you both." She doesn't look either of us in the eye. I wonder how many times she's met Ty—it seems like she already knows him.

We walk by her and start climbing the steps.

Starla Joy has her arms thrown around Dean, who's sitting on his bed holding an ice pack to his cheek.

She turns to us with anger in her eyes.

"Why would this happen?" she asks. And I realize she's looking at Ty, like maybe he had something to do with it.

"It was an asshole prank," says Dean, sitting up. He's changed into a flannel shirt and jeans. I look around the room but I don't see his paint-covered clothes anywhere. "It's okay," he says. "At least I had a good excuse for skipping the sermon."

He grins and he looks ten years old, which makes me want to run up and hug him too. So I do.

"Is this what it takes to get you both in my bed?" asks Dean. "Worth it!"

I smack his leg. "Stop joking," I say. "We want to hear what happened. Who did this, Dean?"

He sighs and hesitates for a moment, looking up at Ty. Ty nods. *Did he just give permission for Dean to tell his two best friends in the world what happened?*

"It was Geoff Parsons," Dean says. "I went into church early to work on some Hell House set stuff, and he was already there, in the art room where my prop supplies are."

Dean stares at the red paint still lingering on his hands. "At first I thought he was just going to talk smack, like usual. He started in on my nail polish and saying I was fat and stuff, but I just ignored him and turned around to work on painting the set piece I'm finishing up. That's when I saw it—the red 666."

I feel a chill pass through me. This is so not okay.

"I thought it was just on one of the gravestones I built for the drunk driving scene," Dean continues. "But then I saw that he had painted it all over the wooden bridge I'm building for Heaven."

"Heaven's bridge?" I whisper out loud. It seems so insane that Geoff would do that. To Dean, maybe, but when Heaven's bridge is involved, it's like he's doing it to God.

"When I yelled at him, he said I'd probably done it myself when I was under the influence of Satan," Dean continues. "The guy's so stupid, though. He still had the red paintbrush in his hand."

Ty shakes his head, laughing a little.

"But what happened to your face?" I ask.

"When Geoff said that about Satan, I walked up to him and pushed him—hard," Dean says. "Turns out I'm not really a good pusher, though. He pushed me back even harder and I fell backward. That's when the side of my face hit the edge of a chair."

"And Geoff just left you there?" I ask.

"Yeah," says Dean, looking down. "People were shuffling into church, and I thought I'd wait it out. You know how the moms get. I figured they'd make it worse."

"How did you—?" I start to ask Ty.

"I slipped out of the service to go to the bathroom and when I passed the art room I saw Dean in there," he says.

"And then Ty rescued me," says Dean.

Ty laughs. "That's me," he says with mock conceit. "The savior of art geeks."

His face gets serious again quickly though.

"Tell them what he said," says Ty, encouraging Dean.

"What who said?" I ask.

"Geoff," says Dean, glancing up at me, then Starla Joy. "He said . . . he said if I didn't paint it, maybe the devil himself did. He said he knew I believed the 'born gay' lie, and that I would burn in hell."

I recognize that—we all do, except maybe Ty. It's a paraphrased line from the gay marriage scene in Hell House.

"He's throwing demon lines at you?" I ask, disgusted.

"That asshole!" Starla Joy shouts, her voice cracking. "I can't believe he'd do this—"

"Or that he'd push you so hard!" I add, standing up and feeling a surge of anger, of disbelief. "Isn't that illegal or something?"

"Exactly," says Ty. "We're going to file charges against Geoff for assault. Aren't we, Dean?"

Dean winces a little.

"I don't know," he says. "I mean, we were all fired up in the car but I pushed him first, and—"

"Wait a minute," says Starla Joy. "Why didn't you come get us and tell us what was going on? You just left us listening to Pastor Frist during all this?"

Dean looks down like he's sorry, but also confirming that yes, that is what happened.

"It's a guy thing," says Ty. "You don't want girls to see you all shaken up." He looks at Dean. "And I *thought* we made a plan to press charges."

"We did," Dean says. "It's just that you don't know this place, Ty. Lacey, back me up—Geoff Parsons is golden. I mean, his uncle *is* the town police. There's no way it'll work."

"Is that why you were talking to my dad?" I ask, looking at Ty. "Because you want Geoff out of Hell House?"

"You talked to Pastor Byer?" asks Dean with a groan. "Oh man, now Geoff's really gonna be pissed."

"I don't think so," says Ty bitterly. It's the first time I've seen his blue eyes darken.

"What do you mean?" I ask.

He looks at me intently. "I think your father's going to let Geoff slide," he says. "He didn't even seem to consider taking Geoff's name off the cast list for Hell House."

"You don't know that," I said. "I'm sure he'll want him out of the show."

"I don't need to cause any trouble," Dean says. "It'll just make things worse for me."

He's backing down but I can hear the anger in his voice.

"You're really going to just let it go?" Starla Joy asks. "You want him to get away with it?"

"He's been getting away with it for months," says Dean. He punches his pillow. Hard.

"What do you mean?" I ask, sitting back down on the bed and taking Dean's hand gently. He looks like he could cry, though I know he's fighting it.

"You guys don't see!" he says, yelling, I think, to block the tears. "You didn't hear him and his friends last year when I got fat.

You didn't watch them stick out a foot as I walked by or whisper 'Boom!' under their breath in class when I sat down. You didn't hear them laugh. Laughing all the time behind my back. And then in front of my face."

We're all silent for a few seconds as things sink in. I knew Dean was having a rough year—that he'd changed his clothes and grown his hair out and maybe was trying to hide from the world. But I figured it was just normal stuff. I mean, he *never* talked about it with me and Starla Joy. We're his best friends.

"Why didn't you tell us?" asks Starla Joy, her thoughts echoing mine.

"I don't know," Dean says, done talking. What he just said is probably the most he's ever said to us about anything serious. He's always joking around or making fun of us or just, you know, being Dean. Kind of dark sometimes, but a good best friend.

And I realize that I haven't been the same for him. Sure, I knew he got picked on, but I had no idea it affected him so much. Or that it would turn into this awful 666 thing. A better friend would have seen it. Ty's known Dean for like two weeks, and he saw it. He knew. I feel my lower lip start to quiver.

But then I stop, and I find my voice. It's low and strong, with a tinge of anger that surprises even me.

"Don't worry, Dean," I say. "Geoff won't get away with this."

When Ty drops me off, I rush into my house, looking for my father.

Mom's in the kitchen, apron in place with the mixer on high, no doubt making a dessert to take to someone else's home. "Where's Dad?" I shout over the machine's whirs.

She stops the mixer and looks up with concerned eyes. "Honey, how's Dean?" she asks.

"He's okay," I say. "Where's Dad?"

"He's out back on the porch," she says. "But tell me—"

I'm already through the sliding glass door. I see my dad in his porch chair reading the newspaper, and I walk right up to him.

"Dad, you have to take Geoff Parsons out of Hell House," I say. "He doesn't deserve to be in the show after what he did to Dean!"

He lowers his paper and raises his eyes above his half-glasses. It makes him look quizzical, but I know he can't be questioning me on this point.

"He defaced church property!" I continue. "He really hurt Dean!"

"Sit down, Lacey," Dad says, patting the plastic-cushioned couch next to him.

When I sit, I hear the *squish* noise that used to make me laugh when I was a little girl, sitting out here and listening to my father practice his children's group sermons on me. But today the *squish* doesn't sound funny.

"I'm really sorry about what happened to Dean," he says. "Boys can get a little rough sometimes."

"A little rough?" I ask. "Dad! He pushed Dean onto the ground and hurled a line from Hell House at him—he practically accused Dean of being a sinner."

"Now that's not quite what happened," says Dad. "I've talked to the Parsons, and they say Geoff and Dean have been trading barbs since last year. Everyone's excited about Hell House, so of course the script is on people's minds—it was carried into their argument, and things just got a little out of hand this morning."

"Hold on," I say. "Are you giving me a 'boys will be boys' line?"

"Lacey Anne, watch your tone," Dad says, and I can see his face getting more serious. "This isn't a big deal. Geoff has been going through a hard time lately. And Dean's fine, right?"

"Well, he's not going to *die,* if that's what you mean," I say. "But I don't think I'd call him fine."

"Boys are more resilient than girls," says Dad. "Dean will be at the first day of school tomorrow with a crazy story, an exciting lunch topic. And we don't need to go recasting Geoff's role in Hell House. He's perfect for the part of Suicide Boy—you should have heard his audition. It was inspired."

Dad's looking up to the sky, like it was God Himself who "inspired" Geoff's performance. I feel a flash of real anger, not at God, but at my father. I don't know that I've ever felt this way, so upset, so sure that my dad is . . . wrong.

"Dad, Geoff *hurt someone physically,*" I shout. "Dean! My friend, who you've known forever. A fellow church member. And he did it at church!"

"Lacey, I've told you," Dad says, his tone getting harsher. "This was a back-and-forth situation between the two boys that's been going on for a while. Dean isn't innocent here. If we take Geoff Parsons's role away, Dean will have to be banned from working on Hell House too. And I hear he's got some great ideas for set design."

Dad rustles the paper back into position in front of his face as my head drops down. *He's not going to hear me. He thinks what happened is okay.*

I stand up and walk back into the kitchen in a daze.

"Lacey, are you all right?" Mom asks.

I look at her. Bright smile, purple polka-dot apron, blue flowered mitts on her hands as she gets ready to take a cake pan out of the oven.

"No," I say, grabbing her car keys off the pegboard by the kitchen phone. "I'm not."

"Lacey!" she shouts as I stomp toward the front door. I want to go talk to Ty.

My mother stops me in the entryway and holds out her hand.

"You can't just take the car," she says. "I need it later today to go see Mrs. Harrison."

Mrs. Harrison is in my mother's Bible study group, and she's been in the hospital for foot surgery, but she got home this week. That must be why Mom's baking like crazy today.

I hesitate for a minute, considering just leaving anyway. What will my mom do—physically stop me? But then I realize that I'm not mad at Mom, and I'm not mad at poor Mrs. Harrison, who maybe needs a homemade cake after her ordeal. I feel some anger leak out of me and I hand my mother the keys.

Then I stomp upstairs to my room. I turn the radio on my clock alarm up all the way—Dad hates loud music—and I tune it to the heavy metal station. I never understood the rebellion that teenagers feel toward their parents, but in this moment I'm ready to break something.

Chapter Eleven

The next morning, Tessa and Starla Joy pull into my driveway and I hop in the back of their big old truck. Tessa's been driving us to school since last year when she got her license.

"Nice shoes," says Starla Joy.

"Thanks," I say, glad that she noticed the one new thing I'm wearing.

Even though I consider reinventing myself somehow each year, I never actually do it. Today, I'm in my favorite jean shorts and a yellow tank top for the first day of school. Nothing's new, except my leather sandals.

I notice Tessa's flowing orange-print sundress. It sits up on her tanned shoulders with a braided halter neck and then falls down almost to her feet in a graceful wave. She always looks fresh as a daisy.

When we get to school though, everything looks stale at West River High. Same brown metal lockers, same gray-green linoleum, same indescribable but completely distinct smell in the main hallway. The same groups are gathered in the stairwells before the first bell, the same loud kids toss balls down the hall and knock into the same smaller, nerdier kids who duck and weave to avoid the fray.

"Hi, Lacey," says Laura Bergen. She's a YL member who's also a violin player, and she's always in at least four of my classes.

"Hey, Laura," I say.

"How was your summer?" she asks. She's always asking boring questions like that—expected questions—which maybe is why we're not closer friends.

"It was . . . ," and I pause.

Normally, I'd say, "Nice. It was nice." But something's different for me today. I'm not feeling very nice.

Laura assumes I said "nice," though, and starts chatting about how *her* summer was incredibly fulfilling because she went to music camp up in New England and it was amazing and she learned a new bow position and blah, blah, blah. I smile and hope our schedules aren't as aligned this year as they've been since seventh grade. I don't know how much of this I can take. Funny that earlier this summer I defended Laura to Starla Joy and Dean, who like to pick on her and call her "Bore-a." That nickname springs to my thoughts now and it's a wonder I don't say it out loud.

Just as I think I can take no more of Bore-a Bergen's "nice" talk, I spot a familiar silhouette coming down the hallway behind her. Tall, blond hair, bold purple polo for the first day of school—a strong statement. Everyone knows who Ty is by now, that he's the Tyson Davis who moved away way back when, and as he walks toward us he smiles and slaps a few hands along the hallway path, like he's a West River fixture who never left.

He's so good with people, I think, as he swoops in and puts his arm around my shoulder, a move I've grown to love despite the fact that it confuses me to no end. I turn around and leave Laura Bergen with her mouth hanging open. Music camp, schmusic camp. I smile as we walk down the hall together, knowing that my summer—at least the tail end of it—was the one that was really special.

When I see Dean after first period, though, that I'm-actually-maybe-with-a-guy high plummets. His eye has a purple-and-green bruise around the edge. And when I notice Geoff Parsons walking by with a smirk, I feel like smacking his face.

"I'm gonna go say something!" I tell Dean. I'm leaning against his locker and waiting for him to grab a Fiber One bar. We've got second period precal together.

"Don't," he says, grabbing my arm tightly, like it's very important to him that I not say a word. "Please let it go."

I look down, feeling embarrassed. For me, for Dean, for my father. Things just seem wrong right now. But it's not fair to put that on Dean, and I know God works in mysterious ways.

I think of Hebrews 11:1: "Now faith is being sure of what we hope for and certain of what we do not see."

I lift my head up and smile at Dean, linking arms with him as we walk to class. I know that things will be okay.

By Sunday's Youth Leaders meeting, my confidence is fading. All week I waited for some sort of discipline to fall on Geoff Parsons, for my father to apologize to me and tell me that of course Geoff was out of Hell House. For something, *anything* to show me that life is fair and just.

But nothing happened. And now I'm in church with all of them, and it's the first rehearsal of the show I've been looking forward to since I was a little girl. I finally have a bigger role to play, I'm finally going to help save souls directly. But it doesn't feel like I expected it would.

Pastor Frist is leading us through a warm-up before rehearsal. We're doing a personal prayer to rile up our energies, and everyone's eyes are closed. I hang my head back as the pastor starts us off, slowly letting his personal prayer language take over his tongue and waiting for the spirit to move us.

It begins as a soft rumble, and I can't tell who goes first. Once the silence is broken, though, more and more people join in with wild yelps and joyous shouts and tangled cries. This is speaking in tongues, finding our own connection to the Holy Spirit through a language known only to us.

I've often been moved by these moments—where I'm gathered among my friends, my pastor, my father—and we're all unselfconsciously conversing with the Lord, letting him truly hear us. I've joined in myself many times, always wondering if I was doing it right, if what I was feeling was real and true and genuinely His presence. Starla Joy and Dean and I, we talk about everything, but we've never talked about our faith. It doesn't seem to be something to ruminate on or ponder. It just is.

But today, as everyone around me feels the spirit, I'm silent. My face is raised to heaven, and the voices of my peers rain down on me, but my mouth isn't moved to open. The sounds seem strange, somehow foreign, and instead of comforting, they menace. I let a little light creep in between my eyelids, and I lower my head so I can look at the faces of the other Youth Leaders. Starla Joy is singing through nearly closed lips, but definitely holding a tune and vibing with everyone else. Geoff Parsons is thrashing wildly, his head going back and forth until little bits of spit fly out of the corners of his mouth as he howls in the name of God. Dean, far across the pews from Geoff Parsons, is whispering softly, finding his own quieter personal prayer language for today's warm-up.

When I spot Laura Bergen, I feel guilty for calling her "Bore-a" in my head all week, and I quickly, silently ask for forgiveness. Her mouth opens and closes very rapidly as she shrieks nonsensically, and it amazes me that she's never this loud in school. I peer at Tessa, who's right next to me, getting ready to speak her first lines as Abortion Girl, and I feel less envy than admiration for her golden glow, the way her rosebud lips move around the words she's found, the spirit she feels. Even with the hint of a tear in her eye, she looks lit up from within, and I wish I could get to that place.

I scan the room once more. Not a single mouth is still, not a single eye is open.

I feel a flash of guilt, like I'm breaking this communal experience by peeking, by cheating, by not wholly trusting.

I'm about to throw my head back again, close my eyes, and give myself up to my own personal prayer language when I see another observer in the crowd. Ty is looking straight at me. He's here because he's a member of YL now, even though he still says he doesn't want to be a part of Hell House.

He catches my eye and smiles. It's warm and friendly, like we're both in on a joke that no one else gets. He rolls his eyes a little, and I know he's trying to make me laugh, to join him in mocking this moment. But the thing is, this is something that's a big part of my life. I know that some people think speaking in tongues is a totally weird thing to do, but it's actually meditative and cathartic.

I shut my eyes and let my chin drop down, feeling suddenly self-conscious. I start to chastise myself. *Is my worry about a boy watching me getting in the way of my personal prayer? Isn't my love for God and my desire to feel His presence bigger than my fear of embarrassing myself in front of Ty?* I ask myself these questions, but I don't add to the sounds of my friends' fevered chanting. I stay quiet, still, praying that I'll feel the spirit and be moved like I'm supposed to be. Praying that I can find my language of faith.

Rehearsal goes smoothly, but Tessa still has a stomach bug and Starla Joy has to take her home early. I run my scene without a lot of emotion—I'm sitting in the front seat of an old Toyota with Zack Robbins, who's playing a drunk driver coming home from a party—and I can't even work up the energy to scream, "Look out! Look out!" with any feeling. But I convince Pastor Frist that I'll build up to it as we get closer to the performance next month.

When it's time to go home, Ty offers me a ride. I'm about to accept, but then I feel Dad's hand clamp down on my shoulder. "I'm almost done here, Lace," Dad says. "I can take you."

I shrug at Ty, but he's not looking at me. His eyes are on my father.

"Pastor Byer, I'm happy to drive Lacey home," he says. "I have a book I want to lend Lacey from our library—a spiritual tome—and I'd like it if she and I could swing by and get it before I drop her off."

My dad looks down at me, and I can see that he's torn. He

doesn't trust Ty, that much is clear, but he doesn't want to be *that dad*, the one who's overbearing and restrictive to the point that his daughter can't pick up a book on a Sunday afternoon.

"All right," he says. "I suppose that would be okay. But be back for dinner at six p.m. sharp."

I'm surprised. And glad.

Ty bumps me gently with his shoulder as we walk out to the car. I can feel my father staring after us, but I don't care. And that surprises me too.

Dad and I have reached a silent truce about the Dean incident, which basically means that we haven't talked about it since that day on the porch. It's unusual for me to feel this disconnected from my father, this unable to express how I'm feeling. But I haven't brought it up again and neither has he. I still haven't been able to forgive Geoff Parsons, though, and I wonder if Dad knows that and thinks I'm holding hate in my heart. I wonder if I care.

The BMW revs loudly as we head up the gravel driveway. There's no sneaking around in this car. I've never been over to Ty's house before, but I know which one it is—it's a modern-style residence set back in the woods where the Geldings used to live. The driveway is long, and I see PRIVATE PROPERTY signs posted everywhere as Ty eases the car down the road. The front of the house is all huge windows that look out on the trees.

My own house is a modest ranch with just two bedrooms. As we walk into Ty's I see that there's an entrance hall. I don't think I've even been in a house with anything you might refer to as an entrance hall before. The ceiling is vaulted—it's at least twenty feet tall—and the walls are bright white, which makes it feel kind of cold and impersonal.

We walk up a couple of steps and Ty leads me to the living room, where one entire wall is a bookshelf. It's so tall that there's a ladder next to it, and Ty climbs up three steps to grab a book, which he brings down to me. I thought the book thing was an excuse to hang out with me more, but maybe Ty really did want to deliver this. Maybe that long day together in the park meant less to him than it did to me.

"Here," he says.

I turn the book over in my hands. *Finding Purity.* I take a sharp breath in and my face flushes—it's all about avoiding physical contact before marriage! I may start hyperventilating. *Is this why he hasn't kissed me? Is he more conservative than I thought?*

"Is this supposed to tell me something?" I ask quietly, looking down at the cover of the book.

Ty takes it from my hands and starts laughing. And I mean really laughing. He's got tears in his eyes when I finally look up and face him.

"Oh, man," he says, gasping for air, "I didn't even look at which book I handed you."

"You didn't?" I ask, not understanding.

"No, Lacey Anne," he says, tossing the book onto a love seat in the corner. "I just wanted to give you something to take home in case your dad asked about it. That shelf is the spiritual section."

He reaches back up to the row of books and hands me one full of eighteenth-century prayers instead. "Here," he says. "This'll be better."

I laugh. "So what did you want from me then?" I ask.

Ty turns more serious then. "I wanted to talk to you," he says. "Alone."

I stare up at him, hoping to read something in his eyes, to get up the nerve to tell him that I like him as more than a friend.

Suddenly my phone starts ringing. It's a Katy Perry song, so I know it's Starla Joy. I silence it.

"What did you want to talk about?" I ask. And then the phone starts ringing again. I push the "go away" button roughly.

"Do you need to get that?" Ty asks.

"No," I say. "It's probably just Starla Joy being obsessive about some new YouTube video."

But then I think about what happened to Dean, and how things with my friends feel a little more intense now somehow. When she calls a third time, I sit down on the couch and answer.

"What's up?" I ask, as Ty slides into the seat next to me.

"It's Tessa," says Starla Joy. I can barely hear her because she's speaking so quietly, but I know her voice. I can tell she's crying.

"What's wrong? What happened?" I ask.

Ty looks over at me curiously.

"I can't tell you on the phone," she says. "Can you come to our spot?" I hear the strain in her tone.

"I'll be there in five minutes," I say.

When I tell him Starla Joy was crying, Ty insists on coming. I let him, partly because I want to stay with him, to let this afternoon linger longer between us. Besides, I reason, he seems like one of us now. He's defending Dean, he's philosophizing with me, he's concerned about Starla Joy. We've become four.

Chapter Twelve

Starla Joy is already sitting on the log, rocking back and forth, when I get there. She's no longer crying, but it's clear she's in some sort of shock.

"Hey—is Tessa okay?" I ask her. She doesn't look up at me.

I grab her shoulders and make her look me in the eye. When she sees me, really sees me, a tear falls down her cheek.

"Oh, Lacey," she says. "My sister's pregnant."

I gasp, my hand covering my mouth. I feel sick to my stomach, like someone just punched me and all my lunch is about to come up. Tessa the perfect. Tessa the smart. Tessa who held it together for Starla Joy when their dad left, even though she's just a year older. Tessa who gives me advice on everything and is so, so beautiful.

I look over at Ty, and Starla Joy follows my gaze.

"What is he doing here?" she asks, turning on me angrily.

"I was at his house when you called," I say. "I thought he could help. I thought . . . I didn't know."

Ty looks around self-consciously and puts his hands in his pockets, turning to go.

Starla Joy's anger deflates quickly. "Well, everyone will know by tomorrow," she says hopelessly.

Ty faces us again and perches gingerly on the edge of the log next to me.

"I'm so sorry, Starla Joy," he says.

"Momma's sending Tessa to Saint Angeles," says Starla Joy, ignoring him.

West River has one of the highest rates of teen pregnancy in the state—at least a few girls in town each year get sent to the Saint Angeles Home, which is a place where they can go for a few key months when they get in trouble. Some of them come back with babies, some don't, but the home is what the church recommends, because we condemn abortion. And most of the girls who choose to give their babies up for adoption come back and slip right into their old roles as cheerleader or student council member or whatever. It's a good ending to a bad story. At least, that's what it seemed like to me, until it involved Tessa.

"When?" I ask.

"Tonight," she answers.

"And this is why Tessa was sick . . . ," I figure out aloud, as the words spill from my mouth. Then I want to know something else. "Was it Jeremy?" I ask.

"Of course," she says.

"I didn't mean—" I start, realizing I made it sound like I thought Tessa was sleeping around or something. Of course she wasn't. I guess I'm just surprised she was with anyone at all. She wears a purity ring too. We all do.

I don't know what to say, so I just look at Ty, and he has so much sadness on his face that you'd think it was *his* sister who got in trouble.

I look over at Starla Joy and see that she's resumed her rocking back and forth. I wonder if this isn't the time to have someone new—even someone old-but-new—in our special spot.

"Um, Ty," I say gently. "Maybe you could just let me and Starla Joy hang out for a while."

"Sure, sure," he says, standing up quickly and putting his hands back in his pockets. "Do you need—?"

"I can walk home from here," I say.

"Okay then." He heads off without saying more.

I put my arms around Starla Joy, who crumples now that I'm here—really here—and let her cry.

I kneel down in the dirt and hold her hands in between mine as I lift my head to the sky. I pray for Tessa, I pray for Starla Joy, I pray for Mrs. Minter. I pray for everyone who faces this challenge. And I pray for me.

Chapter Thirteen

After she broke down for a while, Starla Joy finally calmed enough to give me some details. Tessa's already six months along, so she's due in November. I've heard of people who didn't know they were pregnant, like those stories about girls giving birth on prom night or in their bathrooms, but Starla Joy said her mom's pretty sure Tessa was just hiding it from everyone. I try to remember if her clothes got looser in the last few weeks, but Tessa's always worn a lot of free-flowing dresses so it was probably easy to obscure her stomach for a while.

When I get home from the woods I go right to my room. I'm not sure I'll be able to sit at the dinner table and not share the news with my parents, so I fake an allergy headache—I get those sometimes when the seasons change. I crumple up tissues on my nightstand to be more convincing.

Mom brings me soup in a cup and lets me eat it in bed. She reaches up to feel my forehead, even though my allergies don't come with a fever. I guess it's a maternal instinct.

"Your eyes are red," she says.

I sniffle. "Allergies," I say.

It's the only word I've uttered since coming back from seeing Starla Joy. Part of me wants to grab my mom and hug her and cry into her lap about how unfair it is about Tessa, how scary this is. I want her to kiss the top of my head and tell me it'll all be okay, that Tessa will graduate this year and go to college and she'll be fine, just fine as a mother, and that maybe she and Jeremy will even get married this fall, if that's what they want. That this is a joy, not a sorrow.

But I don't reach out to my mother, because a bigger part of me is afraid of how she'll react. It's safer to keep things to myself, at least for now.

"Honey, is there anything the matter?" Mom asks.

I shake my head no.

"I hope your father and I didn't upset you about Ty," she says, brushing a piece of hair off my cheek.

I shake my head again.

"You know I trust you, Lacey," she whispers, leaning down to brush my forehead with a kiss. Then she leaves me with the soup and an aspirin, closing the door softly as she exits my room.

I feel a wave of sadness. I wonder when I stopped telling my parents everything.

When I wake up the next morning, I go into the bathroom and open the medicine cabinet for my toothpaste. I brush my teeth, and I'm staring into the mirror at my pale freckles and limp blond bedhead when something occurs to me: I get to take over the role of Abortion Girl in Hell House. I feel a rush of excitement and I watch the hint of a smile cross my face just before a twinge of guilt hits me.

I spit and rinse my mouth, thinking about how Tessa may have known she was pregnant during auditions, and she still went for that part. Did she think it would help her work through having a baby? Was she in denial? I know she'd never consider an abortion in real life.

I'm distracted through breakfast, and Dad notices.

"Nervous about the real work starting?" he asks.

"Huh?" I ask, wondering if he's already worrying about me playing the biggest role in Hell House. I need to learn my lines.

"Now that you're a junior," he says. "It's the most important year to show your academic work is up to State's standards."

"Oh," I say, looking down at my scrambled eggs. "Yeah."

"Don't worry, honey," Mom says, heading over to the table to pour more coffee into Dad's mug. "You're a legacy."

She and Dad smile at each other, and I feel that familiar tightness in my chest again. I haven't told them yet that maybe I don't want to go to State.

I scoop up the last forkful of eggs and grab my bag. "I'm gonna wait outside," I say, pushing back from the table before they can say anything else.

I step through the front door just as Starla Joy's truck pulls into my driveway. I can see her beaming from behind the steering wheel.

She looks bright, happy, upbeat—the opposite of how I know she feels. Her hot-pink lips stay frozen in a smile as I climb into the passenger side of the truck—it's so weird that Tessa's not here—and she swishes her head around so I can see the tiger lily she's pinned into her dark, shiny ponytail.

"Good disguise," I say.

She grins at me, genuinely now.

"Momma always says, 'Face a rough day with color and style,'" she says.

"Your momma should talk to Dean," I respond.

At school, Dean meets us in front of Starla Joy's locker first thing. She called him last night to tell him what was going on. And although we know Dean kept it a secret, it's obvious that the word is out.

How does the rumor mill turn? I wonder. Did Starla Joy's mom call a friend who told her daughter, who told her best friend, who told two people, who each told three, who each told four? My head swims with gossip math. One thing is for sure: everybody knows.

In the hallway, as people walk by the three of us, all chattering about nothing before the first bell rings, I can feel the stares. They're not talking about us overtly, they're just *looking*. Like we have special information, and they want to find out what we know.

I can tell what they're thinking, because I've been them. Who am I kidding? I *am* them. I want to hear where Tessa is, how she is, what's going through her mind, if her heart is breaking. But this isn't the time or place to ask those questions. Starla Joy will tell us later, if she wants to, if she even knows herself.

For now, she and Dean and I huddle together, protecting each other from something we don't quite understand.

At lunch, I finally see Ty. Usually he meets Dean and me after second period to walk to third because our classrooms are close together, but he didn't today. And when I catch a glimpse of him across the courtyard as Starla Joy and I settle into our usual lunch spot near the amphitheater, I can tell he's avoiding us. Or me. Or something.

But when Starla Joy reaches up to wave at him, he comes over with a friendly smile.

"How are you?" he asks, looking at her and not me.

She works her pink lips into a big grin and says, "Just peachy."

"It'll be okay," Ty says, though he sounds unconvinced.

Starla Joy smiles again and returns her gaze to the bunch of grapes she's been picking at.

Ty sits down and we're all quiet for a minute. I haven't known what to say since last night, and today I found myself thinking about Hell House and the lines I'll have to learn before I reminded myself that wasn't appropriate—I should be thinking about Tessa now. Tessa and Starla Joy.

"I wonder when it happened," says Starla Joy. She's staring off in the distance and it's like she's not even really talking to us, but just letting her inner thoughts speak out loud. She looks at her fingers and counts. "March," she says. "Maybe over spring break last year when they drove to the beach . . . or that week-end when Momma and I went away overnight to see Grandma on her birthday and Tessa said she had to finish a history paper . . ."

"Starla Joy, you don't have to—" I start. I was going to tell her she doesn't have to think about this so specifically, that it doesn't matter, but she keeps talking over me.

"It had to be unplanned," she says, with that ghost look still in her eyes. "She wouldn't have planned to have sex, right?"

Starla Joy looks at me now and wants me to confirm that no,

Tessa would never have planned to break the purity pledge. I shake my head. "No, I'm sure it wasn't planned," I say.

"If it was planned," says Ty, "they would have used protection."

I glance over at him, but he's looking at Starla Joy.

"They didn't have any," I say, "because it *wasn't* planned."

"Exactly," says Ty, still focusing on Starla Joy. "You know, at my old school they handed out condoms in the guidance office."

I feel a blush creep into my cheeks involuntarily. "Really?" I ask before I can stop myself.

"Yeah," he says, finally looking my way. "There was a basket there. It wasn't like they put one in every locker, but you could get one—almost without anyone knowing."

I want to ask Ty if he ever got one for himself. He's kind of talking like he did, but I can't believe he would have. Would he?

"Well, I know for a fact that Tessa wouldn't have been caught dead with a condom," says Starla Joy, finally tuning back into us. "I'm sure this was some crazy night gone too far—we've always believed in abstinence."

"Yeah, like that's the only option," says Ty softly. He looks down at his shoes, and I can tell he's about to say something more.

But then we hear Tessa's boyfriend Jeremy's voice, and all of our heads turn in his direction.

I can't make out what he's saying, exactly, but he's shouting and whooping it up with his group of jock friends on the other side of the amphitheater, like he doesn't have a care in the world.

"How can he act like that?" Dean is suddenly standing next

to us, covered in paint because he's coming from the art building, and saying what we're all thinking.

"They always do," says Starla Joy, still holding her lips in a smile shape, though there's no happiness in her eyes. "The guys get to go on with their lives, doing whatever they want, taking no responsibility because they're not physically tied to the sin they've committed."

It's creepy to watch Starla Joy in this moment. She's talking like a robot and it seems like she's not really here. It's like she's gone a little bit crazy. And she sounds like her mom. I wouldn't be surprised if she's quoting Mrs. Minter.

"Not all the guys," I say, not wanting my friend to feel the bitterness that I see in her face.

Ty stands up. "I've got to go finish some chemistry homework," he says. "I have Brenner next period."

I know that's true, because I know Ty's schedule. And Mr. Brenner is one of the toughest teachers. But I can't help but feel like Ty's leaving us because he can't handle it here. Because what we're talking about is too much for him.

He strides into the building, past Jeremy and his friends. Ty's looking down at the ground the whole time, not meeting their eyes, and never turning around to see me watching him go.

Chapter Fourteen

. . . .

When I get home, I see that Dad's car is in the driveway. He must have taken off early from work when he heard the news about Tessa. I hope it wasn't for my benefit.

But when I walk in and find my parents sitting together on the couch, speaking in hushed tones, I know that I'm in for something.

"Hi, honey," Mom says, patting the couch next to her.

I smile, drop my bag, and sit in the armchair across the room instead. I don't want to be lined up like three ducks in a row while we talk about this. I want to face them.

"We knew you'd find out about Tessa," Mom says. "And we just want you to know that we're here to talk if you have anything you want to express. You and Starla Joy have always been so close. It must be very hard on her."

"It is," I say. I'm about to say something more, because my parents seem like they're being pretty calm and sympathetic. But then my dad starts talking.

"Did you know about this?" he asks, a hint of accusation in his voice. Or maybe I'm being paranoid.

"Just since yesterday," I say. "Starla Joy told me."

"Oh, honey, your allergy headache?" says Mom, wringing her hands. "I knew there was something more to that. But you didn't feel like you could—"

"Didn't you think you should tell us?" Dad asks, raising his voice to interrupt Mom.

"It wasn't my news to tell," I say, not really knowing where my father is going with this, but feeling both intimidated and annoyed by his tone, which is getting harsher with each sentence.

"Oh, don't be silly, Lacey Anne," Dad says, standing up and pacing the floor in front of me. "This isn't the time for teenage secret keeping."

He looks at me and I stare back blankly. This doesn't seem like my dad, the children's pastor. He's so angry.

"Don't you know that when something like this happens it can affect everyone, especially friends of the Minter girls, in ways they don't understand," he continues, running his hand through his tuft of graying hair.

I glance over at Mom for help, but she's looking down at her hands, which are folded in her lap. It's like she's willfully bowing out of this conversation because Dad's being loud.

"How am I supposed to be affected?" I ask.

"Well, maybe you'll feel like everybody's breaking the rules, and that it's okay to stray from your morals," he says.

"Oh, yeah, Dad," I say, incredulous. "Knowing that Tessa had premarital sex and got pregnant really makes me want to run off with a guy right away."

Mom looks up sharply, and I feel a pang of guilt for saying something so shocking.

"Lacey Anne," says Mom, recovering, "when girls like that get themselves into trouble, they can affect other girls in the community too."

"Girls like what?" I ask.

"Like the Minter girls," says Dad, softening his voice now and walking toward my chair. "They're lovely, and I know you've looked up to Tessa. But she and Starla Joy are girls without a male role model. They've grown up in a house with a mother who's had different boyfriends. It can get confusing for them, I know."

"But we don't want it to get confusing for *you*," Mom says, looking at me again.

"I'm not confused," I say. "And Mrs. Minter has dated maybe one man since Mr. Minter left." I wonder why my parents aren't blaming Mr. Minter for some of this instead of calling Starla Joy and Tessa *girls like that*.

For some reason, that phrase sets off an alarm bell in my head, and I think of Jeremy today at lunch, laughing and hanging out like every other carefree senior, while Tessa is probably sitting in some gray room at Saint Angeles, scared and alone. What about *boys* like that?

"No one's blaming the Minter girls," Dad says. "Your mother and I just think you should branch out in your friendships a little bit . . . maybe find some other girls, like Laura Bergen or Maryanne Duane, to hang around with."

"I can't believe you're saying this," I say, straightening up in my chair.

"Honey, we're not asking you to drop Starla Joy," says Mom.

"We just think you've spent so much time with her and Dean, and now Ty, that you're limiting yourself. Maybe you should find some other social circles too."

I feel the hairs on my neck start to prickle.

"What does this have to do with Dean or Ty?" I ask.

"Nothing," Mom says, looking quickly at Dad. I know there's something they're not saying, but all I can think about is that they're asking me to avoid Starla Joy, my best friend, when she's in total crisis. And I feel as surprised as if they'd asked me to help them steal a car. This isn't what I've been taught my whole life. John 15:12–13: "My command is this: Love each other as I have loved you. Greater love has no one than this, that he lay down his life for his friends." I almost want to say it out loud to them.

Dad kneels down next to my chair, and I stare at our soft beige carpet, focusing on a tiny faded stain next to the leg of the coffee table. It's from when I was six years old and Starla Joy and I were trying to paint each other's nails. We spilled a whole bottle of pink Frosted Pearl nail polish, but Mom just laughed as she cleaned up the mess, calling us her little beauty queens. That one spot never came out.

As I fixate on it I feel a tear run down my cheek, and Dad thinks it's there because I'm sad, because I'm giving in. He reaches up a finger and brushes my tear away, like he's always done.

But I surprise him by standing up and pushing his hand aside.

"I'm not abandoning Starla Joy," I say. "I don't care what you think."

Dad stands up, his brow darkening. "Careful, Lacey Anne," he says.

"I'm sorry," I say, feeling my anger simmering beneath the surface. "I don't mean to be disrespectful, but I'm also not going to stop spending time with my best friend when she needs me the most. That's not what I was *taught*."

I spit out that last word so they know I think they're not acting Christlike. Then I grab my bag and walk toward the door. "I'm going for a walk," I say calmly.

No one objects.

I wait until I'm out of the driveway and halfway to the woods before I let more tears fall.

When I get to our spot, I sit down on the fallen log and listen to the wind rustling the leaves around me. I watch a black beetle work its way across the forest floor, half seeing it, half lost in my own thoughts.

Whose fault is this? Why did Tessa make such a stupid mistake?

I'm not sure how long I've been sitting here when I hear a familiar shuffle walk.

"Hey, Dean," I say, looking up and seeing my flannel-clad friend standing over me.

He settles on the left side of the log, and I move over to the right to balance our weight. We've fallen off this thing a hundred times, so we know how to share it now.

I notice that Dean's hair is cut a new way since earlier today—it's got this asymmetrical emo thing going on.

"Nice haircut," I say.

"Thanks," he says, but I can tell he's not really looking for compliments.

I'm not sure he wants to talk. We just sit there in silence, and I look down at the black beetle again—now halfway across our log circle.

"Weird day," he says after a minute.

"The weirdest," I say.

"I guess I never thought we'd know someone who—" he starts.

"I know," I say. "I mean, not someone we *really* know."

"Yeah," says Dean. "Tessa was so . . . so . . ."

"Good," I finish. "She was so good."

"She just doesn't seem like the type of girl to do something like this," Dean says.

And there it is again—*the type of girl*. Dean sounds angry when he says that about Tessa, like she let him down personally or something. Which I guess she did. I guess she let us all down.

"Do you think it was, like, a one-time thing?" I ask. I feel flushed just talking about this out loud, but it's Dean, so I let myself.

"Who knows," he says. "They might have done it a bunch of times."

"Did you hear something?" I ask. "Like locker-room talk or whatever?"

"No," Dean says. "Jeremy can be a jerk, but not like that."

"I know," I say. "Jeremy really loves her."

"Maybe that's why she did it," Dean says.

"Because she's in love?" I ask.

"They say passion can do crazy things," he says. "Make people forget who they are and what they know about right and wrong."

"Yeah," I say. "Passion seems dangerous."

"It is!" says Dean, speaking loudly all of a sudden. Then, softer, he says, "At least, I think it is."

We sit together in silence for a few more minutes until the sun starts to set, and then both of us get up to go. As I'm turning toward my house, Dean asks, "So you'll get the part, right?"

"Oh," I say. "Um, yeah, I guess so."

I don't want him to know that Abortion Girl has been in the back of my mind all day. I don't want him to know that there's a little piece of me that's jumping up and down because I'm going to be the star of the show. *Me!*

"Well, congratulations, Lacey," says Dean. "And I don't mean that in a sarcastic way, because of Tessa. I mean it in a real way. I think you'll be really good."

I turn to Dean and give him a hug. He pats my back.

"Thank you," I say.

Chapter Fifteen

"Let's all take a seat," says Pastor Frist, stepping up to the podium in the sanctuary.

It's the Wednesday night Hell House meeting, and the first time we've all been together in church since people found out about Tessa. My stomach has been doing this flipping thing all day.

People are coming right up to Starla Joy to say they're praying for her and her family. I sit next to her and hear her thank them all graciously, even some of the same people we know were gossiping about Tessa in school. I love Starla Joy for being so above them.

"I have a few announcements to make," says Pastor Frist as people quiet down. "Everyone knows that Tessa Minter has had to drop out of Hell House due to personal matters."

A little chatter rises up from the pews, but it quiets pretty quickly as he continues. "According to the Hell House casting, Lacey Byer will take over the role of Abortion Girl, with Laura Bergen acting as understudy."

I try to keep my face calm, but I can feel my mouth stretching out into a wide grin. It's official! It's mine. I got it! I knew this was probably going to happen, but hearing that it's really real makes my heart beat faster.

"Lacey, you'll have your first rehearsal tonight," says Pastor Frist. "Your father says you learned the lines for the audition, so I hope you're ready to go."

"I am!" I say, louder than I normally would in church. I even pop up from my seat a little bit in excitement, and I can tell everyone is surprised.

"Congratulations, Lacey," says Pastor Frist. "We know you'll do us proud."

Someone in the back of the church starts clapping and I look up to see Ty leaning on the back doors of the sanctuary and leading the applause. Everyone else joins in, and soon the sound is thunderous. I can feel my face getting red.

Starla Joy squeezes my hand. "You'll be awesome, Lacey," she says.

I look for a flicker of sadness, a flash of doubt, but I just see encouragement in her eyes. "Really?" I ask.

"Truly," she says. "It's meant to be you."

I grin back at her, so grateful to have such a selfless friend, and even more determined to stand by her side. "Thanks," I say.

Then I see Laura Bergen, who looks almost as happy as I am just to be the understudy. I have to have one, since a couple of years ago Molly Bradford lost her voice in the middle of Hell House weekend. It can happen because of the intense screaming and the emotional strain of the role.

The applause dies down and I watch Ty slip out the back door. He isn't supposed to be in here since he's not in the show . . . I wonder if he came for me. I know he's proud of me. I could see it in his face.

I haven't been able to spend any alone time with Ty in a few days. Part of that is because I've been laying low with my parents. They seem to understand that our relationship is in a precarious place. I'm not willing to talk with them about things I'm thinking, like I normally would. It feels strange, because my father's entire job is to help kids through tough times. But he works with little kids, and this year my life seems more complicated than it used to.

And then there's the fact that I don't wholly trust Mom and Dad anymore.

I look over at Geoff Parsons, whose Hell House script is rolled up in the back pocket of his faded jeans. I know he's excited to have such a big part in the show, but I still can't help but feel he doesn't deserve to be in it at all. It seems the stuff between him and Dean has blown over for everyone but me. I haven't forgotten.

Tonight is the first casual Hell House rehearsal, and after a few minutes of vocal warm-up and prayer, we break up into our separate scenes. I go to the nursery, soon to be decorated like a medical clinic. Dean told me we're getting a real hospital bed that adjusts up and down so I can be sitting in an upright position, as if I'm giving birth. "It'll be more emotional if it looks like this could be a life-or-death scene," he said. I'll have fake blood all over my hospital gown as I scream in pain, both emotional and physical. He and the other prop guys have even figured out how to make a passable first-term baby out of raw hamburger meat, so I know the visuals will be amazing.

Right now, though, we don't have any props ready yet, so I

sit on top of a long table and pretend that it's a bed. Because it's the nursery, there are still toys all around the edges of the room. They'll be cleared for performances, but tonight they actually add something for me. The scene starts with the doctor dropping the fetus into a bucket as I scream and cry. Then I rock back and forth in the bed and say, "I killed my baby! I made a mistake . . . I want my baby back!"

It's a lot to jump into all at once, but I do my best. I think about Tessa, and the choice she might have made if she hadn't grown up in this church community. How regretful she would have been for her whole life if she weren't at Saint Angeles, ready to let her baby live and be raised by a family who's probably been praying for a child.

In the scene, the doctor—played by Randy Miller, who was always really good at that game Operation—just shakes his head at my screaming. But the nurse—that's Laura Bergen—she tells me firmly and somberly that it's too late. Laura Bergen is excellent at being firm and somber.

When my dramatic shrieking winds down, Skyler Gordon comes in as an angel, and she's holding the hand of one of the three younger kids who's been cast to rotate through the scene as the night goes on. Even though little kids can't be in the audience for Hell House, they're allowed to be in the show. Pastor Frist says they're often the most effective actors because of their innocence. Tonight, five-year-old Heather Jenkins is rehearsing with us. She's got brown curly hair and a giant smile that shows a big gap tooth. Pastor Frist tells her she's smiling too much when she delivers her line in my direction: "Mommy, why did you kill me?"

I'm supposed to start wailing at that, of course, but I can't help but smile back when she beams at me as she says it. After a few more times, she learns to do the scene more seriously, and on our last run through, my mind flashes to Tessa and her lovely, freckled face. What will her child look like at five? At least we'll have a chance to know. At least she's not committing another sin by going to a clinic like this.

Skyler Gordon ends the scene by telling me that it's too late for my baby to live but it's not too late for me to repent. As I lay dying, she reminds me, and the audience, that God is always forgiving if you're truly remorseful about your sins. The abortion act always gets the girls in the room weeping—and Skyler is really good at delivering her lines: "Though you have committed the sin of fornication before marriage vows, though you have chosen darkness over light, though you have killed your own child, there is hope. For these actions are in the past, and today, right now, you can choose to take Jesus's hand and start walking into a brighter future. Repent! And his arms will open unto you and welcome you into the Kingdom of Heaven."

She comes over to embrace me, and I scream out, "Lord, forgive me!" just before I die. That's supposed to show that you can give yourself up to God even in the last moments of your life—there is always room for faith and hope. When we're done, I shake Skyler off with a shiver and jump down from the table. We've been working on the scene for an hour and I'm tired, not to mention hungry.

I grab my bag and see Pastor Frist clasping Randy's hand. He slaps him on the back and says, "Excellent job, doctor!" Their synchronized laughter rings out loudly as they leave the room. I say good-bye to Laura, Skyler, and Heather and go out into the hallway to sit on the bench in front of the conference room where my dad's been rehearsing the Hell scene. I can hear the screaming through the door—it sounds like they're really getting into it. Dad can be truly scary when he plays Satan. He whispers in your ear things like "I know what you did," and "I've seen your every sin." Now that I think about it, it's probably even more creepy since he's my father.

I hear footsteps coming down the hall, and I look up to see Ty walking toward me. He's carrying a Subway bag with a sandwich and chips stuffed inside.

"Hey," he says, kicking my toe gently as he sits down on the bench beside me.

"What are you doing here tonight?" I ask with a smile. "I thought Hell House wasn't your thing."

"Well, Aunt Vivian's working late," he says. "I came by earlier and she asked me to go pick up some dinner for her."

He points to the bag.

"Sure," I say. "You weren't curious at all about the rehearsal."

"Maybe a little," he says, smiling. "I'm proud of you, Lacey."

"Thanks," I say, looking at him looking at me.

Just a minute ago I felt utterly exhausted, but now I feel energy racing through my body. It's like I can almost hear my heart fluttering, and I have to concentrate on keeping my breath even. This is what it's like when I'm next to Ty.

"I've been coming here a lot this week, actually," he says.

"Oh?" I ask, surprised.

"Yeah," he says, taking in my expression. "Don't look so shocked."

"Sorry," I say. "But I mean . . . what are you—"

"Just thinking," he says. "It's a really quiet place to do that sometimes, and the light in the sanctuary is pretty great around sunset."

"I know," I say, pleased with Ty. "It's nice that you feel comfortable here."

"Well, to be honest, when I came on Monday after school, I had another motive," he says. "But I found it so peaceful that I've found reasons to come back yesterday and today, too."

"Oh," I say. "What was the other motive?"

"I thought you might be here," says Ty. "I mean, if you had some things you wanted to contemplate or whatever."

"I've been busy," I say, flushed at the thought of him seeking me out. And then I think about how I don't really come to church to ruminate in the way Ty's talking about.

"You know," I say, considering this for the first time, "when I want to really think about something, I go to the woods. The breeze calms me down. And I like the way the light is softer there, muted by the leaves."

Ty raises one eyebrow. "Less of a church girl than I thought," he says. "That sounds downright alternative, communing with nature."

"It's not like that," I say. "I want to be close to God. I just think better outside, under His sky."

And when I say it that way, it sounds right, and true.

Ty smiles and nods. "That makes sense," he says. Then he adds, "Starla Joy's been here too."

"You mean in the sanctuary?" I ask. "After school?" Every day this week, she's told me how she has to rush home to help her mom.

"Yeah," says Ty. "She just sits in there. She likes the back row, but I prefer the light from the front. We haven't talked or anything, really, but it's nice to have someone to share the silence with."

And I wonder why Ty has so much to figure out when it's Tessa who got pregnant. It's not like he even knows the Minters very well, but he's acting like it's his own family who's in trouble. I want to believe he's sensitive, but I wonder if there's something more. Does he like Starla Joy? Doesn't he want to share the silence with *me*?

I shake my head to clear those kinds of thoughts. We're in church, talking about Tessa. I shouldn't let envy creep into my mind.

The conference room door opens suddenly, and a group of guys walk out, laughing loudly. Jeremy Jackson looks over at our bench, and I can feel Ty's body stiffen. I look Jeremy right in the eye, and his smile fades.

"Hi, Lacey," he says. "Ty."

"Hey, Jeremy," I say. Ty doesn't move.

Jeremy's eyes stay locked with mine for a beat, then he turns around and joins his friends in their raucous conversation as they disappear down the hall.

Ty and I look at each other then, and I wonder what he's thinking. I'm thinking that it doesn't seem fair for Jeremy to be hanging out, rehearsing for his role as a Demon Tour Guide, while Tessa is hidden away.

I say that to Ty, and he replies, "He's hurting too, he just doesn't know how to show it."

"How can you tell?" I ask, marveling at how generous Ty seems.

"I can't really," he says modestly. "I'm just guessing that that guy has a lot on his mind. He's not a robot, so he must be feeling something we can't see, right?"

"Hmm, maybe," I say.

Ty opens his mouth to say more, but I hear another sound.

"Lacey."

Dad's voice booms behind me, and the edge in his tone makes me stand up quickly.

"Hi, Dad," I say.

"Hi, Mr. Byer," says Ty, standing up beside me.

"I was just waiting for you—" I start, and at the same time Ty says, "I was just bringing Aunt Vivian some—"

We look at each other and laugh, but Dad doesn't crack a smile.

"Let's go," Dad says to me. "Your mother's got dinner ready."

He brushes past us without another word, and I follow him, glancing back once to shrug at a sullen Ty. I don't know what my dad has against him, other than the fact that he's a boy sitting next to me on a bench.

On the car ride home, I want to ask my dad what's going on, but the air feels thick around us. So I stay silent, wondering why, even though he's just a foot away from me, it feels like the two of us are really far apart.

Chapter Sixteen

. . . .

The next day after school, I go to the woods again. The weather's nice, and it's easy to get my homework done out here. Plus, I don't have to feel the strain at home, or hear Mom's sighs when I walk by her and up to my room without a word. Today, I tried to get Starla Joy to come too. Things at school have been intense for her, I know. Every day people are whispering, wondering about Tessa. I haven't asked her much—I'm waiting for her to come to me when she wants to share something—but I was hoping she'd hang out today, get some fresh air.

"Being cooped up in church asking forgiveness for the sins of your sister isn't productive," I told her. And when she wondered how I knew that's where she'd been, she seemed surprised to hear that Ty told me. She claimed she hadn't even noticed him in church.

Even though it's mean, that made me feel better—less envious that they'd been bonding without me. Truthfully, she has been a walking zombie this week. How can I blame her?

She wouldn't come to the woods though—I couldn't convince her. And so I settle onto the log with Dean, who's already there and reading *A Separate Peace* by the time I arrive.

"I always thought 'separate' was spelled s-e-p-e-r-a-t-e," Dean says.

"You've always been wrong," I say, pulling out a notebook and my graphing calculator.

"Whatever," he says. "I like this book though."

"What's it about?" I ask.

"Guys," he says. "Friendships."

I wait for him to explain more.

He smiles at me. "It might be about love too," he says. "I'm not sure."

I hear leaves crunching behind us, and Dean and I both turn toward the sound. Ty is high stepping his way over some low branches.

"What's up?" Dean asks.

Ty smiles and settles onto the stump across from our log.

"I heard the light was good out here," he says.

Dean looks over at me, and I start to blush. I'm glad Ty's here.

"Hey, man," Ty says, knocking Dean's knee and getting his attention. "I'm sorry about what happened today."

"Don't be," says Dean. "It was great."

My ears perk up. "What happened today?" I ask.

"Yeah, but you'll get it double tomorrow," says Ty.

"Worth it," Dean says, and they share a smile.

"Hello!" I shout, waving my hand in the air. "What happened today?"

"Nothing," says Dean, returning to his book. Then, under his breath, he says, "Same old stupidity."

I look over at Ty, but he's still focused on Dean.

I lean toward Dean and put my hand in front of his book so he can't read it. "Tell me," I say.

"It happens every day," he says. "Just jerks in gym."

"What do they do?" I ask, feeling indignant.

"They call me stuff," Dean says. "It's dumb."

"What do they call you?" I ask, wondering why Dean doesn't talk about this with me, why boys keep these secrets.

"Fat, lazy, flannel, painted-nail geek," Dean says, letting all the insults out in a rush.

"You censored that for Lacey," says Ty.

"I know," says Dean. "They don't really say 'geek.'" Then he smiles. "But today, Ty said something back."

I put my anger on hold as I look over at Ty questioningly.

"I just reminded everyone of kindergarten, when Geoff Parsons begged and pleaded to play Mary in the children's Nativity play," he says, affecting an innocent voice. "Your dad let him be a sheep, but he still kept trying to hold the baby Jesus doll."

"I remember." I snicker.

"He carried that funky Cabbage Patch Kid around for a week!" Dean shouts through his laughter.

"It was Laura Bergen's," I add gleefully. "Her mom had to ask Geoff's mom to make him give it back."

"I told him he has amazing maternal instincts," Ty says, slapping his knee and chuckling.

Dean tries to stifle a guffaw unsuccessfully. I haven't heard his loud, free laugh very much in the last year, but there it is. And it's so excellent that I keep giggling too. He leans forward and the log tilts with his weight shift, so both of us end up in the dirt. That just makes Ty laugh harder, so Dean reaches up and yanks him off his stump and onto the ground with us. We collapse into snorts again.

"What's so funny?"

Starla Joy, in a peacock-blue shirt, her favorite jean skirt, and bright red lipstick, is standing above us. Despite her attempts at dressing cheerfully, she looks stern and sad. But when we tell her the Geoff Parsons story, she smiles a little. And then she claps her hand over her mouth. Dean and I reach for her arms, pulling her down to the ground so fast that her silver bracelets jangle loudly. She falls with us into the leaves, and it's like the way we used to lie in a soft autumn pile and pretend it was a fancy feather bed.

There we are, four in the dappled sunlight. It feels like we're as close as we've ever been, and I wish things could stay like this always.

Chapter Seventeen

. . . .

"You're in a good mood," says Ty, sitting next to me.

"I am," I affirm, smiling up at him. His head is in the perfect spot to block the sun as he looks down at me.

It was nice to have an afternoon where we forgot about Tessa, just for a moment. It's not that I don't want to think about her, it's just that I wish I could turn back time and get the lightness of the past, even late summer, back.

There's one spot where the tightness in my chest doesn't ever bother me. I feel freer when I'm with Ty in Ulster Park. Up on that grassy hill we can say things to each other, talk about anything. Today we spread out the sleeping bag and I lie on my stomach, bending my knees and letting my feet kick in the air.

"Can I ask you about something?" Ty asks.

"Sure," I say gamely, wondering what he wants to know that needs to be prefaced by *can I ask*.

"The ring you wear," he says. "Is it—"

"TLW," I say.

"TL what?" he asks, laughing.

I sit up and take off the silver band, handing it to Ty so he can see the lettering on it.

"True Love Waits," I say. "It's a purity ring. My dad got it for me when I turned fifteen."

"So it's a sex thing," Ty says.

"Ew!" I say. "Did I not just say that my *dad* gave it to me?"

"You did," he says. "Which makes it extra creepy."

"Ty!" I shout. "Stop it."

"I'm just kidding," he says. "Sort of."

"Well, I think it's nice," I say. "It's a reminder that I've pledged to stay pure until marriage."

I feel a blush creep into my cheeks when I say the word "pure." No matter how comfortable I get around Ty, this subject makes me nervous. Maybe because of how much I want to kiss him sometimes.

"So did you take, like, an actual pledge?" asks Ty.

"Yeah," I say. "We all signed it."

"Who did?" asks Ty.

"Everyone," I say. "Me, Starla Joy, Maryanne Duane, Laura Bergen—"

"Not the guys?" asks Ty, holding the ring out to me.

"Guys too," I say, taking it back and slipping it on my finger. "But they don't wear rings."

"Ah," says Ty. He lies back on the sleeping bag with his hands behind his head and gets that smug look in his eyes, like he's purposefully making me confused about my purity ring.

"Well, the guys don't want to wear jewelry!" I huff.

"Lacey," Ty says, smiling at me, "I'm not trying to make you mad. I was just asking a question."

And that's the thing with Ty. He's always asking questions. The kinds that keep me up at night, wondering.

Today, though, he doesn't ask the question I expect him to. I keep thinking he'll ask if Tessa signed the purity pledge. She did, of course. And so did Jeremy.

Things between my parents and me aren't getting better. I've been spending more and more time in the woods with my friends. I feel safe there, almost back to normal, except when Starla Joy gets sad. It's hard to take because her personality infuses everyone around her—it's like her bright colors draw us in and repel us all at once.

Hell House rehearsals are getting more intense as September turns to October, but today is an off day. So Starla Joy and I are having girl time, without Dean or Ty, and it feels just like it used to . . . for a little while. We're down in her basement with popcorn and the DVDs to *Dawson's Creek*, this old show that has a really great love triangle.

"So you and Ty spend a lot of time together," says Starla Joy when one of the boring parent scenes comes on.

I look over at her and smile. I've been waiting for her to ask me about Ty. I haven't felt right bringing it up. For some reason it seems like we should be in mourning because of Tessa, and getting excited about a new relationship, or whatever it is, seems insensitive.

"I know," I say. Then I add, "I really, really like him."

"Do you guys still go to the old playground all the time?" asks Starla Joy.

"Maybe a couple of times a week," I say, being coy.

She raises her eyebrows at me and then wiggles them up and down.

"Starla Joy!" I throw a pillow at her. "We *talk* there. For hours and hours."

I can feel that my grin is Grand Canyon big.

"What do you talk about?" she asks.

"Our beliefs," I say. "Our dreams, our fears."

"Sounds like a philosophy class," she says.

"It's nice," I say. "It feels like real talking. Like the kind we do in church on a really good sermon day. The kind that makes me think about the world and my place in it."

"And when you're not talking, what do you do?" she asks with her evil Demon Tour Guide face.

"We share silences!" I say.

"Oh, Lacey, *boooring*," she says. "Are you telling me that Ty Davis hasn't kissed you yet?"

"He hasn't," I say. Then I think about whether I want to talk about this, and I realize that I do, I really do. So I say, "But I think he will soon!"

Starla Joy squees with delight and I join her.

"Girls, are you okay?" Mrs. Minter calls from upstairs.

"We're fine, Mom!" shouts Starla Joy. Then she whispers to me, "Tell me the minute it happens."

"I will," I promise.

"It sounds really sweet, Lacey," she says, smiling brightly. And then, just as suddenly, her smile fades.

That's been her thing lately—from smiles to distress in under two seconds. I know what she's thinking about.

"How's Tessa doing?" I ask.

"She's okay," says Starla Joy, picking at the blue cotton

blanket she's pulled up around her legs. "Saint Angeles isn't so bad."

"That's good," I say. "Is she, um, happy?"

"She likes it when Mom and I visit," says Starla Joy.

I know they've been going every weekend, even though it's four hours away by car, which must be nice for Tessa.

"But I think she wishes Jeremy would show up," Starla Joy continues. Then she purses her lips.

"He hasn't visited?" I ask, incredulous.

She shakes her head no.

"Not even once?" I ask.

"Nope," she says.

"That's not right," I say.

"None of the fathers are ever there," she says. "It's weird. The place is all teenage mothers and the women who help them out, like church volunteers and counselors."

"Does Tessa have anything to do while she's there, like during the week?" I ask.

"She has a tutor who gets her assignments from school so she won't fall behind," she answers.

"That's great!" I say, trying to make the tone of this conversation more upbeat. "I had no idea they did that."

"Yeah," says Starla Joy, not looking at me. "They also have art classes, and even a pastor on hand to talk to the girls there about why their decision is one made in the light of Christ."

"How awesome," I say. "That must really help her."

"Sure," says Starla Joy. "She'll come back to school next semester with all her work completed and some new oil paint skills, just like nothing ever happened."

"Cool!" I say enthusiastically, trying to be positive. But then

I realize my fake-happy energy isn't exactly matching Starla Joy's mellowness right now, and I get quiet again.

"Um, so is she feeling okay?" I ask, still glad that Starla Joy's opening up, even just a little.

"Physically, Tessa's fine," she says. Then she smiles a little. "We got to see a sonogram of the baby this weekend."

"That's so sweet," I say.

"It's a girl," says Starla Joy.

"Ooh, does she have a name?" I ask.

"I think that's the adoptive family's thing," says Starla Joy, her face darkening again.

"Oh, right," I say, feeling bad for bringing it up. "I'm sorry. I wasn't thinking."

"It's okay," says Starla Joy. Then she looks up at me and grabs my hand. "Lacey, listen, I don't want you to be scared around me."

"What do you mean?" I ask.

"I know everyone at church and school is afraid to talk to me about Tessa, like if they ask too much about her, they'll get pregnant too or catch some crazy slut disease," she says. Then she laughs ruefully before getting serious again. "She's still Tessa, you know. She's still my sister and not some monster."

"Of course," I say. "I love Tessa no matter what."

"I know," she says. "I just wonder what other people think. I hear them saying things about our family."

I look away, thinking about what my parents have said and the thoughts I've let enter my own mind. About Tessa, about her sin. But even in my confusion, I've always felt in my heart that this isn't about Tessa being a bad person or Starla Joy's family being somehow deficient.

I look back in her direction and squeeze her hand. She wipes away a tear that's crept into the corner of one eye, threatening her electric-blue mascara.

Then, as quickly as it came on, Starla Joy's vulnerability is gone. She smiles with her bright pink lips and laughs.

"Let's watch the episode where Pacey tells Joey he loves her!" she says, suddenly giddy.

"Sure," I say. "Cue it up."

That night, I lie in bed and stare at my glow-in-the-dark stars, the ones my dad and I put up there together when I was six years old. I mimed my way through dinner again, answering my parents' softball questions about whether my English quiz went well with a nod and a half-hearted smile. Well, it did go well, because I really liked *The Great Gatsby*.

And now, as I lie here with my iPod docked and playing my mellow playlist, I'm thinking about Saint Angeles. It's weird to me that it's a house of women, where the men just don't visit. I guess I think that Jeremy, who was raised within our church community, should be different. Even if the other fathers aren't there—maybe the ones who don't care about the girls or their responsibilities, or the ones who weren't raised with Jesus as an example—Jeremy should know better. We've been going to the same church all of our lives. Matthew 7:12 is one of the first verses we were taught in Sunday school: "So in everything, do to others what you would have them do to you." I bet he wouldn't like to be sitting there alone in Saint Angeles without Tessa.

The more I think about it, the angrier I get. Why aren't his parents making him visit Saint Angeles? I think about Pastor Frist's sermons about righteousness and spreading God's goodwill. Doesn't Tessa deserve some of that, too?

I fall into an uneasy sleep without dreams, and I toss and turn all night.

Chapter Eighteen

My parents have dropped the notion that I might find some new friends, thank goodness, but I've noticed that the Hell House rehearsal schedule is amped up this year—we're now doing four rehearsals a week, double last year's schedule—which leaves little time for me to have a social life. On my paranoid days I wonder if the extra rehearsals are designed to keep me under my dad's surveillance.

Both Dean and Starla Joy have their own burdens—Starla Joy with Tessa's situation and Dean with Geoff Parsons and his friends, who are ever present, no matter how much Ty stands up for him.

Somehow, though, I find time to meet Ty in Ulster Park. We haven't said it out loud—but it's a spot where no one really goes, so we can be alone.

We're here today after school, and I know my parents think I'm with Starla Joy and Dean. They never ask where I am, they just assume, and that makes it easier because I don't have to lie to them.

This afternoon it's a little cloudy and cooler—fall is definitely in the air.

"Starla Joy said her mom got three Tupperware bowls full of food yesterday," I tell Ty.

He laughs and picks a blade of grass. "That's the church ladies' way, right?" he asks.

"Yeah," I say. "It's nice, I guess. I just always wonder if they're giving, like, emotional support too."

"You mean culinary support isn't enough for you, Lacey Anne?" Ty asks, and he looks up at me with a sarcastic smile, like he understands what I mean.

"I just keep thinking about what God would want," I say. "I think he'd want people to do more than bake for the Minters."

"I'm sure he wouldn't want the behind-the-back talk Starla Joy has to deal with at school," Ty says.

"Exactly," I say. "Everyone seems so judgmental. And then they hug her in church and tell her they'll be there for her."

Ty breaks his blade of grass in two.

I stare at the swing set.

"It just doesn't seem right," I say.

"Have you talked about this with your dad?" asks Ty. "Maybe he can help out Mrs. Minter a little more or something?"

I look down at my fingernails, pretending to inspect the clear polish that's starting to peel. "He's caught up in Hell House," I say. Then I sigh out loud.

"You sound disappointed," Ty says.

"I am."

We're silent for a moment, and I feel like I should explain more.

"It's not that I'm disappointed in God," I say. "But there's something about the way people are acting in His name that isn't sitting right with me."

Ty nods like he understands, and I know he does. And I feel kind of bad saying it, but I'm also glad that there's this place, a place where Ty and I can talk without boundaries or parents who don't take our views seriously and change the subject.

I breathe a sigh of relief at having voiced a thought that a few months ago would have scared me to even think: I'm disappointed in the church.

The next day, I'm thinking about disappointment and Tessa and Jeremy and my father. My thoughts are swirling as I sit at my bedroom desk, and I get frustrated, trying to pinpoint a moment in time when things started feeling so off. I stare at my driver's license, wishing I could go back to that day. That was the day I first saw Ty—and he's what I'm looking at in the photo, not the camera. I blush at the memory. I imagined he was a mysterious stranger, but he's Tyson Davis. Sweet, funny, thoughtful Tyson Davis.

And I might go crazy if he doesn't kiss me soon.

I look back down at my math homework and erase the problem I just tried to do—I know the answer's wrong. I start to work through it again, but my thoughts keep wandering to Ty's lips. He puts his arm around me, looks for me in the halls and at church, basically makes it seem like he's my boyfriend in every way but one.

I shake my head to get Ty out of it, and I look back down at the penciled equation I've written, trying to focus. He *did* have that *Finding Purity* book . . . maybe he does think you shouldn't kiss before marriage. I know a lot of people who talk about how their first kiss will be on their wedding day.

There's *no way* I can wait that long.

I look at the clock—time for work. Math has to wait. I close my book and pick up my bag, shoving my blue ruffled apron into it. I've got the late-afternoon shift at Joey's. Mom and Dad don't like me working during the school year, but I convinced them that one weekend shift is good for my character.

It's also somewhere I can meet Ty without them acting weird about it. Because they don't have to know.

"Bye, Mom," I say, grabbing the Honda keys from the peg-board in the kitchen. We've agreed that I get the car for work, because I've told Mom that I don't get off until eight p.m. and it's getting dark by then.

I don't wait to check that she's heard me, I just go. I know she'll hassle me about what time I'll be home and whether Mel the cook can follow me to be sure I get back safely. It's like she thinks vampires come out at night around here or something.

When I get to Joey's, I spend extra time setting up the tiny table in the back corner by the window. It's the one where Ty likes to sit with iced tea and a book. He's been coming here for the past three Saturdays, and even though it's unspoken, I'm sure he'll be by again today.

Around five thirty p.m., like clockwork, Ty strolls in. Mel is out talking to Mrs. Patterson at her table, and I see him notice the smile I give to Ty as I lead him to the corner table, where I've put the best daisy in the center bud vase.

When we get back into the kitchen, Mel grins at me.

"What?" I ask innocently.

"Your boy's here again," he says, teasing me.

"He loves the way you brew that tea," I say, grabbing the plastic pitcher so I can pour Ty a glass.

Mel *humphs* and goes back to his barbecue, but I can tell he likes Ty. Everyone does, except for my parents.

Throughout my shift, there are only a few customers. Saturday's really not a big afternoon at Joey's, and everyone from school goes to the Starbucks in the next town over to hang out on Saturday nights, late night.

I try not to linger too much at Ty's table, even though I refill his iced tea after practically every sip. It's not like we're even talking much—we're just coexisting in this space—but it still makes me giddy. He's become one of my best friends. A best friend that I want to kiss. A lot.

By six, it's clear that this shift isn't going to get any busier. I head into the kitchen and give Mel my best puppy dog eyes.

"Okay," he says. "Go."

I beam at him in thanks and untie my apron. Then I walk over to Ty's table for one last refill.

I have two hours until my mom will even start expecting me home.

"I'm done!" I say to Ty.

"Let's go," he replies.

We take both of our cars and drive out to Ulster Park.

Even though I've told my mom that my shift lasts until eight p.m. on Saturdays, it really only goes until seven. It's a dangerous lie, because my parents know Mel, of course, but they trust me. That makes me feel half-guilty and half-confident in my deception.

This is the third Saturday in a row that Ty and I have spent the evening out at Ulster Park. We catch the end of twilight, when the sky gets that dusty filter and the fireflies flicker. We've mostly just been talking about faith, life—all these big questions and concepts that feel so new the way Ty looks at them. But tonight I plan to ask him why he hasn't kissed me. If I can get up the nerve.

Ty spreads his old sleeping bag on top of the hill in what I've come to think of as "our spot," in the same way that the fallen log in the woods is my friends' spot. This one, however, has romantic potential.

Usually, I leave a foot between us on the sleeping bag. Tonight I edge more toward Ty. In a burst of confidence I lean my head on his shoulder.

I feel his breath quicken but he doesn't push me away. We sit like that for a few moments, and then I say, "I like being with you."

It sounds so simple and innocuous on one level, but so forward and flirty on another. And his silence after I say it means that my own voice is echoing in my mind, taking on a hundred different interpretations and connotations and making me feel more insecure by the second.

Finally, Ty sighs and moves his shoulder from under my head.

I stare forward into space, not wanting to face him as he pulls his knees up to his chest and wraps his arms around them.

"I like being with you too, Lacey," he says. Which is the right thing to say, but the way he's all curled in a ball, like he's protecting himself from me, tells a different story.

"Okay," I say. And I'm so tired of us sitting here, talking about everything, things I don't even talk to my best friends about, that I turn to face him now with renewed energy, silencing the doubting voices in my head.

"So what is it?" I ask. "Do you like me, but you're not attracted to me? Or maybe you like Starla Joy? Or someone else entirely, like . . . ," and I think about how I saw Ty talking to Bore-a Bergen in the halls earlier this week, and I let out a small gasp. "It's not Laura Bergen, is it?"

He chuckles and shakes his head at me. "No," he says. "It's not Laura Bergen. It's not Starla Joy. And it isn't that I'm not attracted to you. You've got the prettiest face I've ever seen, Lacey Anne. And you keep getting prettier."

I look away from him now, embarrassed but also the good kind of nervous, because I can feel the electricity between us. And he just admitted to feeling it too, in his own way.

He reaches for my chin, bringing my eyes back to him and holding my face tilted upward like he did once before, but this time he follows through with what I expect—a kiss. It's soft and gentle, but I can also feel the longing within it. Tingles pass through my body and down to my toes, and I'm not sure I'm breathing.

When we pull back, I open my pale eyes and look into his bright blue ones. I can feel that mine are shining with happiness—this is what I've wanted—but I also want to see that feeling reflected in his. What I see instead is something more like sadness, or nervousness, or fear. I watch his gaze dart to the right as he straightens up.

"I shouldn't have done that," he says.

My heart sinks like an overweight fishing lure.

"It's okay," I say. "I wanted you to."

"Lacey, it's just—" he starts, and then stutters a bit. "You just . . . you don't really know me."

"I know you, Tyson Davis," I say, smiling at him, still hoping to savor this moment. "I know you love trains and know all about them, you always shared the glue, you add a packet of sugar to already-sweet tea, and you aren't quite ready for Hell House. It's really okay."

"You used to know me," he says. "And maybe you know who I'm trying to be. But there are things—"

The beams of two headlights flash into the parking lot, and we both turn to look. It's just someone turning around, but it breaks the moment.

Ty stands up and starts to gather the sleeping bag while I'm still sitting on it. I fall over sideways as he pulls it out from under me.

"Sorry," he says. "I have to go." He tucks the sleeping bag under his arm and leaves me stumbling after him, brushing grass from my jean skirt and fighting back the tears that are starting to sting my eyes.

Ty doesn't look back again, just revs up his loud engine and flees, like he's robbed a bank and needs to get away as fast as possible.

I stand in the parking lot, staring after him for a minute before getting into my car. A wave of shame washes over me as I sink behind the wheel, and when I get home and walk in the door, I drop the keys on the front table and go straight to my room. I text Starla Joy but she doesn't respond and I figure she has enough to handle without me whining to her. I consider calling Dean, but I'm embarrassed to talk about this with him.

A few minutes after I get home, Mom knocks on my door to offer leftovers, and I just shout, "I ate at Joey's. Doing homework."

She pushes the door open anyway, bringing in a cup of

butternut squash soup and a piece of toast on a tray. I sit up and try to look normal.

"Thanks," I say softly, hoping she'll put it down and go.

But she sits on the edge of my bed, staring at me like I'm a mystery.

"Are you okay, Lacey Anne?" she asks.

I want to tell her that I don't even know what's going on with me. I don't even know if I'm okay. But I just say, "I'm fine, Mom."

I take a bite of the toast to confirm it, and she looks down at her hands.

"You know that you can talk to us . . . ," she starts. "To me, I mean, about Tessa. If you're upset or if there's something you need guidance about."

I stay quiet.

"I know your father is normally the one who gives advice," she says, turning her head away from me.

And I realize it's true. It's always been Dad who's there with a sermon-ready lesson or a parallel Bible story to explain away any confusion I've had in the past. But this feels beyond him.

I suddenly feel a rush of affection for my mother, and I reach over the tray to take her hand just as she stands up to go. She doesn't turn around, doesn't see that I reached out, and I take my hand back.

"Thanks for the soup," I say, as she opens the door to go.

"You're welcome, honey," she says quietly, slipping out into the hallway.

When she closes the door, I wonder. If I had taken her hand, if she had stayed . . . would I have told her about my feelings for Ty?

I lie back on my bed and stare at the ceiling, at my

glow-in-the-dark stars. I feel a tear trickle down the side of my face as I wonder what happened. I got what I wanted—the kiss. I thought it was what I wanted, anyway. I guess I only wanted it if Ty wanted it too.

And he didn't.

In the morning I wake up feeling like a slut. I don't even like thinking of that word, but it's what I hear in my head when I think about what I've done. How could I have pressed Ty into kissing me? He obviously didn't want to. He obviously felt sorry for me after I practically threw myself at him. Maybe he even thinks I've gone out there with him to Ulster Park—alone and on a *sleeping bag* for goodness' sake—just so we could hook up.

The thought makes me sick to my stomach, and I wait until the last minute to get in the shower and get ready for church. When they ask me about me missing breakfast, I tell my parents that I'm tired from work, and I grab an apple to eat as the three of us head out the door.

When we walk into the sanctuary, I look down at the floor until we reach our row. I don't want to catch Ty's eyes, not after I shamed myself so wholly last night. I'm unable to concentrate on Pastor Frist's sermon, and when I stare up at the stained-glass windows behind the pulpit, all I see are muted colors and messy imperfections in the glass.

We have a Hell House rehearsal today, and I'm thankful to see Ty and Miss Moss exit the building after the service. That means there's less chance I'll run into him this afternoon. I wonder if he's avoiding me as much as I'm avoiding him.

As Mom and Dad get caught up in their Sunday greeting

rituals, I pass Starla Joy's row and nod. She follows me out the back doors and around the side of the church facing the woods.

"What happened?" she asks. "Lacey, you look awful."

"I feel awful," I say. And then I just come out with it: "Ty and I kissed last night."

Starla Joy's eyes open wide and she grabs my arm. "You did *not*!" she says.

"We did."

"And are you happy?" she asks, dropping her grip.

"Well, I was," I say. "But then he ran off and said, 'We shouldn't have done this' or 'This was wrong' or something like that. He just left me there."

"In Ulster Park?" asks Starla Joy.

"Yeah," I say. "It was a total disaster. He didn't even say hi to me today."

"I saw you barrel past everyone with your head down when you walked into church," says Starla Joy. "I don't think you gave him much of a chance."

"Still . . . ," I say. "He's the one who kissed me and then ran away like I'd shot at him."

Starla Joy sighs and looks at me seriously.

"Do you think he's super conservative and thinks that kissing before marriage should be off limits?" she asks.

"That's what I wondered!" I said. "Before the kiss, I mean."

"And after?" Starla Joy asks.

I flash back to his warm lips on mine, the way our bodies folded toward each other as our mouths touched ever so gently.

"I don't think so," I say, starting to smile. "He was too into it."

"Until he stopped," she says.

"Yeah," I say, smile fading. "Until then."

"And he just bolted?" she asks.

"Yes," I say. "It was bizarre. It was like we'd committed a major crime and he had to flee the scene."

"I know what you should do," says Starla Joy.

Relief floods through me, because she always knows how to handle things, and she's so nice to focus on my problem, even for just a few minutes.

"What?" I ask gratefully.

"You should talk to him and ask him why he freaked out," she says.

"What?" I say. "No, no, no. I don't want to ask him that. I already put myself out there to kiss him and he ended up running away from me like I was a serial killer."

"It's the only way," she says firmly.

"Lacey Anne!" I hear my mom's voice calling from around the corner, and I peek my head out.

"Rehearsal is starting," she says.

"Okay!" I shout. "Coming!"

"You can't know until you ask," says Starla Joy, pressing me. "And you have to ask him straight, without the *ums* or *wells* or *uhs*. Those get in the way."

"I'll think about it," I say. I link arms with her as we walk back into the sanctuary for prayer warm-ups. "Thanks," I whisper, hugging her arm close to me.

"Anytime," she says back. I see her look down at the ground, her heart heavy with a sadness much greater than mine, and I wish with all my being that I could make things better for her.

Chapter Nineteen

. . . .

On Monday at school, I decide to be brave like Starla Joy wants me to be. I wait by Ty's locker, and when he walks up and smiles it just comes out, almost easily.

"I like you."

"I like you too," he says. "I'm sorry."

"Can we just—" I start.

"What if we—" he says at the same time.

We laugh and both look down. Then Ty catches my left palm lightly and looks at my hand. He fingers my ring.

"I guess I'm afraid of temptation too, Lacey Anne," he says.

I blush, not sure what to say. "People deal with it," I mutter.

"We could have rules," says Ty. He sounds like he's half-joking and half-serious.

"Like what?" I ask.

"We'll make them up as we go along," he says. "But kissing should definitely be on the list."

Then he leans in and gives me a quick peck on the cheek. We *are* in the hallway after all.

I nod in agreement and float to my class, feeling his warm lips next to my skin all through first period.

For the rest of the day, I'm walking on air. I had a library lab for chemistry and we were supposed to be doing online experiments, but instead I took a million quizzes, trying to figure out if Ty is the one for me. I can't stop thinking about what my skin feels like when he touches me. The moment our lips met replays in my mind a hundred times—I acknowledge that I might be insane. I never thought I'd feel like this, like those girls who can't hold back and keep thinking about a guy. But when I get home I plan on replaying movie kisses on YouTube to make sure I'll do it right when it happens again. I can't seem to get Ty out of my head.

After school, I see my dad's Taurus station wagon in front of the main building as I walk out with Dean. My first thought is that I'm in trouble somehow. Strange that that's where my mind goes these days.

But then I see a broad smile across his face, and I peer behind him through the window of the car and spy two fishing rods in the backseat. I walk up to him warily.

"Hi, Dean," my dad says.

"Hey, Pastor Byer," Dean says back.

"You'll have to come over soon and help me work on the model some more."

"Oh," says Dean. "Uh, sure." He hasn't been over to see my dad since before school started.

Then Dad turns to me.

"I got the boat from Mr. Tucker," he says. "Mom knows we're going to try to catch dinner."

I raise my eyebrows in a question. It's rare for him to want to take me out on a school night. Fishing is usually a summer thing, maybe weekends, but never Mondays.

"How come?" I ask.

"Well, your Saturdays are taken up at Joey's, and I just felt like getting out on the water with my little girl," he says. He looks more like my father than he has in a few weeks. There's no tense line for a mouth, just a wide, open smile.

I shrug. "Okay," I say, moving toward the car. "Dean, I'll see you tomorrow."

"Cool," he says, already making a beeline for the student parking lot to meet Starla Joy. I suddenly panic that my dad found out that Ty and I kissed—that someone saw us in the hallway!—and now we're going to have to have a sex talk on the boat, where I can't escape or close a door or even really turn away from him. My heart races.

But then I realize that Mom would be the one to have that talk with me, and I calm down. Sort of.

When we get out to Otto Lake, the water is glassy and sparkling. It's still warm out for fall, so the sweater I wore to school is sufficient, and Dad brought my bright yellow rain shell for me too. I put it on so I won't get splashed.

We pick up the old motorboat and put Dad's tackle box in the middle. My light rod is pretty easy to set up, and we use artificial lures—not real live worms or crawlers. Even though I can unhook and clean my own fish, squirming bait has always made me squeamish.

By the time we get to our favorite spot—Satterwhite Cove—I'm feeling renewed. It's pretty hard not to see God everywhere when you're in the middle of nature. Sure, the engine is kicking up small waves and making noise, but soon we stop to coast and start casting out our reels. The late-afternoon sunlight dances on the surface of the water as the waves lap up against the boat in a rhythmic beat, and I feel a sense of peace settle over me that I haven't experienced in a while.

If Dad is trying to win points with me, it's working. Out here, we're father and daughter, two fishermen with the same thoughts and goals.

After four casts, I feel a bite, and I jerk my rod up to hook whatever's nibbling on my bucktail jig. I start reeling it in but I can tell it's a small one, and when my dad sees it's a tiny sunfish he says, "First catch of the day is still first catch of the day."

He brings it up to the side of the boat and gently unhooks the little guy, who promptly swims away.

I remember the first few times I tried unhooking my own fish. Dad made it look so easy—his hands were so gentle. But for me, it was tougher. The hooks have barbs; they're made to stay attached. You have to remove them quickly, so the fish aren't out of the water too long. And sometimes it's bloody.

I lost a few fish in the beginning—they died while I was trying to release them—and it always used to make me tear up. But my dad would say, "Ashes to ashes, dust to dust. They are a part of the circle of life."

Once we sat where we could see the floating dead body of a fish we couldn't keep—it was a tiny one and in my six-year-old mind I imagined that the fish, too, was probably a six-year-old, starting first grade at its "school." (I took most words literally back then.) I had hooked it and worked to get it free, but it died while I was trying to untangle it, and I started to cry.

Dad sat there with me as we watched it bobbing on the surface of the water—and soon birds came over and started picking at the fish. Finally, a big bass jumped up and swallowed it in one joyous gulp.

I guess that might have been traumatic for some kids, but for me it was proof that my dad had all the answers. It's okay that fish die, because they provide food for other fish, who then get a hearty meal. One fish's death may even save another fish's life with its sustenance. It's all in God's plan.

Every question had an answer back then, and my dad could shed light on any doubting darkness that crept into my mind.

"Lacey Anne," Dad says, speaking in soft tones like we tend to do out on the lake. "I wanted to talk to you."

"Okay," I say, concentrating on my cast. I fling my rod forward and get a good distance—about twenty-five feet. The lure drops into the water and I reel in a tiny bit of line. Then I wait. Nervously.

"I want to apologize," says Dad.

I look at him now, surprised.

"Your mom and I shouldn't have suggested that you rethink your friendships," he continues. "We know that you and Starla Joy have been close since you were babies. And we both love her, too, and Dean as well."

Ty's name is noticeably absent, but I nod anyway. In recognition, in acknowledgment of the apology. In silent thanks that he doesn't seem to know about the kiss.

"We were scared," Dad says then, and when I look over at him his face is shining like it does when he speaks to the children's group at church. Like he's being honest. Like he's imparting wisdom. "This business with Tessa hits close to home, and we didn't want you to get caught up in it. But we went about it the wrong way, and I'm sorry. We both are."

Dad's rod starts to jerk then, and he smiles as he reels in a keeper—it looks like a three-pound smallmouth. I set down my rod to help him unhook it, and it flops around the boat for a minute before Dad picks up the bonker and clubs it twice. The fish twitches, then stops moving. We throw it in the bow of the boat, where there's a container for catches.

Dad casts out again, and I pick up my rod too. I want to acknowledge his apology, even though the moment has passed.

"Thanks, Dad," I say.

"Thank you," he says back. "You're becoming an expert at unhooking."

"No, for the other thing," I say.

He smiles at me. "It's important for us to talk, honey," he says. "To be honest with each other. It's harder now that you're sixteen, but it's a priority."

I look out at my line and reel it in a little more, wondering if I should open up to my dad now, wondering if he'll be able to talk to me the way he used to, when things were more simple.

"Dad?" I say, and my voice is so soft that I hardly hear it myself.

"Yes, Lace," he responds.

"How come some people suffer for their sins, but others just get to sin and then go on living their normal lives like they didn't do anything wrong?" I ask. And I know it sounds cryptic, but I'm not sure how to broach the specifics with my dad. I've tried before, at breakfast, but never really gotten the words out.

"You're talking about Tessa?" he asks, cutting through my vague question.

"And Jeremy," I say, feeling suddenly brave. "She's sent away, dealing with her choice every day in a very real way. But he's just going to school, rehearsing for Hell House, hanging out with his friends. It doesn't seem right."

"I know this has been on your mind, Lacey. But it sounds like you're presuming an awful lot," says Dad. He reels in his lure and casts out again before he continues. "It's plain to see how Tessa's affected because there's the physical manifestation of pregnancy, and also because she's gone. But how do you know that Jeremy isn't going through something on the inside that we just can't see?"

"That's what Ty said," I say.

"What?" Dad asks, his head jerking up quickly.

"Ty said that too," I say again. "That Jeremy might be feeling things he isn't showing."

"Well, yes," says Dad. He seems flustered at the mention of Ty, and I want to ask him what's wrong, why he doesn't like Ty, but he continues and I don't have a chance. "It's important that we remain supportive of Jeremy in this hard time. He should be taking his mind off of things, and normal activities, like Hell House, will do just that. He's got a bright future, that boy. With basketball and—"

"And what about Tessa and *her* bright future?" I interrupt, feeling my skin prickle a little. "We should remain supportive of her too, right?"

"Of course," Dad says. "That goes without saying."

"Does it also go without *doing*?" I huff. I turn away from Dad to face the water.

"Lacey Anne, I've been very kind to Mrs. Minter, as has the entire church community," Dad says. "Did you know that Pastor Frist helped facilitate a spot for her at Saint Angeles? It's not easy to get in there, you know."

I frown and jiggle my rod.

"I've also seen to it that the Minters' fridge is full of church-baked casseroles as they face this difficult time," Dad adds.

"It's good to know that even *girls like that* get the church's culinary support," I say sarcastically, and I realize I'm quoting Ty. I no longer want to accept my father's apology. What he's saying seems so unfair, so one-sided. How does he not see that Jeremy gets to do *everything* he wants to do while Tessa is locked away like she's contagious until after she has the baby?

"I thought we were understanding each other," Dad says. "I've told you I'm sorry and that you can continue your friendship with Starla Joy. The more we thought about it, the more your mother and I figured that you'll be a good influence on her. We've raised you well—you're a smart girl. Church is a wonderful resource, but for a rebellious teenager without a father, peers have a big effect too. You can help her set her life on the right path."

"Oh, well, thanks for the permission to choose my own friends," I say, turning back to face Dad. "Starla Joy doesn't *need* a good influence, by the way. She's already a wonderful person on her own, father or no. And you're right, I am a smart girl. I'm smart enough to see the unfairness, Dad. Tessa and Jeremy aren't being treated equally."

"Lacey, when a girl is pregnant it's impossible to treat her equally to a boy who is not," my dad says, his temper flaring. "Besides, a boy has desires that girls don't understand—it's more her responsibility to keep this from happening."

"Are you blaming this on Tessa?" I ask. Anger rushes through me so quickly that my hands start shaking and I reel in my tackle with a force that rocks the boat.

"Of course not," Dad says, steadying his own rod and turning back to the water. "But generally, the girl does have more self-control, Lacey. That's just the way it is—that's nature, as much as the birds in the sky and the fish in the sea. Don't forget that."

I flash back to Saturday night with Ty. I don't think my dad knows *anything*.

I unhook my lure. "I'm ready to go home," I say. I can't believe my father—my rational, patient, kind, devout father—is saying this. And I can't believe it's true. I won't believe it.

Dad doesn't argue. We're at an impasse. And when he took me out here trying to fix something between us, I'm afraid he broke it even more.

Chapter Twenty

I close my eyes and hold out my palms, waiting for the spirit to move me.

There are just three weeks left until Hell House officially opens for a three-night run, and today at the Youth Leaders meeting we're watching a couple of the scenes in a run-through. Because I'm in the Abortion scene, I haven't yet had a chance to catch the others or see what people are doing with their characters.

We're in the sanctuary doing the warm-up, which includes my dad and Pastor Frist leading us in our personal prayer language. I go through the motions with everyone else, but I'm not feeling it. Plus, Ty's here with us today, and I already know that he's not exactly into personal prayer. I haven't had a chance to be alone with him since we basically talked about the fact that we should definitely kiss again soon.

I feel guilty for not participating—I know how silly and small-minded my worries about Ty are, but they feel so big right now.

I whisper to God inside my head. *Lord, please forgive me for not channeling your power today. I'm confused about how best to serve you, and I'm unsure of my own thoughts and feelings. But I still deeply love you and wish to do the right thing. Help me to walk in your footsteps with grace and humility.*

It's a prayer I think up on the spot, but I'm pretty proud of it as it runs through my mind. I wish I had some paper to write it down. I think even Dad would like it, though we haven't talked—aside from the required niceties—since the lake. We came home that night and cooked up Dad's fish, each having a little bit. Mom sparkled with conversation about how proud she was of her two fishermen, and she talked so much about the new novel that Mrs. Harrison had loaned her that I'm not sure she even noticed Dad and I hardly saying two words to each other.

Even with my eyes closed, I can feel that tonight during personal prayer everyone is energized. I peek a bit and see that Geoff Parsons has sweat pouring off his brow. I wonder how someone so mean can be so feverish with the holy word.

Suddenly, I hear a loud cackle, and Geoff yells, "Get the devil out of Dean Perkins!"

My eyes snap open and I see that Geoff's eyes are rolling up into his head, and he's pointing at Dean, who looks confused as he breaks his own personal prayer language to see what's going on.

Some people are still chanting and swaying, lost in their connection to God, but others have stopped to watch Geoff, who's now heading toward Dean, arms outstretched.

"Get the devil out!" he shouts again, as he grabs Dean's shoulders and starts to shake them.

Dean looks completely bewildered, and I turn to the pulpit to see what Pastor Frist and my father are going to do, how they'll handle this. They're both still chanting, still enrapt in their holy connections.

No one's ever broken personal prayer like this, and Geoff Parsons looks possessed by a spirit. I study his face, sweaty and contorted into an angry mask, eyes still rolling around in his head, showing more white than I care to see. It's frightening.

And then I look at Dean. He's surprised, he's shocked, he's clearly afraid. I glance back up to my father, who still looks lost in his personal moment. But someone has to do something. Didn't he hear Geoff yelling?

Then a strong, authoritative voice fills the sanctuary. "Stop it!" Ty shouts. All eyes turn to him as he jumps over a pew to reach Geoff, prying his hands from Dean's shoulders. He restrains Geoff, who shakes Ty off with a fierce arm swipe, but Ty positions himself protectively in front of Dean, who falls into the pew. He sits there, his breath coming out in short gasps. Starla Joy and I run over to Dean to make sure he's okay.

I look around and see that everyone has broken their personal prayers, thanks to Ty's booming voice. They're all staring. Not at Geoff, but at us: me, Starla Joy, Ty, and Dean.

And in this moment, I don't care.

"What were you *doing*?" I snap at Geoff Parsons.

He holds his hands up in front of his chest, smiling. "I was just joking around," he says with a chuckle. "Dean knows it's all good, right, D?" he flicks a nod at Dean, who glances up for a second and then lets his eyes hit the floor again.

I look up at my father, challenging him to intervene, hoping he won't tolerate bullying in church.

"Now, boys," Dad says, as if Dean or Ty had some

involvement in this too. "Personal prayer time is sacred. It's important that we all concentrate and gear up for Hell House together."

"In other words," says Pastor Frist. "Leave the outside world outside, and come into this House of God without grievances or even casual jokes."

"I'm sorry, Pastor Frist, Pastor Byer," says Geoff, looking contrite. "I was honestly just kidding. You know, trying to get us in the mood for the devil tonight."

Dad chuckles and puts on his Satan voice. "The devil hates an exorcism!" he booms. People start laughing, and the tension in the room breaks.

How can Dad make this into a joke? I stare up at him, my eyes burning. I want to shout at him and tell him he's being unfair, he's being *cruel.* But I'm afraid he won't hear me. Dad doesn't meet my gaze and I let my eyes drop.

I see Ty shake his head and walk out of the sanctuary. He's the hero of this moment in my eyes, but no one follows.

"Now," Dad says, clapping his hands together. "Let's take five and gather back here to watch our opening scene together. Dean, you come with me and we'll talk about how the props are coming along."

"Are you okay?" Starla Joy whispers to Dean as people start to disperse.

"I'm fine," he says, straightening his shirt and heading toward my father. I can see that he's still visibly shaken though.

I'm hoping they'll talk, that my dad will give Dean some strength, a lesson from the Bible to hold onto about how jerks are all around, but Christ faced them down and came out a better man because of his trials. I know there are parts of the Bible like that. Dad used to quote Jeremiah 29:11 whenever I had a bad day at school: "'For I know the plans I have for you,' declares the Lord, 'plans to prosper you and not to harm you, plans to give you hope and a future.'"

Starla Joy and I walk out into the hallway together and we head into the ladies' room, checking under the stalls for feet before we exhale.

"What was that?" she asks.

"I have no idea," I say. "Geoff seemed possessed! And then it was a joke?"

"He shouldn't be joking about the devil being present in Dean," says Starla Joy, turning on the water at the end sink and wetting a paper towel.

"It's vicious," I say. "And sacrilegious."

"What does he have against Dean?" she asks. "We've all known Geoff Parsons since we were in the church nursery."

"They used to be friends," I say. "Remember? Back in elementary school."

"Yeah," says Starla Joy. "What is Geoff's deal?"

Starla Joy starts reapplying her pink lipstick and I lean on the sink and look at my face in the mirror. My eyes look tired, with puffy bags and dark circles underneath them. I'm having trouble sleeping lately.

"Can I borrow some of that?" I ask Starla Joy, thinking maybe a hint of pink will wake up my dreary face.

"Sure," she says, handing me the lipstick tube.

I apply a little, but I end up wiping most of it off. Bright makeup always looks clownish on me for some reason. I sigh.

"Come on," I say. "Let's go see what Gay Marriage is like."

When we gather in the sanctuary again, everyone has calmed down.

"What did my dad say to you?" I turn to Dean, hoping he'll tell me that my father imparted some helpful wisdom.

"We talked props," Dean says. "He wanted to go through the checklist and see when things are getting delivered."

"Nothing else?" I ask.

"When we were done, he did say something," Dean says.

"What?" I ask, still hopeful.

"He said that if I had the devil in me, he'd know," says Dean. "I wasn't sure what he meant. Like, I couldn't tell if he was in character as Satan or if he was being Pastor Byer."

I hold my breath for a second, thinking about what Dean just said. There are moments lately when I don't recognize my father either.

Ty hasn't come back. We're moving into a Hell House rehearsal tonight, so he probably would have left early anyway, but I have a feeling he cut out because he's upset. My leg bounces up and down. I'm still irritated by Geoff's outburst, but as we all sit down to watch the opening scene of Hell House, I see that Dean is back to normal. He even looks excited to watch the show. I guess if he's okay, I'm okay.

Mr. and Mrs. Sikes are the couple in the first scene. They're the only adults in the production besides my dad as the devil and Pastor Frist as Jesus. They walk down the aisle, and beside them is Jeremy Jackson. Through the whole show, his role as the Demon Tour Guide is to be both a guide for the audience and the devil's mouthpiece, so Jeremy says things to exacerbate the situation.

Paul Rich plays the officiant in this scene, and as he whispers the traditional marriage vows to the gay couple, it's Jeremy's job to overpower Paul's voice, yelling over the officiant with his own version of the vows. He turns to the Sikeses and says, "Do you promise to fornicate unnaturally with dozens of people in a direct challenge to God's will, forsaking all that is normal and sealing your fate for a painful and horrific death?" His eyes glow as he recites the lines, and everyone can see that he'll be one of the favorite tour guides this year—he's feeling it.

I think about Jeremy in this role that condemns promiscuity—as if he hasn't had a lapse of his own—but I push the thought out of my mind. This isn't about Jeremy and Tessa, it's about two men marrying, which is wrong in a different way.

The actors move from the pulpit up onto the sanctuary stage. On the left is a bedroom scene with red fabric draped over lamps. "We've got leopard print sheets coming for the bed," whispers Dean.

"How do you know what sheets gay people like?" asks Starla Joy.

Dean frowns and says, "I was guessing. I want every scene to have the right atmosphere."

I think leopard print gets the point across that it's a wild person's bedroom, so I see where Dean is coming from. In any case, the props aren't ready yet so we're just watching Mr. and Mrs. Sikes hug and run their hands up and down each other's backs in the left corner of the sanctuary, which to be honest is pretty gross, even though they're married. They're old.

On the right side is another part of the set. It's a hospital stretcher, and after a brief blackout for the actors to change positions, Mrs. Sikes stretches out on the stretcher, moaning in pain. She's supposed to be dying as she reaches for Mr. Sikes.

It's hard to think of them as a gay couple while she's wearing a flowery blouse and khaki shorts, but when we do the real performance, she'll be in a suit and wearing a fake mustache, just to be clear.

As she lies on the stretcher, the Demon Tour Guide speaks. "This is Adam. He thought his homosexual lifestyle was fun and *fabulous*, but now he's dying of AIDS." Mrs. Sikes, playing Adam, writhes on the bed, screaming in agony. This is just a rehearsal, but she's really getting into it.

A chill passes through me and I turn to look at Dean and Starla Joy, who are both riveted to the scene.

Jeremy finishes his final condemnation of the marriage by saying that the couple has been "believing the born-gay myth" and calling their wedding a "matrimonial abomination."

"Whoa," I say, letting out a breath. This script is more intense than usual.

"Yeah," says Starla Joy, sharing my emotion.

"I think I'll try to find an old disco ball for the bedroom," says Dean, his eyes lit up as he turns to us, only props on his mind.

Starla Joy leans in to me and whispers, "You can't say he's not dedicated."

We both laugh and stand up and head into the choir room, where we'll see the second scene of the show—Domestic Abuse. We crowd along the back wall and when all of us are crammed into the audience space, we watch a drunk husband beating his screaming wife. The way that Graham Andrews and Susan Casper play it out, it's hard to watch. She's crying and cowering, while he picks up a chair and throws it down at her. Of course, today he just pantomimes doing that, but Dean says that on performance day we'll have a chair that's made to break up into pieces and can easily be put back together for each successive presentation. And since the scenes are played out about twenty times per night, we'll get our money's worth out of that prop even though it cost like fifty dollars.

Everyone claps at the end of the domestic violence scene, and we split up into smaller groups so we can rehearse our own parts. We'll see the rest of the show later.

I've gotten good at my lines—and I can conjure up emotion on cue now. Plus, I'm still managing to draw angst into this scene through my thoughts of Tessa. It's amazing to be in this show, to finally have a movie moment of my own, where all eyes are on me.

I cry real tears during the last run-through, and after I finish my screams and the room goes quiet, I see my father standing in the doorway, beaming.

When I jump off the table to head out, he walks up to me and gives me a hug. "I'm so proud of you, Lacey Anne," he says.

"Thank you," I say coldly, brushing his arm off my shoulder as we walk out of the room. I'm still mad at him, and I feel frustration welling up inside of me because I want to hug him back. I want to share this Hell House experience with him fully. I tell myself I'm going to try to talk to him again, that we must have misunderstood each other out on the water. And that he *would* have stepped in to defend Dean today if Ty hadn't said something first.

But then I see Geoff Parsons in the parking lot. My father gives him a thumbs up and a "Great job tonight, Geoff," and I feel a rush of anger. I hate seeing my father so buddy-buddy with him—acting like he's done nothing wrong—and I feel something harden in my heart.

Chapter Twenty-one

Corner of Oldham Road at 11, I text. I don't know what Ty will think—probably that I'm dying for more kissing, which I am—but really, right now, I need his ear. And I know he'll be there.

I keep my shoes off until I get outside the house. I've never snuck out before, but it's surprisingly easy. Maybe that's why it's easy—my parents have no reason to keep their eyes or ears at attention. I'm a good girl. Or I was anyway.

As I walk down the driveway, I check the time—five till eleven. I would never have thought of going out this late last year. I walk three blocks up to Oldham. Ty is already there, engine off, waiting.

"Hey," I say as I get in the car.

"Hi," he says back.

I close the passenger door gently and say, "Go anywhere."

He drives to Ulster Park, but this time we don't get out of the car. It feels late, it feels risky. The fireflies aren't out and laying down the sleeping bag in this deep darkness would be strange.

As soon as he cuts off the engine in the empty parking lot, I expect him to turn to me and ask why I called him, what I want. Instead, he rolls down his window and leans his seat back to almost horizontal, putting his right arm behind his head and closing his eyes.

I stare at him for a minute, taking in his light eyelashes and full lips, then letting my eyes run over the hard muscles in his arm that peek out from his short-sleeved yellow polo. His skin looks soft and still so sun-kissed from summer that I have the urge to reach out my hand and run it over his bicep.

But I stop myself, remembering to hold back, and then I roll down my own window and recline my seat to match his angle. When I put it back it far enough, I can see the moon through the windshield. It's almost full, bathing the car in a white glow. The air is silent except for the bugs singing around us.

"I may be the devil," I say to Ty.

His laugh cuts through my serious statement.

"You certainly are not," he says.

"I'm serious," I say, sitting upright. "I feel so much anger lately. And today . . . today, it felt even darker. Like . . . hate. Actual *hate* for Geoff and Jeremy."

Ty doesn't say anything. His eyes don't widen in surprise; his jaw doesn't drop in disbelief. He keeps on leaning back, eyes closed, and I think I see a hint of a smile playing on his lips.

"Ty Davis, are you taking me seriously?" I ask.

He opens his eyes and grins at me.

"Of course," he says. "Always."

"Well, even if you're not, I still want to talk to you," I say.

I can talk to this boy. I can talk to him like I've never talked to anyone. Not my pastor, not my best friends . . . not my father.

I'm afraid to show spiritual weakness in front of anyone in town, especially those closest to me. We've never questioned anything or anyone related to the church. You just don't *do* that in West River. But here's Ty, a bit of hometown, a bit of the bigger world. Somehow I think he understands.

So I open up to him again. I tell him how I'm confused about my parents' unwillingness to discuss Tessa or Jeremy with me, how I'm so angry at Geoff Parsons for tormenting Dean while being a member of Youth Leaders and a star of Hell House, and how Pastor Frist's sermons are echoing more and more hollow with every passing Sunday.

"And today, when Jeremy was saying his lines about having sex recklessly, I couldn't help but think of how *he* did that," I say.

"How did I miss a reckless sex scene?" asks Ty.

"No!" I say, swatting his arm. "It's the gay marriage scene. I know that makes it different—they're talking about gay sex so it's not the same as with Jeremy and Tessa, but—"

"I thought you said that sins were sins, Lacey Anne," Ty says, tripping me up with the words I said this summer.

"They are," I say. "But regular premarital sex is one thing and homosexuality is just . . . different."

I shudder, thinking about men kissing men, or really about Mr. Sikes kissing Mrs. Sikes, which is almost as icky.

Ty looks at me, silent.

"I mean, being gay and having lots of sex is like a double sin," I continue, sensing that he's not seeing my point. "Because you're not married, so you can't be making love in a holy way, and you're also going against nature by doing it in a gay way, so you're sinning twice."

I smile, satisfied with my mathematical explanation.

"What if you live in Vermont and you *can* get legally married if you're gay?" asks Ty.

"We don't live in Vermont," I say. "And around here, gay sex isn't the same as premarital sex between two normal people. It's immoral. And gay marriage isn't legal."

"But it *is* in some places in our country," Ty says. "And you at least have to admit that the morality of gay marriage is open to interpretation. Unlike, say, the morality of child abuse. Can you imagine some states legalizing that?"

"No, but it's not the same thing," I say.

"Ah, but your earlier logic says it is," says Ty. "Hell House shows one scene after another—Gay Marriage, Domestic Abuse, Abortion, Suicide, Cyberporn—and it puts them all on the same level."

"Well, they're all bad," I say.

"And we're back to this circular conversation again." Ty sighs.

"Leviticus 20:13 says 'If a man lies with a male as he lies with a woman, both of them have committed an abomination,'" I say.

"Lacey," says Ty, sighing a little and looking exasperated. "I'm not gay, but even *I'm* tired of hearing that verse come out of the mouth of the church."

"Well, it's in there," I say.

"So is the subjugation of women, vengeance, and the murder of children," says Ty. "It's an amazing book, and it has tons of good lessons, but it's also got some pretty messed-up passages."

"Like what?" I ask.

"Leviticus 20:9," Ty says. "If anyone curses his father or mother, he must be put to death."

"Well, it's all in how you interpret things," I argue. "That's really just an extension of honoring your father and mother."

"Okay," says Ty, smiling at me now. "I'm glad you're aware that there are different interpretations and not everything in the Bible is *literal*. I knew you were a smart one."

"Ty!" I shout, exasperated.

"I'm joking, Lacey," he says. "I am. Can we just stop talking about this, though, for right now?"

"Okay," I say quietly, wondering if I've offended Ty somehow. Maybe he has a gay cousin or something. I'm only saying what I believe.

"Do you think I'm becoming a bad person? That I've fallen from grace and that's why there's all this confusion in my head?" I ask. And when I say that sentence out loud, I feel a sting of fear, like maybe it's possible.

Ty stays quiet for a moment, and I wonder if he's going to say yes, that he does think I'm losing my path in the light with all this doubt I'm feeling. Maybe I shouldn't speak it out loud, maybe I shouldn't show my fear to anyone, not even Ty.

But then he answers.

"Lacey Anne," says Ty, "the God I know welcomes questions. He welcomes doubts. He welcomes criticisms of His Kingdom when things aren't just or fair. He rewards people who can see clearly enough to right wrongs. That is definitely what you're trying to do, in your own way."

I smile. What Ty just said sounds like something my dad might have told me when I was younger and I asked if I'd go to hell for stepping on an ant or chasing a bird with my bike. It was okay, *I* was okay. So why doesn't the church make me feel that way anymore? Why does it take a boy in a car at midnight with the seats all the way down?

I lean back and look up at the moon again, relaxing into my

confusion, feeling content, feeling accepted, feeling understood.

After a few moments of silence, Ty speaks. "Have I told you how much I adore you?"

Well, that just floors me. After I confess to having hate in my heart, that I might be on the path to the devil, he tells me he's into me. Surprised as I am, though, I don't want to mess up this second chance at something more.

"No," I say. "But I think I gave you a really good opportunity to do that once."

"You're right," he says, rising up and leaning on one elbow, facing me. "I blew it."

I sit up then too, and look into his eyes, my attraction to him almost palpable. "No," I say. "You didn't."

"What were the rules?" he asks, teasing me.

"I don't think we have any yet," I say, feeling breathless.

"Oh, good," he says.

He leans in then, and I make sure that it's *he* who kisses *me* first. We don't have two cars; he can't run away. And besides, as strong as that first kiss—*my* first kiss—was, this one is ten times stronger. As I feel his lips move with mine, I'm keenly aware of everything around me. The moonlight pools on our faces, the bugs sing a midnight hymn, the leather of the car seats squeaks as we move closer and press our bodies together.

I feel a warmth radiate through my chest and down to my thighs, working its way through my body. I gasp as the sensation gets stronger. His lips are the purest touch I've ever felt.

"Lacey Anne," Ty says, pulling back for a second. "You make me feel brave."

I smile and kiss him again. I don't know what he means and

I don't think too hard about what we're doing here. If I am lost, I don't want to be found, at least not tonight.

When he drops me off around the corner from my house, Ty holds my hand and looks into my eyes. "Good night, Lacey Anne," he says, leaning in for one more kiss. I feel like everything has changed.

I walk home and slip off my shoes at the front door. I'm careful not to let the lock click as I enter, and then I pad softly up to my bedroom.

I lie down, but my body is buzzing with energy. It feels almost holy, like when we speak in our personal prayer languages. I don't know how I'll ever fall asleep. And yet somehow I start to drift off. As I'm fading into dreamland, I think I understand how Tessa could have made a mistake with Jeremy, if she ever felt like this.

Chapter Twenty-two

On Wednesday after school at Hell House rehearsal, I let go during personal prayer warm-up. I allow the energy to flow through me, and I hear myself shout while my body jolts and jerks. The movements feel like they're coming from inside my soul, and my awareness almost completely leaves the room.

I remember this connectedness, this nearness to God. I've always loved how it's made me feel. And now, even in my confusion, I bask in the glow of His love. I know it's there for me, no matter what my thoughts. Because He is there even for those who question Him, even for nonbelievers, even for sinners. Ty reminded me of that.

I pause for a moment and I hear my father's personal prayer language—the way he gives himself up to God so willingly, so passionately. I know things can't be right when we're at odds like we are. I know I must have misunderstood things he said to me, I know we can get back to the place where we see things the same way. I pray for that, as I feel God's love warm the room with all of us together, sharing this moment.

When we break to rehearse our individual scenes, I make a quick stop at the ladies' room. Through the window I can hear the strains of Geoff Parsons's Suicide scene happening outside. I haven't seen it yet, and I'm intrigued by what I hear.

When I leave the bathroom, I hear Pastor Frist call out, "Lacey! We need our Abortion Girl in here," but I ignore him. I walk straight to the back exit and outside toward the staff parking area, where the suicide scene is being staged.

Geoff Parsons is sitting on the hood of our Taurus. I almost forgot we were using it in the show. He's holding the prop gun my dad showed us earlier this summer, and it looks very, very real.

"Lord, I'm worthless and useless," he says, and it stops me in my tracks. His voice is shaking. I feel the wind kick up and blow my hair around my face, and I shiver a little.

"My parents tell me I'm a waste of space, I don't have any friends. I have no talents, Lord. I'm a loser, I'm a loner, I don't deserve to live." Geoff Parsons is riveting. He looks devastated, he looks broken, he looks nothing like the bully in the sanctuary who took Dean roughly by the shoulders. And somehow he looks more like a real person, more like himself.

As I hear him say his lines, I feel tears well up inside me, and I start to see why he has to have this role. Why he can't be thrown out of Hell House. Why the work that he's doing by starring as Suicide Boy is bigger than his bad attitude.

The door opens behind me and I hear Pastor Frist call my name again. "Lacey," he says. "We're needing to start your scene."

I take one more look at Geoff, who's still totally in character and putting the gun up to his head. Then I turn and follow Pastor Frist back inside.

* * *

I think about Geoff's scene all day on Thursday. I had no idea he could bring that kind of emotion, that much pain, to the part of Suicide Boy. I've never seen anyone play it that way, and I'm wondering if there's more to my dad's defense of Geoff in this role.

Mom was right when she said Dad is always the one who gives advice—and his door has always been open to everyone, especially me. So why am I running away from trying to understand his point of view? I have to talk to him.

After school, I visit Dad's office at the church. The door is open a crack and I start to knock, but I see that he's in the corner by the window, reading aloud from next Sunday's children's sermon. "Proverbs 17:27," he says. "'A man of knowledge uses words with restraint, a man of understanding is even-tempered.' And so what does that tell us about the times when we're upset with others? How can we peacefully resolve even the little things that happen each day, like when an older brother or sister gets on your nerves?"

I stand in the doorway for a moment, not wanting to disturb him. As I listen to his voice, I close my eyes and remember what it was like when I thought he knew everything, when I thought he almost *was* God. His pitch rises and falls with the rhythm of the lesson, always inflecting perfectly to convey the message of the passage he chose.

It's easier when my father and I are in sync, it's safer when I believe he can do no wrong. I want to believe that he knew what he was doing—and that it was the right thing—when he didn't punish Geoff for bullying Dean. I take a deep breath and I choose to believe in my dad.

"Lacey Anne?" He stops reading and I open my eyes to find him facing me with a smile.

"Hi," I say. "I want to talk to you."

I tell him about what I saw in the suicide scene—that Geoff Parsons is truly meant to be in Hell House, that I know he's not being punished because he is God's voice in that scene, because he will save a lot of souls with his passion.

"I understand," I say.

He folds me into a hug, and I squeeze back. When I heard the words coming from my mouth, part of me hesitated and felt unsure, but the hug from my father feels so good that I let go of the doubt. I'm so happy in this moment. I want the trust I have in my dad to be strong again, I want to know that he does have reasons for doing what he's done with Geoff. He's thinking of the bigger picture of Hell House, the one in which Geoff Parsons is a tool for saving souls.

That night at dinner, Mom, Dad, and I sit down to pray.

"Lord, thank you for bringing this food to our table so we may enjoy time as a family and the sustenance of you, our God," my father says. "We thank you for another glorious day. For good friends, long chats, and the understanding that comes between fathers and daughters when they do your holy work together. In Jesus's name we pray. Amen."

"Amen," echo Mom and I.

We dig into big platefuls of spaghetti, talking excitedly about Hell House and how great this year's performance will be.

"Have you seen Ron Jessup in the Cyberporn scene?" Dad asks.

"No!" I gasp. "I've only seen Gay Marriage, Domestic Violence, and part of Suicide."

"You should walk through it all this week, Lace," Dad says, so animated that he's talking with his mouth full. "We'll have

Laura Bergen rehearse Abortion Girl so you can get the whole picture."

"That would be great," I say.

"Can I have a sneak peek too?" Mom asks.

"Sorry, Theresa," Dad says. "Creatures of Hell House only, I'm afraid."

They both laugh and I join in, happy to be smiling with them again. I want to believe that Dad is working toward something larger than my friends and I can see. I know Dean and Starla Joy will understand—we're putting on the most incredible Hell House this town has ever experienced.

The next day, I meet Dean, Starla Joy, and Ty in the woods. I have to tell them about Geoff, about why he has to be in the show no matter what. I want to explain; for my dad, for myself. I feel like if I say it out loud and my friends affirm my feelings, I'll be able to shake this shadow of doubt that still lingers in my head.

"You guys, I have to talk to you about something," I say, once we're all situated on balanced logs. "I had an epiphany about Geoff Parsons, I think. Or at least a serious realization."

"Did you realize that he's a jackass?" Ty asks. "Sorry, Lace, but he deserves a J-word."

I can't disagree, but I think back to seeing Geoff in his scene, the pain in his eyes that looked so real out in that parking lot.

"No," I say, staying calm and trying to figure out how to talk to them about this. "I think I realized that he's human and that he deserves a little understanding."

"What?" Ty asks, looking disturbed.

Maybe it wasn't a good idea to bring him out here.

"Lacey, he picks on me in *church*," says Dean, speaking softly as he drags a stick in the dirt by his feet. "School is one thing, but I thought that church was different. Like a safety zone. Like I'm on base in a game of tag."

"It should be like that," I say, not wanting to hurt Dean.

"Not that that guy has the right to pick on you anywhere," Ty says.

"No," I say. "Of course not."

"And to do it so publicly, during personal prayer time," Starla Joy says. "It just seems . . ."

"Bold," Ty says. "Geoff Parsons hasn't been punished; he hasn't had to answer for anything at all."

"He can't just keep doing this," says Starla Joy, sticking to the topic at hand. "Lacey, have you talked to your dad?"

"A little," I say. "I mean, not exactly about that, but—"

"Why not?" Starla Joy asks.

"I saw Geoff's scene last night," I say. "The Suicide scene."

"Too bad that real-looking gun isn't a *real* gun," Ty says. I look up at him harshly, and he says, "Kidding, kidding."

Then I turn back to Dean. I take in his black-markered nails and his baggy black sweatshirt, and I can't see his eyes under his asymmetrical hair.

"So how was it?" asks Starla Joy. "How was the Suicide scene?"

I take a breath. "It was amazing," I say. "Like Geoff knew that character and his pain inside out."

"He probably does," Dean says. "Even in first grade I remember thinking that Mr. Parsons was pretty much a giant bastard." He looks at me. "Not that I thought in those terms back then."

I can tell by the look in Dean's eyes that he's wondering how to feel about Geoff Parsons. Wondering if his pain grants him some kind of pass. I remember my father telling me that Geoff's going through a rough time at home, which could mean anything. Or nothing. I wasn't really listening when he said that—I was upset about Dean—but after seeing him act out such raw hurt, I can tell that he knows what pain feels like.

"There's something else," I say finally, pretending like I'm on a stage, about to make a big speech. "Something bigger."

"What is it?" asks Starla Joy.

"I think we're focused on the day-to-day of Hell House right now," I say, purposefully not addressing Ty. "So we can't see the larger picture."

"Believe me, I know every scene and the position of every lamp and table," says Dean. He smiles and I see a hint of his normal self again.

"Very nice, prop master," I say. "Beyond that, though, we have to remember the true purpose of this outreach. I think that's why my dad has been so permissive with Geoff."

I see Ty shift in his seat out of the corner of my eye, but I don't look at him. I'm talking to Starla Joy and Dean now—I'm not sure Ty will understand.

"You guys, Geoff is *really* compelling in the Suicide scene," I continue. "It's like he grabs the audience—even me, and I was mad as heck at him!"

"He must have really gotten to you to make you near-swear," says Dean, and I smile back at him.

"He did," I say. "I think when people walk through Hell House his scene is going to shake their souls."

"Like he was shaking Dean's shoulders?" Ty asks sarcastically.

I glance over at him for a moment, and I flash back to our

night at Ulster Park. I felt so close to Ty in the darkness, but in the light my confusion seems weak. It's the church and Hell House that have been my whole life, not Ty. He's not my audience right now. Dean and Starla Joy are listening to me, and I know they'll understand where I'm coming from.

"You're saying it's for the greater good," says Starla Joy.

"Right!" I say. "If Geoff's scene is a linchpin for people, one that's going to convince them that Jesus is their Lord and Savior and they are going to walk through this performance and recommit to Him, then we need Geoff in the show. And no matter if he acts like, forgive me, a major jerk outside of Hell House, Geoff Parsons is going to save some souls!"

"You sound like your father, Lacey," says Ty. I ignore his warning tone and keep looking at my friends.

"I hadn't thought of it that way," Starla Joy says.

"I hadn't either, until I saw Geoff with that gun to his head," I say. "I almost melted to the floor."

"It was that intense?" asks Dean, peeking through his veil of dark hair and looking right into my eyes.

"Yes," I say honestly.

Starla Joy exhales. She looks over at Dean.

"For the glory of Hell House, I shall put aside my Geoff beef," he says, holding up his arm in a power fist.

He breaks up laughing, but I know I've won him over. I smile and reach in to hug him.

"Wait till you see him in the scene," I say, getting excited.

Ty scoffs with a snort through his nose, interrupting me.

"Are you *serious*?" he asks, sounding disgusted.

"What?" I ask him, leaning back from Dean and crossing my arms over my chest.

"You guys think that because he's a good actor he doesn't have to be a good person," says Ty.

"That isn't it," Starla Joy says. "Maybe you don't know because you've been gone for so long, but it's important for Hell House to be amazing."

I nod in agreement.

"It saves lives," I say, uncrossing my arms and reaching out to Ty.

He pulls away. "It's extreme," he says.

"We understand that feeling," Starla Joy says. "Pastor Frist has told us that the media and some people misinterpret what we're doing, but it all comes down to saving souls."

"Yeah," Dean says. "It's not like we don't know that it's shocking. I'm shaping hamburger meat into the form of Lacey's baby for a prop!"

The three of us laugh then, but Ty doesn't even smile. He looks hard at Dean. "Do you hear yourself, man?" he asks softly.

"I'm joking around," Dean says. "Come on."

"Remember what my dad said to you that first day?" I ask Ty, interrupting them. "*You've gotta shake 'em to wake 'em?* It's really true."

"Kids get adults talking to them all day long about what they should learn and how they should be," Starla Joy says, jumping in. "But Hell House is *our* chance to show people our own age what the consequences are if you don't accept Jesus into your heart. And it's shocking—it has to be so they'll pay attention."

Ty doesn't move, and now he's not looking at any of us. I wonder if we're losing him, if I'm losing him.

Then Ty turns his face toward us, still not meeting

anyone's gaze. His own blue eyes look a little teary, like he's fighting back a strong emotion. But his mouth is hardened and angry.

My heart aches because I know I've probably encouraged Ty's doubt with my own. I never should have shared that with him. The devil waits for doubt and then makes it spread and fly like dandelion seeds on the wind.

"Lacey," Ty says, turning to me, "I thought you were opening up. I thought we understood each other."

I feel Starla Joy and Dean staring at me, wondering what Ty means. I can't tell them that I, too, have had doubts about the House of Enlightenment, my father, and Pastor Frist.

"I understand that you're lost right now, Ty," I say. "And we're here. We're always here to help you come back to true believing."

I grab Starla Joy's hand, and she grabs Dean's. The three of us stand there, facing Ty together.

But Ty turns and walks into the shadow of the woods without another word. Starla Joy, Dean, and I stand there for another few seconds. I have the urge to go after Ty, but I don't want my friends to wonder what I was opening up to him about. I don't want them to think my faith is wavering.

"I hope he sees the light and love that I'm trying to send his way," I say. "I hope he feels it."

"I'm sure he does," says Starla Joy.

Dean says that he should get going, and we separate then, heading back to our own houses.

I sit through dinner with my parents, bowing my head for prayer and smiling at all the right moments. It feels good to have the tension between Dad and me out of the way.

But later, as I lie in bed and look up at my stars, I let myself think about Ty and what happened this afternoon. The closeness I've felt to him is real, and so were the doubts I shared. But they were clouded by my own self-involvement; I wasn't seeing the bigger picture. Right?

Chapter Twenty-three

A few days go by where Ty doesn't show up at school. It's like he's hiding from the world. I'm not sure if he's still upset with me or if he feels ashamed or what. But I'm determined to talk to him. I know he's a believer deep down; I know he's good.

After four unanswered texts, he finally replies to the fifth and agrees to meet me at Ulster Park on Saturday after my shift at Joey's. I'm anxious all day—I spill iced tea on Mrs. Sharp's silk flowered blouse, I get four orders mixed up during the lunch rush, and I burn my fingers on the hush puppy fryer when I forget to grab a rag to take them out of the hot oil. After that, Mel lets me leave early.

"You're doing more harm than good today, Lacey," he says. "Must be all those Hell House rehearsals. I hear it's gonna be a whopper this year."

"You got that right," I say, smiling. I'm glad I've thrown myself back into the performance without reservation. I can see things from all angles now, and I realize that I'm working for the greater good. I just have to convince Ty of that too.

I take off my apron and head to the car. I figure I'll get to Ulster Park a little early and wait. But when I drive up, the red BMW is already there. Ty's leaning back in his seat and the radio is blasting an old Rolling Stones song through the open windows.

I walk up to the driver's side and lean in. "Hey," I say.

Ty starts. "Oh! Hey!" he says, smiling and laughing at his own jumpiness. "I was really feeling the classic rock for a minute there."

I laugh at him and move aside as he opens his door, relieved that it already feels easy between us, that he isn't acting mad.

When he steps out of the car and stands up, I give in to the urge to hug him. I put my arms around his waist and rest my chin on his shoulder. I close my eyes and stand there for a minute, until he wraps his arms around my shoulders and holds me back.

When we break apart, he looks more serious, and he goes around to the trunk to grab our sleeping bag. We set it up on the hill without talking, just going through the motions.

I keep a paraphrase from the book of James in my head: "Let every person be slow to speak, quick to listen." That's how I want to approach this day. I want to listen and really hear Ty. Because I know we're on the same side. I can feel it.

We sit for a few minutes in the shade. The leaves have turned now, their summery green changed to fall's brown. I take a few deep breaths, slowly and quietly, hoping Ty will go first. But I asked him to meet me here, after all. I guess I should start.

"So why haven't you been in school?" I ask, avoiding the hard part.

"I just had to do some thinking," Ty says. "You know how school gets in the way of that."

He smirks a little and I grin back.

"Yeah," I say. "School hasn't exactly been easy this year for any of us."

"Especially for Dean," he says, looking at me.

"Yeah," I say, hoping we don't have to talk about Geoff Parsons again.

I can feel Ty looking at me intensely now. It's like the right side of my face is heating up under his gaze. "Do you get it, Lacey?" Ty asks, his tone getting harder. "It's like Dean's never going to be able to be himself in this town."

"Dean's himself," I say. "He doesn't conform. He's always been a little weird, but in a good way. I mean, look at his nail polish!"

I laugh again, trying to lighten the mood, but Ty's done smiling.

"He's *trying* to be himself," Ty says. "In little ways, like with the nails or his hair or even the way he dresses in all black. It's all these parts of him trying to get out, but here they're all stuffed up inside of him."

I remember that Dean and Ty have a friendship too. That they hang out and play video games, and they went to see the new slasher movie together with Graham Andrews when Starla Joy and I deemed it too bloody for us. What have they been talking about?

"What do you mean?" I ask. "Do you know something about Dean?"

"I don't know anything about Dean that anyone with any common sense wouldn't wonder," says Ty.

"Do you think Dean is gay?" I ask. And I'm surprised when I hear the word come out of my own mouth. I've never asked anyone that, never said it out loud. It gets hurled at Dean sometimes, as an insult, a word that hurts. People here don't always get that he's different so they try to assign a label. But now that I'm asking, I'm not sure how I feel about it, if it's attached to my friend for real.

"I don't know," Ty says. "And that's not the point anyway, Lacey."

"Well, it's a pretty big word to throw around!" I say.

"I didn't throw it around," Ty says. "You did."

He's right, but he knows he planted the seed in my head.

"But did he say something to you?" I ask, looking up at Ty curiously.

"Lacey Anne, this isn't for us to talk about," he says. "It's Dean's business, and I have no idea. But the thing is, in this town, I don't think he'll ever know."

"What do you mean?" I ask.

"I mean that if he *is* gay, or questioning, or whatever, he'll never have a chance to find out," Ty says. "He'll squelch that part of himself because he'll see himself as evil. Because you all see it as evil."

"That's not true," I say. "Hate the sin, not the sinner."

"So you wouldn't hate him for being gay unless he actually 'acted gay'?" Ty asks. "If he never did anything 'wrong' by your standards, could you still be friends?"

He uses air quotes when he says "acted gay" and "wrong," and I don't like how he's making me sound like a zealot.

"The born-gay myth is pervasive," I say. "But homosexuality is a choice people make, and it's a choice to sin. Dean would never make that choice, because he's a good person who lives his life with God."

"Are you quoting a pamphlet?" Ty asks.

He looks at me with such disappointment that I turn my eyes to the grass so I don't have to see his face. The truth is, I *am* quoting what I've learned in church. Not a pamphlet, but my father and Pastor Frist for sure. They've always been the voices in the back of my head. I try hard to find my own words so Ty will know what I believe.

"Even if he did make that choice," I say, thinking about Dean possibly being gay, possibly exploring that world, "I know he would come back to the church."

"And you would forgive him," says Ty, sounding distressed.

"Yes!" I say. "We would welcome him home."

"As long as he gave up the gay lifestyle," says Ty, "and denounced who he is."

"Do you really think he's . . . *gay*?" I whisper it this time, almost convinced now that it's true.

"No," Ty says. "I don't know. I don't think he knows. But I'm his good friend and I want him to be able to be who he is, either way."

"Oh my gosh," I say. "Dean might be gay."

"Lacey, don't get caught up in that," Ty says. "It isn't what I wanted to say. I was just using that as an example of your 'bigger picture.'"

"What do you mean?" I ask.

"The church," Ty says. "I just . . . I have these doubts."

"I know, we've talked about doubts," I say. "And I've had mine too—you know that better than anyone else." I think about how to phrase what I want to say, and I feel like I'm in a class, discussing big thoughts and ideas, trying to get my head around it all. It feels exciting.

"The doubts are just because of these tiny things," I start again. "Things in our own lives that we're caught up in because we're sixteen and self-involved."

"Now you're quoting *my* father," Ty says.

"Well then, he's right," I say, smiling again, urging Ty to see things my way. "We're worried about the day-to-day drama, but God's got the whole universe on His mind. Like you said—it's the bigger picture. Even our Hell House isn't a huge part of that plan, but it's much, much bigger than the trivial things going on at school with Dean. Or even Dean being gay." I can't help but smile uncomfortably. "Ty, seriously, do you think he is?"

"Lacey," Ty says, staring mock sternly at me. "I'm trying to talk to you right now and you're stuck on that. It was just an example."

"Okay, go on," I say, stifling my nervous giggles.

"With Tessa, then," Ty says, "is it trivial that everyone at school talks like it was her fault alone that she got pregnant, like *she* sinned and Jeremy somehow didn't?"

"No one thinks that," I say, though I know they do. And I was fighting with my father about this very thing.

I shake my head to clear my thoughts—this isn't about Tessa. I'm trying to stay calm, almost like I'm channeling one of Pastor Frist's sermons, because this moment feels important.

"Okay," I say. "Maybe some people do say that about Tessa. But God has a bigger plan—He doesn't have time to care for each of our issues individually. That's why some unfair things happen in this town . . . I mean, that's why people *starve* sometimes. And kill.

There's a higher power at work, and there's not time for every issue to come out right."

"And it's our job to work on this higher level with God instead of paying attention to the individuals right in front of us, the ones we can care for and comfort now?" asks Ty.

He's so good at this—at talking and throwing ideas back at me. He reminds me of my father right now. I feel exhilarated and frustrated at the same time. I want to hold my own.

"It's our job to bring people to God," I say. "So that *He* can care for them and teach them how to act in His image."

"Well, Geoff and Jeremy are in the House of God all the time, but they sure don't 'act in His image,'" says Ty.

More air quotes.

"Well, it's probably harder for some people than others," I say. Then I smile. "Or maybe Geoff still wants to play Mary like he did in kindergarten."

I nudge Ty, and his lips turn up a little bit but he won't give me a real smile.

"I'm kidding," I say. "You remember joking around?"

Ty smiles then, and I can tell he's picturing Geoff carrying around that Baby Jesus doll.

The air feels lighter around us for a moment, but then Ty frowns again.

"Lacey, this is serious," he says.

"Ty, I'm trying to understand you," I say, sighing.

"I know," he replies. "It's just that there's so much you don't know."

"I may not know a lot about the world outside of West River yet," I say. "But I know *you*. I know you're a good person." He turns his head away from me but I can tell that he's listening.

"I know you think Hell House is extreme," I say, trying to get the conversation going the way I want it to. "You're right—and it's meant to be. That's how we get people to understand how important having Jesus in their lives is."

"Lacey Anne, there are other ways," Ty says.

"'Others save with fear, pulling them out of the fire,'" I say, quoting Jude.

"Stop coming at me with other people's words," says Ty. "I want to hear *your* words. What do *you* think? How do *you* feel?"

"That *is* what I think," I say. "Those words tell the real truth of how I feel, without my own self-involvedness confusing me. That's what the Bible's there for. For me to lean on when I get in my own way."

Ty looks at me and his eyes go sad. His mouth slacks into a disappointed line.

I replay what I just said in my head. "That's what the Bible's there for. For me to lean on when I get in my own way." Sometimes I wonder why I don't trust my own thoughts. Should I be more brave? More confident, like Ty?

Before I can express any of this, though, Ty speaks.

"You're not the person I thought you were," he says. Then he stands up and walks away, leaving his sleeping bag with me.

I'm alone in Ulster Park, and I sit there for another few minutes, thinking about what Ty said, thinking about Dean, thinking about Tessa, thinking about God. I've always had these words, other people's words, in my head. They've reassured me, they've guided me, they've helped me choose the right path so many times. The Bible leads me, my pastor teaches me, my father reassures me.

But where are *my* words? No one's ever asked for them before. Ty is the first person to wonder what *I* think, deep down. How *I* feel. I thought I knew, but now I'm so confused.

How can I love this boy? He asks me questions and wants real answers from deep inside me. He challenges me and fights with me.

He kisses me. He makes me think outside myself. And maybe deeper inside myself too.

Did I mention that he kisses me?

I wonder how much the kissing scrambles my brain.

I watch the sun streaking in bright pinks and oranges, and I wait until it's dipped below the horizon before I get up to go home.

Chapter Twenty-four

Ty isn't in school on Monday, and I consider showing up at his house after classes—I'm not giving up on him—but then Dad calls a special Monday night Hell House rehearsal. We spread the word through our texting tree; each of us has to text two other YL members. He puts in a few understudies—one for me in Abortion, one for Graham Andrews in Domestic Violence, one for Ron Jessup in Cyberporn—so some of the primary cast can walk through and see the effect of the scenes from the audience's perspective.

Starla Joy offers to be the Demon Tour Guide for the night, and I'm so proud of her as she gets into the role. Usually, the demons are all guys, so it's a big deal that she got this part. She's breaking boundaries. I make a mental note to tell Ty about that aspect of the show this year, how it's progressive.

Gay Marriage is still powerful—though I cringe a little bit knowing that Ty feels the way he does about the issue, and I can't help but let my mind wander to Dean again. I look over to where he's watching. His hands are tucked into the pockets of a black sweatshirt, but his hood isn't up, at least. His new haircut has been growing out, and I know he's taking a little teasing because of the asymmetrical thing—the standard around here is pretty close cropped. But I've always been proud of Dean for being who he is. I don't like thinking that he might be hiding something. I push that thought from my mind. Ty said himself that Dean was just an example. He's not really . . . he can't be.

After Mrs. Sikes takes her dying breath—which I think is a little overacted, to be honest—Starla Joy leads us into the choir room.

Domestic Violence is even better now that Dean has the breakable chair prop ready. He's been using the art room at school to put together a lot of the props, and he painted the chair bright red to make it stand out in the white-walled room.

Cyberporn is hard to watch because the understudy, Brian Crosby, has to act really degenerate and simulate touching himself. "That's right!" yells Starla Joy, egging him on. "Your perverted desires will lead you straight to hell, and you won't be able to log off from what Satan has in mind for aberrations like you."

When we get to Abortion, Starla Joy starts the lines that people hear in the hallway, on the way into the nursery, where my scene is staged.

"You've seen movies and read books about *young love*," she growls. "I want you to believe in that! I want you to believe in that feeling, that rush of sick pleasure that goes through your body when you're touched by impure thoughts!" Her voice is getting louder now, and she's practically yelling at us. I hadn't heard this lead-up to my scene performed, and I flash back, guiltily, to the night Ty and I were kissing in his car.

I wonder if Starla Joy is thinking of Tessa and Jeremy, of the way their relationship has gone. There *is* young love, isn't there? It isn't always wrong and dirty. Half of our parents were high school sweethearts. I try to catch her eye, but Starla Joy is too far gone. She's in character, and she's playing it well.

"Are you ready to see the *slut?*" she shouts, spit flying from the corners of her mouth. "Are you ready to witness a *whore* making a *choice?*"

I feel my chest tighten a little, and when we walk into the room, I see that the hospital bed has arrived. I watch Laura Bergen say my lines. "It's my choice!" she's screaming. "It's my choice!"

"That's right," Starla Joy says, and now her demon voice is in full effect. She's rasping and snarling. "Kill your baby. Sin and belong to *me*! It's your *choice*."

She hisses, and I can't see anything of my friend in her eyes. She's transformed. It's a little shocking to see her this way. She's always been bolder than I am, but I had no idea she had this kind of dramatic energy inside of her.

Watching the action from this side is intense. The doctor, Randy Miller, is running around while Laura lies dying on the table. Dean has a new kind of fake blood this year that he promises looks completely real. It will be dripping down my legs as I slowly die from the procedure. I mean, not me, Abortion Girl. Seeing Laura play the role makes me all the more determined to do it justice. She's screaming, but it sounds softer than I want it to—I'm going to shriek like a banshee when I'm in that hospital bed.

Then there's the drug scene, where a guy who's become a junkie convinces his friends to shoot up with a needle. The script calls for the evil guy to be goth, with eyeliner and white powder on his face, but Dean objected to that and got Pastor Frist to agree that evil comes in many forms. "Regular-looking sinners are even more dangerous," Dean argued, and everyone saw his point.

The drug scene is followed by Drunk Driving, which is the first outdoor scene. We'll have a tent ready in case it rains, but the air in October is usually crisp and clear. We walk into the parking lot behind Starla Joy as she snarls, "Have another beer." She's facing Zack Robbins, who's stumbling around like he's been drinking a lot already, and Demon Starla Joy continues to entice him. "You'll fit in. You'll be cool. You'll be one of *us*." Then she cackles maniacally, and we watch as Zack gets behind the wheel of a car with two friends in it.

This was the scene I was originally cast in, and Jessica Thatcher is now in my role as the drunk guy's girlfriend. She's in the front seat, laughing and smiling until the moment that Zack acts out driving into a tree. Everyone in the car screams, jerking forward and backward, and the sound of breaking glass startles me. I didn't know that part was ready yet, but I look over at Dean and smile. "I have some of the audio rigged early," he says, and I can see he's really proud of his work.

Suicide is the scene we see right before heading into the Judgment part. We're out in the parking lot, and Geoff is just as powerful as he was when I saw him the other night. He's shaking with pain. I lock eyes with Starla Joy and I know she sees it too—how good he is, how right this part is for him. She says her lines to him. "Your parents hate you, you're a bottom feeder, you're trash. No one loves you. Where's your Jesus now?"

Geoff writhes and cries, holding the shaking gun up to his head. Starla Joy screams, "Do it!" and there's the sound of a single gunshot. Maryanne Duane jumps again, but the rest of us were ready for it. Geoff slumps over onto the sidewalk, and we hear the sound of loud hand clapping coming from the back of the parking lot.

"That's my boy!"

It's Mr. Parsons, Geoff's dad. As he walks toward us and into the light, everyone can see that he's stumbling drunk, his car keys jingling in his hand.

I hear Ron and Graham whisper back and forth nervously. "What's he doing here?" asks Ron.

Geoff looks up at his dad, and I think I see fear in his face. No one moves.

"I liked that, boy!" shouts Mr. Parsons, clamping a hand on Geoff's shoulder. Then he clenches his teeth and growls, "I like you telling the world how useless you are."

Maryanne gasps, but the rest of us just stay frozen.

"Dad, come on," Geoff says, standing up. "Let's just go home, okay?"

He reaches for the keys, but his dad jerks his hand out of reach. "You get your grubby hands away from my car!" shouts Mr. Parsons.

"Dad, please," Geoff says. And I can hear the desperation in his voice, see it in his eyes as he looks around and knows we're all watching, seeing, listening.

I knew there was something going on with Mr. Parsons, like that he's gotten into trouble at the local bar a few times and that he's not usually at church on Sundays, just sometimes, like on Easter. But now that I'm seeing it, what it really is, I feel a wave of sympathy wash over me. I look to my right, where Dean is standing. I can tell he's feeling it too.

There isn't another adult out here—no one's sure what to do. I look to Starla Joy, but she's just watching them.

I hear the back door of the church open and I see the outline of Pastor Frist's figure. He must be coming out to see why we haven't moved on to the next scene. I watch him scan the parking lot, and he sees what's going on instantly.

"Jimmy Parsons!" he says, jovial as always. He walks over to Geoff and Mr. Parsons and puts an arm around "Jimmy."

"Pastor Frist," says Mr. Parsons. "I'm gonna drive my boy home now. It's time for him to come home."

Geoff stares at the ground like the blacktop of the parking lot is the most interesting thing he's ever seen.

"The kids have rehearsal now," Pastor Frist says. "Let's go get a cup of coffee in the lobby. How does that sound? A nice cup of coffee."

Mr. Parsons lets Pastor Frist lead him inside, and Pastor Frist nods at Starla Joy as he passes her. "Keep going," he says.

I look back at Geoff, still staring at the ground.

"Now you will face your judgment!" howls Starla Joy, and I jump a little, not quite ready to get back into Hell House. But Geoff follows along with us, I guess to see the rest of the show, and I see Dean nod at him as they pass. Geoff just stares ahead, looking hollow.

Little Tate Jenkins, a seven-year-old who'll be dressed as an angel, motions for us to come inside, into the crafts room, which has been staged as the judgment scene.

Vivian Moss is in this part—she's playing Saint Peter at the pearly gates. A senior, Joey Turner, had been cast originally, but he's had some trouble with his grades, and his parents punished him by making him give up Hell House. I think Pastor Frist was nervous about casting a woman as Saint Peter, but Ty's aunt has charmed everyone and she was happy to step into the role. She has a giant book of names in front of her as she stands at a pulpit set up among the tables full of glue and glitter. Dean will move those on show night, of course, and white curtains will be hung on the door on the left side of the room. The door on the right is covered in black garbage bags, and red light leaks out from underneath it—that's the entrance to Hell.

Vivian stands at the pulpit with her reading glasses on, wearing a shirt that says I ♥ BOOKS. Though she's not dressed for it, she's fully in her role, glancing at each of us as we walk into the room and line up in a row along a blue piece of tape on the floor.

"This is the Lamb's Book of Life," Vivian says ominously. "It contains a list of all the names of people who've accepted Jesus as their Lord and Savior." She pauses. "Is *your* name in this book?"

"As I say your name, please step forward," she says. The Demon Tour Guide, Starla Joy, has fallen silent. That's her role in the more godly scenes—it's supposed to symbolize how her strength weakens in God's presence. Then Vivian begins to read from a piece of paper, and she says each of our names out loud. "Lacey Anne Byer," she reads, and her eyes sit on me. She stares extra long at each person when they step forward, and then after we've all been called, she pauses for what feels like an hour, looking at each one of us individually.

This is the part in the show where people start to get really squirmy. They've seen all the sins—which is exciting and kind of cool in a gruesome way—but now they're being stared down by God's representative.

I get a chill as her eyes fix on me.

Finally, Vivian says, "It is not your time today." She points to the door to Hell and continues, "But when it is your time, the choices you have made on this earth will affect your afterlife for eternity. Choose wisely."

She walks to the door on the left, where the white curtains will hang on show night, symbolizing her exit to Heaven.

We watch her go, and then suddenly I feel my father's hand on my shoulder. I almost jump, though I should have known that was next.

"Come with me, little darlings," he says, using the voice he's perfected over the years, Satan's sound.

We walk through black garbage bags hung over the entrance into Hell, also known as the Sunday school room. Dean isn't quite done with the staging, but the usually cheerful kids' area is definitely transformed already. There's a red light pulsating in the corner, and the walls are draped in black paper. Chains hang from the ceiling, some with lost souls attached, and the stereo system is playing a continuous track of screaming and moaning to set the mood. There's also a space heater that, judging by the massive heatwave that hit me as I walked through the door, is working overtime. I start to sweat.

My dad parts the crowd and goes to stand in the corner, and though he's not in full makeup, he does have on his hooked nose extension and the long nails he likes to wear as the devil. He uses them to creep people out by dragging them along cheeks and shoulders, and it's so disturbing that sometimes kids shake when he gets close to them.

"Some of you know where you are," my father says, his voice deeper and darker than I remember it sounding even last year. "Make no mistake. This is the *gate to hell.*"

He throws up his arms and pauses for dramatic effect before continuing.

"This is my domain, where I have the ultimate power over you because you have stolen, you have lusted, you have coveted, you have *sinned* . . . and I know everything. Your actions, your deeds, your thoughts—there's nothing I didn't see. You turned away from Jesus, and I am what you turned to. Welcome to hell!"

As I watch my dad, I start to feel uneasy. I've seen him in this role a dozen times and I've always loved the way he dramatized the devil. But tonight, I'm feeling guilty about the doubts I've had, the doubts I still have, about the church.

"God says you can join him in his kingdom, that you can sit by his side by simply following his footsteps? Never!" Dad continues, gesticulating wildly. "I will run with fire through your lives, burning up your relationships and making them sick and twisted, fattening your greed until it destroys your ambitions, killing your unborn children. I'll harness chaos and murder humanity with wars and hunger and disease. I want every one of you to rot with me down here *forever!*"

He puts his left arm out, and with a sweeping motion, the flashing red light stops pulsing and burns bright, casting an evil spotlight on the center of the room where kids hang from chains. I look over and see Dean smiling, so I nod at him in approval of the effect.

"Meet my minions!" Dad screams. They're all screaming and weeping; they represent souls who have sinned and are in hell for eternity. They whine, "I can't take it!" and "Let me out of here!" Then one—Brooke Ross—distinctly calls for Jesus.

"Silence!" shouts Devil Dad. "His name is not welcome here. I hate everything that He loves. And He loves you. But to me, you are nothing."

"Demon!" he shouts at Starla Joy. "Remove this scum from my presence."

She grabs Brooke by the arms and pulls her away, kicking and screaming, like she knows she's being led to even worse torture.

Then Dad—Satan—laughs and turns his eyes on us. "This is a glimpse of what you are headed for if you keep doing what I know you've been doing and thinking about doing."

Usually the devil goes down the line, saying something to every guest that may or may not resonate. I always remember, it's not Dad—it's the devil. When my father is in this role, he disavows himself of any responsibility, he goes for it. And he uses what he sees to divine sins that really might be there, under the surface.

He walks up to Dean and puts one long nail under Dean's chin. "What sins lie within your mind, Dean Perkins?" he asks. "In the darkness of a sixteen-year-old boy's room there are many temptations." Then Dad howls and breaks into demonic laughter. He always uses people's names when he knows them—it just makes the scene more effective.

I'd worry about Dean, but I know he knows the drill—this is Hell, and there are no holds barred for this performance.

Dad makes his way to Maryanne and gives her some generic

lashing about respecting her parents. I thought that was the one he was going to use on me, but I guess not.

When he does get to me, I'm nervous. He's never turned this on me before, never looked at me and tried to see sin. I close my eyes for a second as he approaches.

"Look at me, Lacey Anne Byer!" he screeches.

I open my eyes and see the devil staring me in the face.

"When you deceive, you sin," he rasps. "And even if you don't get caught, you know in your heart that you have sinned."

I feel a trickle of sweat drip down the side of my forehead. *Does Dad know I've snuck out? Or is he just fishing for a sin and coming up with this one?* I stay very still, trying not to react.

"And why deceive, if not to cover up more deep, dark, and ugly sins? Sins of betrayal, of doubting your Father, of *lust*?" he says that last word with feeling, and my face starts to redden. Luckily it's dark in here. When he said "Father," did he mean God? Or himself?

How does he know?

Then he moves on, quickly, to Ron Jessup, whom he hits with greed. I relax my shoulders in relief that my confrontation with him is over, and I remind myself that it's all an act, and it's all in the name of God.

Soon Dad backs away, facing all of us at once, and talking about breathing deceit into our souls so that he can one day own them.

Then, a white floodlight pours into the dark room. "Satan, these are not your children," says a calm voice. It's Pastor Frist, who always plays Jesus. I think it's an excuse to let his hair become a mullet and grow a beard, but he does resemble Christ. He's wearing a white choir robe and there are two little kids at his side dressed as angels with golden pipe-cleaner halos. I hope he talked to Mr. Parsons. I hope he gave him lots of coffee.

My father, the devil, starts shrieking—it's the most hideous sound I can imagine hearing—and he shrinks to the back of the room as Jesus leads us out of Hell. I'm glad to get away from that space heater—it's really cranked up. We walk into the hallway, where there are more angels waiting to greet us with warm handshakes as we head to the library, which is staged as Heaven.

Dean built one of those small garden bridges from Home Depot, and it's positioned over a kiddie pool that I'm pretty sure came from Maryanne Duane's house. There are cotton clouds hanging all around the room, and Jesus marches in front of us, then sits upon His throne and welcomes us to gather around.

All of the angels smile at us—it's their job to make people feel welcome.

"My children," Jesus says, "this is but a glimpse of what awaits you in heaven if you accept me as your Lord and Savior. I died for your sins, and though sin still exists in the world, all you must do is invite me into your heart and you will be saved."

There's audio of birds tweeting, and a projection of a rainbow appears over Christ's throne. Dean is going all out on this room! We stay a minute more, as angels come around and hug us, and then a very humbled and quiet Starla Joy leads us out and into the main lobby of the church.

On Hell House nights, this lobby will be the room where our junior pastor, who hardly ever gets to talk in church, asks people to pledge their lives to Jesus. He'll do a prayer with everyone and then ask people to fill out cards with their contact information if they've committed or recommitted to Christ tonight. Over the course of three nights of Hell House, we collect hundreds of cards, and each one represents a saved soul.

Tonight, though, the lobby is just the lobby, and Starla Joy takes off her demon mask. "Pretty crazy, right?" she says, finally talking in her mellow normal voice.

"Yeah," I reply.

Chapter Twenty-five

As I walk out into the parking lot after the run-through, I feel about a thousand emotions. I know this outreach will bring people to God—it's more intense than in past years—but there's a knot in my stomach too. I notice that Mr. Parsons's truck is still here. Maybe he's talking to Pastor Frist some more. I hope so.

Dean catches up to me and Starla Joy. We're already whispering.

"Mr. Parsons was wasted," says Dean.

"That was scary," I say.

"It's over," Starla Joy says. "I'm sure Pastor Frist gave him some coffee and a talking-to."

"Starla Joy!" I say. "That was serious."

"Lacey, everyone knows Geoff's dad is like that," she says. "It's sad and weird, but that's the way he is."

"To see it, though," I say.

"Yeah," says Dean. "And Geoff's face while his dad was there."

"It was awful," I say.

"I know," says Starla Joy. "But that's not our problem right now. Geoff isn't an angel either."

Dean and I stay silent

"Oh, come on, you guys!" says Starla Joy, starting to head toward her truck. "Let's go get cheese fries and debrief!"

Dean loosens up then, smiling a little.

"You can say it," he says. "I'm the King of Prop."

He looks back at me. I feel like we should talk more about Geoff, maybe even try to find out if he's okay. But then again, I don't think he'd do the same for any of us. I give in to my friends.

"You're the King of Prop," I say to Dean. I head for the truck too.

"And I'm not even halfway done," Dean says excitedly. "Wait until we get the smoke machines and the fake blood and the porn projection screen! Seriously, you guys, I might want to make this my thing. Like, creating sets and environments and stuff."

As Dean rambles on, we get into Starla Joy's truck, me in the middle. I told Dad I was going out with my friends, and he agreed that I could stay out half an hour past curfew. He knows we're all excited after tonight. He even told Dean how proud he was of the amazing prop work this year, and how he hoped they could work on the model in the garage again after Hell House is over.

"Ooh, it's already eight thirty," Starla Joy says. "I'm starving."

"Do you want to call your mom?" I ask her. I know Dean doesn't have a curfew, but Starla Joy usually checks in.

"Nah," says Starla Joy. "She's so preoccupied with other things that she doesn't even notice when I get home anymore."

"Oh," I say. But Starla Joy doesn't seem upset—she's still high from her amazing turn as a Demon Tour Guide. "You really ruled the realms of hell tonight," I tell her.

"Are you saying I'm a natural beast of Satan?" she asks, raising her eyebrows as she pulls out of the parking lot and heads to Diner. It's a diner, obviously, and it's uncreatively, but aptly, named. I think in the early days of small towns things were incredibly simple, and this place has been around forever. It's the only spot open late night besides the Starbucks one town over.

"I'll say it," Dean says. "You were terrifyingly evil!"

"Why, thank you," says Starla Joy.

"I didn't know you had it in you," I tell her.

I look at her profile to see if she reacts at all.

"Well, I am a demon," she says matter-of-factly.

I'm about to ask her if those lines about young love make her think of Tessa and Jeremy at all, but I hesitate and then Dean jumps in.

"Wasn't the disco ball cool?"

"That is the gayest gay apartment ever," I say. Dean beams.

"I just want it to look authentic," he says.

"Yes, Dean," Starla Joy says. "I'm sure every gay couple has a disco ball above their bed."

We all laugh.

"Hyperbole in Hell House is a good thing," says Dean.

"There's a lot of over-the-top stuff this year," I say, turning again to look at Starla Joy. "That stuff about young love before the abortion scene is pretty intense."

"Yeah," she says. "It's awesome."

I face the windshield again, still not sure what I think. Where everything used to seem so cut and dried—sinner or saint—I see new complexity. I wonder if my friends do too. But I don't want to press Starla Joy or remind her of Tessa right now, when she's in this untouchable good mood. She deserves it. And I'm sure we'll save a lot of souls, so how much does it matter if a few lines seem off to me?

We pull up at Diner and Starla Joy and I pile into a corner booth while Dean goes to the restroom. The seats are wooden and there are years of names carved into them: "Oscar loves Carolyn," "Russ + Quinn," "Tommy Walker rulz." A small TV in the corner plays highlights from the high school football games.

Starla Joy takes the salt shaker from the edge of the table and pours out a little bit so she can do her trick where you balance the edge of the shaker on the loose crystals.

I decide that I need to ask her about her lines. They just reminded me so much of Tessa. I know she had to think about that.

"Starla Joy, is Hell House hard for you at all?" I ask.

She doesn't look up at me—she's concentrating on the trick.

"No," she says. She's blowing me off, but I press her.

"I just mean like seeing Jeremy there as a Demon Tour Guide too," I say. "And the lines you have to say outside the abortion room. They must kind of make you think about—"

"Stop," she says, grabbing the shaker and brushing the salt crystals onto the floor, abandoning her efforts. "I'm okay. It's okay."

"What's okay?" asks Dean, sliding into the booth next to me.

"Lacey was saying that all the 'slut' lines must remind me of my sister," say Starla Joy.

"That is *not* what I was saying!" I say.

"I know, I know," Starla Joy says, waving her hand to calm me down. "I'm kidding. And okay, that part is a little bit hard for me, to be honest."

"You were so good," I say. "I mean, I could hardly recognize you."

"That's what I do," she says. "It's like I feel what I feel and even if it's upset or sad or whatever, I can turn it into anger."

"That's good for the role," Dean says.

"I know," says Starla Joy. She smiles at us and I envy her strength. I don't know how she does it.

Doris, a waitress who's worked here since way before we were born, comes over without menus.

She puts three waters in front of us and says, "Cheese fries."

We nod our heads in affirmation, and Doris starts to walk away, but then she turns on her heels, like she forgot something important.

"Did ya hear?" she asks.

"Hear what?" I ask.

She leans in to our table and starts to whisper. "Turns out that Tyson Davis—that boy I hear you've been hanging around with lately, Lacey—the one who moved out of town and then came back . . ."

We nod, and I'm afraid for her to continue but more afraid for her not to.

"Seems that while he was away he got himself in some trouble," she says.

"What kind of trouble?" Starla Joy asks.

"I don't like to spread gossip," Doris says, contradicting everything we know to be true about her, "but I heard he got in a car accident last spring and was arrested for driving under the *in-flu-ence*."

She practically stretches each syllable of "influence" into its own sentence.

Then she looks around the diner like she hasn't told every table this already and whispers, "Drugs."

None of us react, which isn't what Doris expects.

"Well, that's the word anyway." Doris turns and walks back to the kitchen.

Dean and Starla Joy and I look at each other.

"Do you think it's true?" asks Dean.

"Yes," Starla Joy says immediately. "Didn't you guys always feel like Ty was holding something back? Like he couldn't tell us about a part of his life."

"The truth always finds you," Dean says.

"You sound like Oprah," Starla Joy says.

"But he's right," I say.

"Did you know this, Lacey?" asks Starla Joy, looking at me intently.

"No," I say, thinking that I wish I had, feeling like I *should* have known. He should have told me.

"It doesn't seem like Ty," Dean says. "He's not a drunk-driving type."

"What *is* a drunk-driving type?" I ask. "I mean, what does that mean?"

"Bleary eyes, bad grades, a who-cares attitude," says Dean. Then he smiles. "Okay, I know I sound dumb. You're right. It's like in Hell House where the script calls for the drug guy to be goth. So stupid."

"He's just Ty," I say. "He's the same person we met again this summer." I want to talk to Ty, want to find out what the real story is.

"I need to go," I say.

Chapter Twenty-six

Starla Joy takes me straight to Ty's house, and neither she nor Dean ask to come in. They know I need to talk with Ty alone.

As I head up the walk, I turn my phone to silent. I don't want to be interrupted. I notice again how big and foreboding this house is, especially at night. But before I even ring the bell, Ty opens the door and warm light floods out from inside the entry. He looks rumpled in his pajama pants and a white undershirt, but he also looks extremely adorable. His hair is sticking up on one side.

"No polo shirt?" I ask.

"Not when I'm off duty at home," he says, frowning.

I see Vivian Moss appear just past Ty, but she nods and makes a quick exit. I hope she won't tell my dad she saw me here, but even that fear can't distract me from the conversation I want to have with Ty. I have to find out the truth—where he's been and what really happened.

"Can I come in?" I ask, realizing that Ty's not going to offer that.

"I guess," he says.

I follow him into the large living room.

"It's kind of late for you to be out on a school night, right?" asks Ty, sitting down on one end of the brown leather couch and grabbing a throw pillow. He pulls it up into his chest protectively.

I choose an armchair where I can sit up straight.

"I needed to talk to you," I say.

"Let me guess," Ty says. "You finally heard . . ." His voice drops off. We sit there quietly for a moment, and I realize that I'm going to have to start this thing.

"What do you think I heard?" I ask.

"I guess you heard why I wasn't at school," Ty says. "I can tell by the look on your face that it's ruined."

"What is?" I ask.

"The image that you have of Ty Davis, the sweet little boy who's into trains," he says, a rueful smile playing on his lips.

"Is that an illusion?" I ask.

"It's an outdated perception," he says.

"Ty, what did happen?" I ask.

"What did you hear?" he asks.

"Just that you got arrested for driving under the influence," I say. "That you were in an accident."

"That's right," he says.

"It doesn't seem like you," I say.

"Who does it seem like?" he asks. "Geoff Parsons?"

"Maybe," I say too quickly, thinking of Geoff's dad. "Anyway, it doesn't seem like *you*."

"Well, I'm not really the person you think I am," Ty says.

"Isn't that exactly what you said to me the last time I saw you?" I ask. "That *I'm* not the person you thought I was?"

"Could be I was projecting," Ty says, smiling a little. "Ever since I got here I've been trying to be someone else, to forget what happened."

"That's why you came back?" I ask.

"My parents thought that if I moved in with Aunt Vivian, here where things were safe and good, that I'd be able to leave the 'bad influences' behind," he says.

"Bad influences? That sounds intense," I say.

"Yeah, well, that's my dad's term but DUIs are intense," says Ty. He picks at the corner of the throw pillow he's holding. He looks like a lost little boy.

"Ty, what happened?" I ask again.

"It's a boring story," he says, but I don't believe him for a second.

I stay quiet, wanting him to continue. I know he will. This is what he wanted to tell me when he brought me over to his house the day we found out Tessa was pregnant, what he's been trying to tell me all those evenings at Ulster Park. He's been listening to my thoughts and feelings, pushing back and challenging me gently, but I haven't been listening hard enough to him. I didn't know there was something he needed to say.

But I know now, and I'm not going to talk around it. I'm just going to listen.

"There was a party," he says after a while, leaning back into the arm of the couch. He runs his hand through his mussed-up hair. I almost wish I were lying with him in his arms. Maybe that would make it easier to tell. But I stay still.

"It was pretty normal for everyone to be drinking," he continues. "I thought I was fine to drive home. I'd done it before."

I nod, consciously keeping any judgment off of my face.

"This time I wasn't okay," he says. "There was a sharp curve on the road, and I lost control of the car. We spun out and hit a tree. Totaled my dad's Lexus."

"We?" I ask.

"My ex-girlfriend was in the passenger seat," he says.

"And everyone was okay?" I ask, pushing down the jealousy that flares up at the word "girlfriend." Of course he would have had a girlfriend before. It's normal. Nothing wrong with that.

He closes his eyes, and I feel my own start to fill with tears.

"She's okay," he says quietly. "She had a broken leg, but she's fine now. I saw her last week."

"That's good," I say, feeling relief at the well-being of the ex-girlfriend I'd been jealous of thirty seconds ago.

"Yup," he says. And I see his mouth shut in that way that guys close their lips when they don't want to say any more. I can see some sort of pain on his face, but I don't understand what it is, and I need to.

"Ty, it's okay," I say. "I'm still here. I'm still your . . . friend. I know you're sorry. I know God's forgiven you."

I think about the scene I just saw in Hell House with Zack Robbins—the one I was originally cast in. Pastor Frist told Zack to play his character, the drunk driver, like an oblivious jerk. A sinner who doesn't care that he has his friends, his girlfriend, in the car. That character isn't meant to be forgiven—he gets dragged into Hell by demons during the show. But that's not who Ty is. The truth is much more complicated than that.

"I didn't mean to," Ty says. "I knew better."

It's like he's not talking to me now. He's looking somewhere to my right, out the big windows and into the woods.

I see a tear slip down his face and I have no idea what to do. I've never seen a guy cry like this before. It's quiet and still. It's terrifying. But I want to be strong. So I sit and wait for him to keep talking or to start crying harder or something. I don't move, I don't let myself think. If I think, I might want to run away, and I need to stay, because my dad's always told me that being there is sometimes the most powerful thing you can do for someone. And I want to be there for Ty.

"Afterward, it was like I had taken a baseball bat to her leg myself," he finally says. He wipes away the few tears that slipped out. "These guys—my former friends—threatened me. The girls stared at me like I'd intentionally hurt her."

He looks over at me and I can see a mix of sadness and raw anger on his face. He snorts a little now, a choked laugh. "Lacey, all of them had done the same thing every weekend," he says. "They'd just never gotten caught."

He looks back out toward the woods. "I can't take the double standard," he says. "I can't stand the hypocrisy. I did something wrong, and I'm being punished for it. I can take that. But why just me? Why do some people get to go on with their lives like nothing happened?"

I stand up, not sure where I'm going or what to do, but I head to the kitchen and pour myself a glass of water. Watching him in so much pain, feeling so much confusion myself, makes me feel weak. My shoulders start to shake and, on impulse, I drop to my knees by the refrigerator.

"God, please help me get through this moment. Please help

me to understand Ty, and what happened, and how to move forward and how to do the right thing. God, please help me to act in your image, to know what that is and to believe in it fully. To—"

I fall silent. The relief I'm looking for isn't coming. My own words are scaring me. So I stop praying and I stand up.

I turn around and walk back to the living room, heading straight for Ty. I put my arms around him and he doesn't push me away. I lean against him, holding him close to me. We're both letting tears fall.

We stay there for a long time, hardly moving except for the rhythm of our breath.

Later, I sit with Ty and hold his hand. I want to tell him that everything is okay, that he's forgiven and he can move on. But I'm not sure what the rules are in this situation. So I tell him the one thing I know for sure. "I'm still here," I say.

It's two a.m. by the time I leave. Ty drives me home in his aunt's car so we won't wake my dad, but I already know that I'm in trouble. I have twelve missed calls.

Sure enough, the living room light is on.

"Do you want me to go in with you?" Ty asks. "I could explain or—"

"No," I say. "I'll handle it."

I walk up the front steps feeling empty, hollowed out by the emotional wallop I experienced tonight.

When I sit across from my dad in the living room, he puts down his book slowly and takes off his reading glasses.

"I was at—" I start.

"I know where you were," Dad says. "So don't bother telling me you were with Starla Joy."

"I wasn't going to, Dad," I say. "I was at Ty's."

"Well, that's an honest beginning," says Dad.

"How did you know?" I ask.

"Vivian called around ten thirty," he says. "She wanted me to know you were okay."

"Oh," I say. "Well, I'm not sure that I am."

"She also updated me on Ty's . . . *situation,*" he says. "And she told me that you were counseling him through some of his grief about his transgressions."

"I was being a good friend," I say. Then I look in my father's eyes. "A good Christian."

"I know you were, Lacey," Dad says. "You should have called—you know that—but I was proud to hear that you were helping Ty tonight."

My heart softens a little and I smile at my father. "I learned it from you," I say.

He smiles back, but it's a tight-lipped version of his usually wide-open grin.

"Well, now I'm going to have to say something to you that you won't want to hear," he says.

"What?" I ask, my spine straightening.

"I don't want you spending time with Ty Davis anymore," he says.

My mouth opens in objection, but Dad holds his hand up and silences me with a motion, just like he does with rowdy kids in Sunday school.

"I know that you two have become close," he continues. "I don't object to a friendship."

"Then what do you object to?" I ask, my skin prickling a little.

"Lacey, I know you've been out late at night with Ty," he says.

I look down at the carpet.

"You've been deceiving your mother and me," he adds. "I don't know what else has been going on, but that's enough evidence to tell me that you're getting too close to a boy who has a history of problems."

"A history?" I ask. "Dad, he made a mistake! He's asked for forgiveness, Dad. And you should see how sorry he is."

The words tumble out of my mouth and even I'm not sure how I feel about them. I find myself wishing I could talk to my dad, be open with him about the confusion I've felt, which is only getting bigger instead of smaller.

"That's between Ty and God," Dad says. "I'm glad he's seeking forgiveness, and I will happily be there for him should he need my counsel."

"So why can't I be there for him?" I ask. "What if he needs *my* counsel?"

"I'm sorry, Lacey," Dad says. "But you've changed in these past few months. My little girl would never sneak out like you have, she would come to me with problems and talk to me about things that are going on in her life. You've become a mystery to your mom and me. You've been deceptive. And it all started with Ty's arrival."

"I'm sixteen," I say. "I'm finding my way."

And when I voice that, I know it's true. And then it's like I'm channeling the words to say to my father.

"You've raised me with God and the church and a huge

network of community support: good people who saw me grow up, friends I've known since I could crawl, a safe small town to explore," I say. "But you've also shown me the way all along—*your* way."

Dad starts to interrupt me, but I use his hand trick and it works.

"It might be my way too," I say, "but it might not be. I can't go on being protected and sheltered from life. People I care about are in pain. I have to be able to make my own choices about how to respond and who to help. You should trust me to do that."

Dad pauses, lost for words for a moment, and I think I've gotten to him.

"You're very eloquent, Lacey," he says.

"That's from you too," I say, chancing another smile.

He frowns. "Unfortunately, you're also sixteen, you've been lying to us, and you're just not emotionally equipped to deal with some of these things right now."

I feel my heart cramp. *He doesn't hear me. He doesn't trust me.* I find myself wishing I hadn't snuck out, wishing I'd just been honest with my parents all along. But they wouldn't have let me spend time with Ty. I know they wouldn't have. And I don't regret that. It's like I can't win.

I'm so tired tonight, so emotionally drained. When Dad stands up and holds out his hand to me I take it, and join him on the walk upstairs.

"Good night, sweet daughter," he says to me when we reach the landing. He kisses the top of my forehead. "We'll let tonight go, okay?"

I look at him, and I realize he thinks he's giving me a great gift. A pass. He won't punish me for being out late with Ty, but he's also banning me from being near him. Dad thinks it's a fair trade.

"Good night," I say.

I walk into my room and close the door. Then I lean against it and sink to the floor. What I said to Dad tonight may not have gotten through to him, but it rang very true within me. And I won't abandon my friends when they need me.

Chapter Twenty-seven

. . . .

The next day at school, I'm relieved to see Ty in a Carolina blue polo shirt, smiling and laughing as he walks down the hall. The news has spread, slowly and then rapidly, like a fire racing through a forest, by now—everyone knows about his accident. But I know he's sorry. I know better than anyone.

I just hope Dean and Starla Joy can understand.

"So?" Dean says when I sit down in the courtyard for lunch. "Last night?"

Starla Joy stares at me intently.

I try to think of how I want to describe it, how I can convey the sympathy that I felt without sounding like a pushover. But I also don't want to tell them everything—I don't think Ty would like the crying part to get around.

"He was at a party, drinking," I say. "His judgment was impaired and he drove his ex-girlfriend home. They hit a tree and she was hurt—a broken leg."

Starla Joy shifts in her seat, but I ignore her.

"She's okay now," I continue. "Everything's fine."

The three of us are outside having lunch on campus. Dean's mom packed a bag of carrot sticks and a Fiber One bar, so Starla Joy hands him half of her sandwich.

"You're not upset that he kept that from us?" Starla Joy asks. "From you?"

"Of course I am," I say. "But he's asked for forgiveness and he's here to start over—or start from the beginning again. He's trying to do the right thing and be the person he really is."

"I don't get it," Dean says. "You're the girl who gets upset when I say 'shit' but you're going to let Ty off the hook for keeping this secret?"

"Dean, don't curse," I say.

"I was making a point," he says. "And I think you just made it even stronger."

"Truthfully, Dean, did you know?" I ask him.

"Me?" Dean asks. "No! Ty and I hang out sometimes, but we don't really talk or anything. I mean, not about serious stuff like this."

"More about how to get to the next level of *World of Warcraft*?" I ask.

"Yeah," says Dean, laughing.

"Well, now we all know," I say. "And if someone really wants to be forgiven, and is truly sorry, how can you deny them that?"

"Are you giving us the WWJD talk?" Dean asks. He laughs again and swats Starla Joy's arm. And that's when I notice she's looking down, her face drawn.

"You're right, Lace," says Starla Joy. "He's trying to find himself again, back here, where his past lives. When bad things happen, I think people want to go back to before . . . like with Tessa."

Dean and I both look up at the sound of Tessa's name. Starla Joy's eyes sparkle a little, wet with tears that aren't falling.

I reach out for Starla Joy's hand. She pulls away as she grabs a napkin from her lunch bag and dabs at the corner of her eye.

Dean and I are still silent.

"She wants to pretend it never happened," Starla Joy says. "I can tell when I see her. She talks about school; she wants to hear gossip and find out what's going on with the winter basketball season and whether prom planning has started yet."

"Isn't that a good sign?" Dean asks. "She'll come back to normal here, and it'll all be okay."

"She's not acknowledging reality or being honest about what's happened," I say, understanding. "Just like Ty wasn't."

"Maybe she just doesn't want to talk about everything out loud," Dean says. "Did you guys think of that? Maybe she wants to have a normal conversation with her mom and her sister without being surrounded by reminders that she's different, that she's somehow tainted. I'm sure she gets enough of that just being at Saint Angeles!"

I'm surprised at how worked up Dean is getting. From across the field, Laura Bergen waves at us. I'm the only one who waves back, but it breaks the tension a little bit.

"We should go see her," Dean says.

"I go every weekend," says Starla Joy. "It doesn't help."

"You have to go," I say. "You're her sister. But Dean's right—we should all go. We can let her know that she's okay, that this is okay."

"Right," Dean says. "She's still Tessa to us—not some slut or sinner or whatever dumb thing people are saying."

Starla Joy looks down.

"Not that they're saying that," I say hurriedly, throwing a look at Dean.

He shrugs. "It's just the truth," he says. "We all get called stuff."

"It's okay, I hear it too," says Starla Joy. She tears at the napkin in her hands and we let her think for a minute.

"Please, Starla Joy," I say after a while. "Let us go see her. We can go on Saturday before the evening Hell House rehearsal."

"Okay," she says. "I think she'd like that."

I nod. This is important.

"Let's invite Ty," I say. "He'd want to come, I bet."

"Yes," Starla Joy says instantly.

"Cool," Dean says.

And I feel a surge of affection for my friends. They're forgiving, they're understanding, they're caring. And we all understand that Ty is Ty is Ty. And he's our friend.

"I'll talk to him," I say.

I don't see Ty for the rest of the day. I figure he avoided us at lunch because he wanted to give us space—time for me to help Starla Joy and Dean understand.

I call him as soon as I get home. It rings and rings, but voice mail picks up. I don't leave a message, I just wait ten minutes and then call again. This time, when I hear his simple, "Hi, it's Ty. Talk to me," I don't hang up. I don't want to seem crazy by letting him see multiple missed calls from me, so I just say, "Hey, it's Lacey. Starla Joy and Dean and I want to go see Tessa on Saturday. Are you in? Call me back."

I try to keep my voice light.

It works. Two minutes later, my phone rings. I grab it quickly.

"Hey," I say.

"Hey," Ty says. "Are you really going to see Tessa?"

"Yes," I say. Though the way he asks makes me remember to be nervous. I'll have to lie to my parents again. I'm afraid they'll tell me I can't go.

"I'm in," says Ty, interrupting my worrying.

And that's all that matters at this moment. Ty's in.

Chapter Twenty-eight

The plan to see Tessa is in full swing. Starla Joy will pick me up on Saturday for a "precal cram session." I haven't figured out how I'll explain possibly getting home late that day, but I don't want to lie. That's why I'm avoiding it altogether. Besides, we'll be back by seven, in time for the dress rehearsal of Hell House—we all have to be there.

When I slip into the tiny backseat of Starla Joy's truck on Saturday morning, I can't help but feel excited. I've never been on a road trip. Well, except for with my parents to see my grandmother and my cousins, but that hardly counts.

Dean turns around from the passenger seat.

"I have a box of Fiber One bars, a cooler full of Mountain Dew, and two bags of Doritos—regular and Cool Ranch," he announces.

"I've got to be honest," says Starla Joy. "That sounds like a fartfest waiting to happen."

I join in their laughter as we head to Ty's house. He's waiting at the end of his long driveway, backpack in hand.

"I told Aunt Vivian we had a project to work on all weekend," he says, slipping into the seat beside me. "Dean, I'm spending the night at your house."

"You may want to rethink that after you hear about his snack choices for the day," I say. Dean smirks, holding up his bars and Doritos for Ty to see.

"I guess we can pick up some fruit or something," he says.

"No, man," Ty says. "You got it right. Road trips are made for junk food and McDonald's!"

"And fiber?" I ask.

"Hey, the guy's got daily dietary needs," Ty says. "It's cool."

Starla Joy turns up the radio as we get on the ramp to the highway. I look out the window and stare out at the flat plains around us.

"Adios, West River," says Dean. He leans around with his hand in the air and Ty gives him five.

Dean and Ty go back and forth through the whole car ride, sharing snacks, debating the merits of the new *Star Trek* movies versus the old, arguing over radio stations (Dean wants metal, Ty wants classic rock). I'm surprised that Starla Joy doesn't chime in for the music part—she usually insists on country while we're in her truck—but she's just being quiet, like I am, taking it all in.

We stop at McDonald's, and I get the two cheeseburger meal, eating one while we're there and tucking the other into the seat pocket when we get back to the truck. As we pull onto the highway again, Starla Joy says, "If I find that cheeseburger in a week, you're going to be cleaning this entire truck."

"Don't worry," Ty says, grabbing it. He looks at me and grins, asking for permission as he unwraps it.

"Sure," I say, smiling.

He takes a huge bite and part of the bun sticks out the side of his mouth. I laugh.

Ty seems wholly himself, like a weight's been lifted off of him. The slightly brooding moments have left this week—and the confidence that was 90 percent there before shines fully now. I see what forgiveness and honesty can bring. I think of Isaiah 1:18: "'Come now and let us reason together,' says the Lord. 'Though your sins are like scarlet, they shall be as white as snow.'" And I smile.

A few minutes later, the sky turns gray and it starts to rain a little bit, just enough so Starla Joy puts the windshield wipers on the low setting. I hear the *squeak, squeak, squeak* every time they go across the glass.

Dean reaches for the radio.

"Dean, if you touch that dial while Van Morrison is still singing I will throw your fiber bars right onto the highway," Ty says, snagging the box of bars and rolling down his window.

Dean puts his tuner-reaching hand up in the air.

"Put the box down," he says. "There's no need to take this out on the health food. I am ready for some Metallica though."

Ty snorts.

"Man, I stayed up all last night working on the Hell House props for the dress rehearsal," Dean says. "They have to be ready to go tonight or I'm in deep you-know-what."

"You're tired?" asks Ty. "That's why you need Metallica?"

"It refreshes me," Dean says.

"Oh, fine," Ty allows, and Dean reaches forward to hit the preset for Rock 88, a hard-core metal station.

"Hey, this is it," says Starla Joy, and suddenly music takes a backseat. We're getting into the right lane to exit, heading into the town where Saint Angeles sits.

We have to drive about ten miles off the highway. We pass an antiques shop with painted posters that tout china sets, oriental rugs, and rocking chairs. Two farm stands by the road have handmade wooden signs advertising squash and corn and potatoes in bold red paint. Each spot we pass looks a lot like West River, but it feels different somehow.

We've all gotten quieter and quieter, and by the time we get up to the driveway of Saint Angeles, we're downright silent.

When we get out of the truck, our door slams echo loudly in the October rain. It's misting, not pouring, and the sky is that yellow gray that shows up when a storm isn't bad yet but is going to roll soon enough.

The building sits unimpressively in front of us. Somehow I imagined it like a castle out of medieval times, with large spires and double-thick oak doors. But it's actually just a one-story ranch house—larger than most—with tan vinyl siding and a glass entrance. It could be an insurance agency. I feel mildly disappointed.

"We have to check in," Starla Joy says.

The three of us follow her through the flimsy glass doors and meet Dottie, an older lady with one of those beehive hairdos, in the reception area.

"Starla Joy, honey," she says warmly, stepping out from behind her desk to give Starla Joy a hug. Then she eyes the rest of us from under blue-shadowed lids. "Where's your mama, baby?" she asks.

"She couldn't come today," says Starla Joy. "She had to work, so some friends of mine—and Tessa's—decided to drive here with me."

I'm in awe of Starla Joy's skillful white lies. They come so fast and free.

Dottie gives Dean a once-over. He's wearing normal jeans today but his XXL black sweatshirt still covers most of his body. He pulls the hood off his head and gives Dottie a smile through his greasy-as-usual hair.

Suddenly Ty, with his perfect blue eyes and his crisp lavender polo shirt, runs interference. "Miss Dottie, we're so honored to meet you," says Ty in a honey-sweet voice. He distracts her gaze by taking her hand and kissing it.

Overkill, I think, but it seems to be working. Dottie giggles and I swear I see a hint of a blush on her wrinkled cheeks.

"I'm Ty Davis," he says. "Starla Joy's told us all about the lovely lady who is helping take such good care of our Tessa. Won't you escort us back to see her? I'd love to hear about your work at Saint Angeles."

He holds out his elbow for her, and without a second of hesitation she grabs on.

"Well, I just work at the lobby desk, but I really am on the front lines of who gets to see our girls," she babbles, leading us down the hall.

"He's a genius," whispers Dean as we follow.

"You could've showered," I say back, bumping him playfully.

He leans into the wall and knocks a framed photo.

I stop to set it straight again, and that's when I notice that we're in a hallway lined with baby pictures. Some infants are sitting with their mothers, others are burbling alone on rugs surrounded by colorful toy blocks. It's like the inside of a Sears Picture Studio.

"Former guests," says Starla Joy, noticing my interest and turning back to me.

"Wow," I say, taking a deep breath. These are all babies who might not have been born if it weren't for Saint Angeles, if it weren't for the influence of churches and the work of God. I swallow a lump in my throat because these photos are really moving, but it's not fair for me to cry before I even see Tessa.

"Come on, Lace," says Starla Joy. "Let's catch up before Dottie tries to make out with Ty."

I smile and grab her hand. She squeezes it as we head down the hallway.

I'm so glad we're here.

When we get to Tessa's room, I see her sitting by the window, legs up on a low table, with her back to us.

"Tessa Min-ter," says Dottie in a sing-song voice. "Your friends are here!" She claps her hands together, utterly charmed by Ty at this point, and Tessa turns around, startled.

Her hair hangs down in unwashed strings and I see now that she's wearing a bathrobe and blue fuzzy slippers. As her profile emerges, I gasp. She's so big. I mean, I knew she was pregnant, but it's another thing to really *see* it.

"You didn't know we were coming," Dean says, stating the obvious.

"No," says Tessa, looking at Starla Joy anxiously. She pulls her robe over her blue-and-yellow-striped nightgown and stands up laboriously. Ty reaches over to help her, taking her arm.

"Thanks," she says, her smile starting to return to normal. "Just give me a minute, okay?"

She stops by her closet and picks a dress off a hanger, then walks across the hall and into the bathroom, head held high.

"I'll let you all visit," says Dottie, and she walks back down the hall after an oddly coquettish wave to Ty. He blows her a kiss.

"Ty's got a new girlfriend," Dean says, sitting down in the chair Tessa just left.

Ty laughs. "Someone had to take that fall to get your punk-looking self in here," he says.

I look over at Starla Joy. She's fussing with the comforter on Tessa's bed, which I notice is from their house. It's dark blue with white stars along the edges, and it's more Tessa than anything else in this room.

I glance around. It's sort of like a hospital here, but a little bit nicer. There's bright yellow floral wallpaper and sheer white curtains with ruffles at the edges. The nightstand by Tessa's bed has a cute seashell lamp and a Bible sitting on it, and there's a pretty big bookshelf in the corner filled with old paperbacks. But still, Tessa has to share a hall bathroom and there's a stale cafeteria smell everywhere.

"Why didn't you tell her we were coming?" I ask Starla Joy, walking around one side of the bed to help her straighten the comforter.

"I didn't want her to tell me no," she says quietly.

Then she looks up at the doorway, and I follow her eyes. There's Tessa, still as round as if she had a beach ball under her clothes, but looking much more like her old self. She's wearing an off-the-shoulder peasant dress with colorful blue embroidery across the neckline. Her light brown hair, brushed out now, touches her freckled shoulders softly. And her eyes are sparkling. She still has the blue fuzzy slippers on, though.

"I'd take you guys out into the garden, but the rain looks

like it's going to pick up," says Tessa, cheerful now. "Let's go in the den and see if anyone's around."

She spins on her toes and we all follow her up the hall, like she's our teacher or the field-trip chaperone or something. Tessa is still mesmerizing.

In the den, there's another girl-with-beach-ball reading the Bible at a table that has a chessboard painted on top of it. This place is starting to remind me of a mental institution, or at least what I've seen of mental institutions in movies. But I'm trying to be open minded. I think back to those baby photos in the hall and all the tiny lives that get nurtured here.

"Hey, Sylvia," Tessa says.

"T!" Sylvia says enthusiastically, pushing back her chair to stand up and greet us. "Who you got here?"

"You know my sister, Starla Joy," Tessa says. "And these are my friends Lacey, Dean, and Ty."

Sylvia nods at each of us as she holds the Bible to her chest. "Nice of y'all to visit the fallen one," she says.

I look at Tessa anxiously, but she just laughs, like this is a common joke among the girls here. The rest of us smile nervously.

"Sylvia's family is always here," says Starla Joy. "Her grandma made us the *best* pumpkin bread last weekend."

"They've got my back," Sylvia says. "That's for sure. And it's important too." She gives Starla Joy a meaningful smile. "I'll let y'all catch up," she says. Then she flashes us a peace sign and heads down the hall.

"She seems, uh . . . ," Ty starts.

"Really pregnant," says Dean.

"Dean Perkins!" I chide.

"I was gonna say friendly," says Ty.

"She's both," Tessa says, sitting down on the couch in the center of the room. "Most of the girls here are."

We all stand around, and I feel weird. Visiting Tessa seemed like such a good idea, but now that we're here I'm not sure how to act. Should I ask her questions about the baby or will that make her upset? Should I talk about Hell House, or will that make her think about what she's missing by not getting to star in it? Should I—

"Will you guys stop standing around like we're at a *wake*?" Tessa says. "Sit with me already!"

Starla Joy plops down on the couch and I perch on a love seat to her right. Ty sits next to me and Dean slinks into a chair across the coffee table. Tessa puts her feet up in Starla Joy's lap and leans back against a pillow.

"This is the week of surprise guests," she says.

"We didn't mean to—" I start.

"It's okay, Lacey," Tessa says, turning her warm smile on me. "I'm glad you came." She looks around the room at Dean and Ty, then at her sister. "I'm glad you all came. It's been pretty empty here since Monday—three girls left last week, so we're waiting for the open rooms to get filled this weekend."

"Who else staged a surprise drop-in?" asks Starla Joy.

"Jeremy," Tessa says, looking right at me.

"He came," I whisper.

"Thanks to your dad, Lace," says Tessa.

"Really?" I ask, surprised.

"Jeremy said that Pastor Byer encouraged him to visit me after they prayed together one afternoon," Tessa says. "I guess he said it would be good for us to see each other and talk."

"Oh," I say, still caught off guard.

"He's such a good man," Tessa says.

I'm guessing she's talking about my dad and not Jeremy, because Jeremy's not really a man yet—more like in guy stage—but I'm not sure. I'm also contemplating the news that my dad talked to Jeremy. Why didn't he tell me that? I wonder if Jeremy came to him. I wonder if what I said to my dad about how Jeremy needed to visit Tessa had an effect? Maybe he *does* hear me sometimes.

I'm so lost in my own thoughts that I miss part of the conversation and I rejoin reality just as Tessa says, "—asked me to the prom too!"

I see Starla Joy roll her eyes. "Yeah, well, he'd *better* ask you to the prom after what he's putting you through."

Tessa's gaze narrows and her voice gets low and angry. "I'm almost out of here," she says to her sister. "Leave it alone."

"Besides," she continues in her usual bright tone, addressing all of us again, "I've always wanted to go with Jeremy to the senior prom, and now I have seven whole months to pick out the perfect dress."

I smile at Tessa warmly, but her cheeriness feels thin to me. Her hands are resting on her large stomach, and I can't help but wonder if she ever thinks about the baby. I mean, she *must.* But it's clear we're not talking about it.

"I hear Hell House is going so well!" says Tessa, nodding enthusiastically. She's making up for the rest of us and our awkwardness by filling the silence. "What's it like playing Abortion Girl?"

She looks right at me, and I wonder if she resents my getting the role. But all I see is sunshine in her smile.

"It's pretty intense," I say. "My voice gets hoarse after rehearsals sometimes because Pastor Frist really wants me to practice my screaming. And Dean's got this great fake blood on order—he says it looks really real."

"It's perfect," Dean says, leaning forward in his chair. "I've got one kind that clumps so we can have that dripping from the fetus—"

"Also known as hamburger meat," I interrupt. "Did Dean tell you how good he is at sculpting with beef?"

"I am," says Dean, all modesty gone. "It's really *real* looking! I found instructions online about how to make raw meat look like a preemie baby. And anyway, the other blood is really liquidy so it'll run down Lacey's legs like syrup while she's on that table."

I laugh at how animated Dean gets when he talks about the props for Hell House. His smile is like a million miles wide.

But when I look over at Tessa, her face is pale.

Stupid, stupid, stupid! How can we all be sitting here talking about a hacksaw abortion when Tessa's about to have a baby, on a table, with lots of blood? It's not exactly the same thing, but it's enough to make anyone weak in the knees.

"Oh, Tessa, I'm sorry," I say softly, and then everyone turns and sees her wobbly smile. She's trying to keep it together but it's clear she's shaken. Starla Joy reaches out to hold her sister's hand, and Tessa closes her eyes for a long moment while we all sit on the edges of our seats.

When she opens her eyes again, she looks straight at Starla Joy. "I'm so scared," she says. I see a couple of tears slip down her pretty face, and I wonder if Ty, Dean, and I should leave the room and let Tessa and Starla Joy be alone.

Ty's already thought of that too. I see him standing up and motioning to me and Dean. "We'll go get a soda," he says quietly to Starla Joy, but she doesn't look up. She's holding her sister and whispering in her ear.

Dean, Ty, and I head down the hallway toward Tessa's room. We passed a Coke machine before, and we stand in front of it now. Ty takes out a dollar bill and presses it against the corner of the machine to get it flat before he tries to put it in the slot. It gets rejected once but some more flattening works, and he presses the Sprite button.

When he opens the can, the noise echoes loudly in the hall. He leans back against the cream-colored wall and takes a sip.

"Maybe we shouldn't have come," Dean says. "It's my fault, it was my idea. And then I went on and on about the blood—ugh! I'm so stupid!" He looks down at the floor.

"It's not your fault," I say. "I'm the one who brought up the blood in the first place. It's just that when you look at Tessa's face, she seems like her old self. It's like you forget—"

"You forget that she's pregnant," Dean finishes for me.

"I think she wants to forget," Ty says. "But she won't be able to. Probably not ever."

I lean against the wall next to him. Our hands are so close that I can feel the heat between us, and I blush at how easily my thoughts wander to kissing him. The girls who are in here felt this kind of heat too, and I understand how it can carry you away a little.

I imagine that we're all thinking about our own lives, and how our experiences relate to what Tessa's feeling right now. Can anyone ever see the world in any other way but through their own personal lens?

After about twenty minutes, Starla Joy and Tessa come down the hall toward us. Ty, Dean, and I look up expectantly, unsure of what emotion is going to greet us from the Minter girls. They've got their arms around each other, and Tessa is leaning on Starla Joy's shoulder. For the first time, in this moment, Starla Joy looks like the older sister.

When they get close, Tessa lets go of her sister and turns to me for a hug. "Lacey, I'm so glad you got the part," she says, opening her arms.

"Thank you," I say, wrapping her up as close as she can get with her stomach in the way. "That means a lot. I think of you every time I—"

And then I stop, realizing that I'm telling her I think of her while I act out having an abortion. It's like I am totally oblivious today.

"It's okay," Tessa says, leaning back from our hug and giving me a grin, like she thinks it's funny that I just put my foot in my mouth *again*. But she doesn't start crying. In fact, her smile looks more genuine right now than it has all day.

Tessa moves around me to give Ty a kiss on the cheek, and then she pulls Dean in for a hug too. He pats her back awkwardly, looking so uncomfortable that I almost want to laugh, but I don't.

"Truly, thank you guys for coming," Tessa says. "It means more than you'll ever know."

"Meet you guys at the car?" Starla Joy says. "I just want to say good-bye to my sister real quick."

"Sure," says Ty, and he leads us past Dottie, giving her one more princely hand peck before we walk out into a gently falling rain. We stand by the truck, without keys or umbrellas, getting wet.

Dean pulls on his hood. We're still not sure we should've come. But when Starla Joy walks out a minute later, her grin is as big as Texas.

She presses the unlock button on the keys and we settle into our seats. Before she starts the engine, Starla Joy turns around to all of us.

"Thank you," she says. "That was the first honest conversation I've had with my sister in forever."

"Really?" I ask. "And it was because of us?"

"Well . . . ," says Starla Joy.

"Was it the blood description?" Dean asks. "Did that make her face the reality of birth?"

"No," says Starla Joy. "That was actually pretty awful of you guys."

"No kidding!" Ty says. "You were rambling while Tessa turned as white as a ghost."

"Hey!" I say. "You were just sitting there."

"Yeah, sitting there horrified!" laughs Ty.

We all start to relax now that we know the visit was a good thing overall.

"So what *did* get Tessa to open up to you?" I ask.

"The fact that my mom wasn't there," says Starla Joy. "Tessa's so afraid, but she told me she feels like she needs to be strong when Momma's around and act like it's not really happening, like she's a normal high school senior who just got waylaid for a few months."

"Is your mom in denial?" asks Ty.

"Big time," says Starla Joy. "She doesn't even like it when I allude to the baby or Tessa's being at Saint Angeles. She just pretends like Tessa's away on vacation or something and she'll be home again soon."

"Wow," I say.

"Yeah," says Starla Joy. "I didn't really think about it before, but I realize now it's my mom who's making the 'it's all normal' charade important. Tessa's just going along with it to keep the peace. But she's really afraid."

"I could see that," I say.

"I think Jeremy's visit opened her up a little too," Starla Joy says. "She was pretending it didn't matter that he hadn't come, but now she doesn't have to do that anymore, because he did show up. He even told her he was going to come to the hospital when she goes into labor. He talked to his parents about it and they said the car would be his when he needs it."

Starla Joy looks at me as she talks about Jeremy.

"That was really great of your dad," she says.

I nod, making a mental note to somehow ask Dad about all this.

"It's good Tessa got to talk to you," Dean says.

"What else did she say?" asks Ty. "I mean, about the baby and stuff."

Starla Joy looks at him and gnaws on her bottom lip a little, like she's not sure it's okay to tell us what her sister expressed. But then she does anyway.

"It was really surprising," Starla Joy says. "She's scared, of course. She's also glad she's giving the baby to a family who's been wanting a child for a long time—Saint Angeles set up the adoption."

"That's so great," I say.

"Yeah," says Starla Joy. "But all that I knew already."

She looks at Ty, then at Dean, and finally at me. We all stay quiet, knowing there's more to come.

Starla Joy bites her lip again and takes a breath. "She also told me she's glad she didn't play Abortion Girl this year—that she wouldn't want the role."

"Why not?" I ask.

"She's not really sure if she believes abortion is wrong anymore," says Starla Joy.

Chapter Twenty-nine

On the four-hour drive back home, Starla Joy explains the details of what Tessa said to her in the Saint Angeles den. Tessa is calling herself "pro-choice and anti-abortion." Ty says he gets that right away.

"But that means she thinks women should have the right to kill their babies if they want to," Dean says.

"I don't understand," I say. "I thought Saint Angeles was a Christian home."

"It is," says Starla Joy. "I think Tessa talked to a lot of the girls in there, and they all come from different places. There was one who'd been abused by her own father, and that's why she's there."

I gasp. "Really?" I ask.

"That's sick," says Dean.

"I know," Starla Joy says. "And that girl wanted to get an abortion, but her family would hate her forever—even more than they do now, I guess. You guys know Tessa. She just sympathizes and empathizes with everyone. And even though she knows abortion would be wrong for her, she thinks it should be everyone's individual choice."

"But that abuse situation is an extreme case," says Dean. "Even then, I don't like that choice. It's a life that's been created by God. Right?"

"Right," I say, but my voice is quiet. That must be a terrible situation to be in.

"I don't know," Starla Joy says. "I got kind of confused too, just listening to her. She just thinks that it's a good thing to be able to make your own choice, I guess."

"The choice to have an abortion?" I ask.

"Yeah," says Starla Joy.

"They do have a choice by law, and I agree with that," Ty says. "Tessa realizes that although she hates the thought of an abortion, it's a choice that some people make."

"Ty Davis, are you a closet liberal?" asks Starla Joy.

"I'm not anything," Ty says. "I just have some thoughts that aren't the same as my parents' thoughts."

He looks at me.

"I have my own thoughts," I say defensively. "But *excuse me* if it still surprises me that Tessa's in favor of abortion."

"Listen harder, Lacey," Ty says. "Tessa's not in favor of abortion. But she does believe in choice."

I sit back, silent for most of the rest of the discussion. It isn't that I'm ignoring my friends. In fact, I am listening very, very closely. But all these ideas are jumbled in my head and I'm not sure how to sort them out. I can't get past the notion that Tessa would be okay with abortion, however she explained it.

We return to West River around six, and when I get to my

house Mom is just about to serve dinner. It seems like she didn't even notice that I'm home pretty late for having left so early in the morning. I don't have to think of an excuse, I just go upstairs to wash up and then come to the table.

Dad emerges from the computer in the living room and we all sit down and hold hands for grace.

"Lord, thank you for bringing this food to our table so we may enjoy time as a family and the sustenance of you, our God," he says. "Thank you for Theresa's fabulous lasagna tonight, and for the cattle who gave us this meat sauce. Thank you for our always sympathetic and caring Lacey, and thank you for helping her to see where the limits lie, for her own well-being. In Jesus's name we pray. Amen."

I want to talk to him about Tessa, and about how he sent Jeremy to her and maybe helped her open up a little bit today. But the prayer that Dad said makes my chest tighten, and I take a few deep breaths so I won't scream. I also don't think Dad would like to hear about Tessa's new thoughts on abortion. And my head is still swirling, so I stay quiet and let Dad go on and on about tonight's rehearsal.

I'm still thinking about his grace, and our hurried dinner, as I walk into the House of Enlightenment. Tonight is our first full-on dress rehearsal, complete with all of Dean's props at "go" so we can test them out. Starla Joy isn't here yet, but Dean and I sit together right up front.

"How are you?" I ask.

"After meeting Dottie and the girls and hearing about Tessa's new politics?" he asks. "Absolutely sure that I'm not having sex until marriage."

I swat his arm and laugh.

We quiet down as Pastor Frist approaches the podium with a mile-wide smile. "Friends, Youth Leaders, tonight we have a very special guest with us," he says. "You know of Pastor Tannen, who is studying our Hell House and considering his own production for next year."

We all nod in recognition—Pastor Tannen's name is famous in the evangelical world.

"He wants to learn why Hell House is such an awesome outreach that has the devil on the run," continues Pastor Frist. "And this week, he's here with us to watch the final seven days of refining before our big shows over Halloween weekend!"

A tall man with a tuft of white hair and a strong stance, despite his age, joins Pastor Frist at the podium—it's Joe Tannen himself. I hear excited titters in the pews. I wonder why he chose our church to visit?

"Hello, House of Enlightenment," says Pastor Tannen, his voice booming even more than Pastor Frist's always does.

"Hello!" the church answers back enthusiastically in the call-and-response instinct that takes over when we're in the sanctuary.

"I've heard tell of a world-class Hell House right here in West River," he says. "And I had to see it for myself!"

"Woo-hoo!" shouts Jeremy Jackson. Everyone laughs and Pastor Tannen smiles too.

"You may wonder why I'm not tending my own sheep in Oklahoma," he says. "Well, I decided to let my fellow pastors handle it so that I could take a sabbatical."

A low, questioning rumble moves through the crowd.

"Now, now," says Pastor Tannen, waving his hand to quiet everyone. "I'm only traveling for a few weeks, but I'll tell you what." He pauses briefly in the way that pastors do. I've always been impressed by their skill at emphasizing meaning with that powerful pause. Dean once said it reminded him of the way wrestling announcers take a breath before shouting out "Wild Willie Wogan!" or whatever.

Pastor Tannen continues, louder than before. "I believe it's God's will that I'm here in West River, to watch this Hell House and gain inspiration to create just as powerful an outreach with my own congregation back in Oklahoma!" he shouts. He does kinda sound like a wrestling announcer.

A cheer erupts in the pews, and a few people stand up to clap.

I look over at Dean, who's glowing with excitement. Everyone is. Laura Bergen is listening to Pastor Tannen almost as if he's an older version of Jesus.

I wish I could be thrilled with this moment too, but I'm still caught up in my own thoughts—about Tessa, about Ty, about the experiences I haven't had, the things I haven't seen. *Is it okay to not know what I believe?*

Pastor Tannen speaks for five more minutes and then he leads us in personal prayer. I stay quiet tonight, and I don't feel guilty about it. It's like my own meditation among all the yelps and high shrieks. Just because I'm not screaming doesn't mean I'm less connected to God.

When I get into the nursery for the full rehearsal, I have to catch my breath. It looks like a real hospital room. The bed that adjusts up and down is waiting for me, made with white sheets that will soon be covered in blood. There's an IV that I have to tape to my arm, and there's even a machine next to the bed—the one that goes *beep, beep, beep* along with your heart.

When I die at the end of the scene, it'll flatline into that eerily long *beeeeeeeeep*.

I change into one of those hospital gowns—this one has little flowers all over it—but I still wear pajamas underneath. We're not getting *that* realistic. As I climb up on the table, I see my dad come into the room.

"Lacey, have you seen Starla Joy?" he asks.

"No," I say. "Maybe she's just helping her mom or something. I'm sure she'll be here."

"Okay," Dad says. "I wanted her to take Pastor Tannen through—she's our best Demon Tour Guide—but I'll put him with Jeremy."

I nod.

He smiles and winks at me, and I smile back. Part of me wants so badly for us to share this Hell House, to be devil and daughter like I pictured when I first got this role. Plus I'm so grateful to him for sending Jeremy to Tessa. But the other part of me knows that our relationship is changing.

I sit back on the reclining bed, which is mostly in an upright position. Abortion Girl watches as the hamburger meat gets taken from her womb. I think about the girl Tessa mentioned, with her own father's baby. My stomach tightens.

Randy Miller and Laura Bergen are in costume, and he's turning on the beeping machine while she tapes the IV to my arm and fastens some tubes to the backs of my thighs—those are for the fake blood.

"Ready?" she asks.

"Yup," I say, taking a deep breath.

We sit there, silent and poised, for a couple more minutes.

Then I hear Jeremy outside, getting closer. The first two

scenes are over and he's leading Pastor Tannen and some other VIPs down the hallway. I can make out his voice, growling the lines I heard Starla Joy say just a few days ago.

"You've seen movies and read books about *young love*," he says, his tone gritty and hard, sounding even more eerie since it's muffled by the door. "I want you to believe in that! I want you to believe in that feeling, that rush of sick pleasure that goes through your body when you're touched by impure thoughts!" He's yelling now, really getting into the demon state.

"Are you ready to see the *slut*? Are you ready to witness a *whore* making a *choice*?"

He's talking about me. I mean, not me. But for a moment I *am* this girl, lying on a hospital bed and scared out of my mind, being judged by everyone around me and subjected to this physical torture. I try to remember how Ty told me this isn't what an actual abortion is like. There's not this much blood. It's not this intense. *I'm in a play. It's a show. It's not real.*

The door swings open and I see Pastor Tannen's face. He's beaming at me. I also see Pastor Frist. And my father. "It's my choice!" I scream dutifully. "It's my choice!"

"That's right," Jeremy says, rasping and snarling. "Kill your baby. Sin and belong to *me!* It's your *choice*."

He hisses, and I feel myself start to cry. It's involuntary—and every time I try to catch my breath and calm down, another sob chokes my throat. Tears stream down my cheeks and blur my vision.

Randy Miller is opening my knees and reaching under the sheets, where the hamburger meat is hidden. I feel a cold spurt of wetness, and I realize that Dean's fake blood is running down my legs now. I see a splat of the clumpy blood drop to the floor as Randy Miller lifts the burger baby up from between my legs and throws it into a trash can next to the bed.

I've rehearsed this scene dozens of times. But now, with the props and the blood and the smiling bobble-headed faces of Pastor Tannen and Pastor Frist and my father and Jeremy sneering in front of me, I watch the room start to spin. I still haven't gotten control of my sobbing—my breath is coming out in short spurts. Jeremy is laughing maniacally and clapping his hands in evil glee—my sin has made me the devil's property. Randy Miller grins warmly at me and says, "That's it, miss. You've made your choice."

And then everything goes black.

Chapter Thirty

When I come to, I see my father leaning over me. The flatlined machine is screaming.

"Turn that off, Laura!" Dad shouts. "Lacey, are you okay? Wake up, honey."

I push myself up onto my elbows and look around. The IV is still taped to my arm. Randy Miller, in his doctor's coat with a stethoscope hanging from his neck, is staring at me, open-mouthed. Laura Bergen is holding my left hand and stroking it. Kind of annoyingly, actually. I see Starla Joy standing by my side, one hand on my leg and the other holding her demon mask. She's out of breath like she ran here.

I look down and see that my legs are splayed open and covered in bright red fake blood, as is the sheet that was white ten minutes ago. In front of me is Pastor Tannen, Jeremy in his demon costume, and Pastor Frist. Everyone is frozen. I must have fainted, but thank goodness I remember where I am—this is a scary waking-up moment. I take a deep breath.

"I'm okay," I say.

And then Pastor Tannen starts clapping. His hands thunder together, and he looks around the room smiling, encouraging everyone to join in. Soon I'm in the middle of my own standing ovation.

"That was the best example of giving it up to God that I've ever seen, young lady," he says. "Ted, you oughta be very proud of your daughter."

Dad beams. "I am," he says.

Pastor Tannen comes over to me, holding out his hand. I shake it.

"It's a pleasure to know you," he says. "I'll be thinking of you when I cast my own Abortion Girl next year."

"Thank you," I say, still a little stunned and not sure how to handle this situation. How can I tell them that it wasn't God that moved me to faint—it was my own doubts and confusion, and maybe the sight of that burger baby.

"I think that's enough for Lacey tonight," Dad says. "Joe, I'm gonna take her home if you don't mind. She needs her rest."

"Absolutely," says Pastor Tannen. "We need to save that star power for the real shows next week."

I give Starla Joy a weak smile and whisper, "I'm really okay," in response to her questioning, worried face. My dad helps me down off the hospital bed. Jeremy slaps me on the back encouragingly as we walk through the doorway, but I don't respond. When we get out to the car, Dad lays a dark maroon towel on the passenger seat so I won't get fake blood everywhere.

"Dean says it's washable, but your mother would kill us," Dad says.

On the ride home, my father goes on and on about how

great I was, how into the scene I got, and how he could see Jesus working through me to convey the horror of abortion. He calls me a vessel for God.

Six months ago, I would have swooned at those words. But tonight, I know they're not true.

When I get home, I wash off quickly and get in bed. Now everyone thinks I'm this iconic star of Hell House. That's what I wanted, right? My movie moment. How can I tell them that I fainted amid a swirl of doubt?

My sleep is fitful, and the next morning I wake up full of angst.

Part of me doesn't want to break the illusion that my father and the pastors are under—part of me *wants* to be the Hell House star that Pastor Tannen raved about and held up as an example of godliness. I've wanted to step out of the shadows for so long, and now I have this light shining on me.

But a bigger part of me knows I have to be honest with Dad—I'm done skirting the truth.

When I come downstairs, Dad is preparing the usual seven a.m. pre-church morning pancakes—whole wheat now, since his cholesterol has been high—and Mom is at the table reading the newspaper.

"It wasn't God," I say quietly, slipping into my chair.

"What?" asks Dad, still staring at the frying pan.

"Last night," I say. "I wasn't channeling Jesus or anything. I was thinking about . . . other things."

"And God came through you," Dad says. "That's a powerful meditation, Lacey." He flips a pancake, smiling, and looks at

Mom. She's beaming too—he must have told her what happened last night. Or his version of what happened anyway.

"No," I say again, louder this time. "It wasn't God. My head was full of doubts—*is* full of doubts."

"What are you talking about, Lacey?" Dad asks.

He brings over a pitcher of orange juice and a stack of dark brown pancakes. I reach for one and start to eat it plain, with my fingers.

"I don't know," I say, my mouth half stuffed with fluffy pancake.

"Chew, honey," Mom says.

I finish my bite and swallow. Then I look at Dad and find my words.

"I don't see things in black and white anymore," I say. "The light and the darkness—they're mixed."

"Lacey, you're not being very clear," Dad says.

"Dad, do you think that Tessa's going to hell for having sex before marriage?" I ask. "Because I don't."

I get goose bumps when I say that because it feels good to express what I think, maybe even better than being in the spotlight at church.

Mom's hands fly up to her neck. "Oh, Lacey," she says. "What *are* you talking about?"

Dad quiets Mom with a hand gesture.

"Lacey, I don't know why that came into your head, but Tessa's situation is a very unfortunate thing," Dad says. He's using his children's pastor voice. "Still, you know that if she truly repents for her loss of purity and lives her life in the light from now on, God will forgive her."

I stare at my orange juice.

"I don't know, Dad," I say. "Maybe you're right. But I don't know. I have to think about it more."

And as I say that, I realize that I *do* want to think about it. I want to think about *everything*. I want to think about Dean, and who he is and what if he *were* gay? What would that mean for him? For his family? For the church? For me? And I want to think about Tessa and her choice to have premarital sex. What if she's in love? Isn't there love before marriage? I want to think about Ty's accident, and how talking about it, and asking for forgiveness, was what he needed. I want to think about Ty himself, and the questions he's brought to me. I wanted to give him answers—solid words and lessons I've read and been taught—but instead he gave me questions. And I am *glad* that I have questions.

"You shouldn't have to think about it, Lacey," Dad says. "You know right from wrong."

I open my mouth to argue with my dad, to tell him that right and wrong aren't two sides of a coin to me anymore—they're complicated ideas. But then I close it again. I'm past fighting with my Dad. And he can't stop me from thinking for myself.

My house is a house of answers, I think. *There isn't room for questions.*

"Honey, if you ever have doubts, you know to return to your Bible," Mom says.

"That's right," Dad says, reaching for the front page of the newspaper and not looking at me anymore. "First Corinthians 6:18: 'Flee from sexual immorality. All other sins a man commits are outside his body, but he who sins sexually sins against his own body.'"

I push away from the table gently. I've moved beyond being mad at my parents. They're not bad people—they just already have their own answers, and they don't have time for questions.

"Thank you," I say, kissing Dad on top of the head. "The pancakes were great."

"Where are you off to, darling?" Mom asks. "Service is at eight."

I look back at the table—Dad is reading the paper now and Mom is standing up to clear the dishes.

"I think I'll attend the second service at eleven today," I say. "I need to go for a walk."

Before they object, I spin on my heels and head out the front door.

They could stop me. They could talk this out with me more. They could ask me about what I'm feeling. But they don't, and I know they won't bring it up later either. They want to dam up the rush of my doubting thoughts with fast answers, and I'm sure they think that's what they've done. My parents will never entertain certain questions with me. So I'm going to talk to someone who will.

Chapter Thirty-one

It's early, but I text Ty from my driveway anyway and start heading toward Ulster Park. It's too far to walk, but soon I hear his loud red BMW behind me. He pulls to the side of the road and leans over, swinging open the passenger door.

"Get in," he says.

I flash back to the first night he pulled over for me, how nervous and rebellious I felt just talking to him. Could that have been just a few months ago?

We drive in silence to Ulster Park. We don't have the sleeping bag with us, so we sit right on the grass. I lean into him and he puts his arms around me. There's a square of sunlight on the ground, and I ease my toes into that spot. Even though it's almost seventy degrees today—a gorgeous fall afternoon—my feet are always cold.

"I heard about last night," Ty says. "Sounds like you were really moved by the spirit."

He's not being sarcastic, but I can tell he's wondering what I'll say, how I'll interpret the fainting incident.

"I lost it," I say. "All the blood and Jeremy's angry lines and Pastor Tannen—and the burger baby!"

"The burger baby!" howls Ty, and he laughs so much that I have to readjust my position.

"Dean is really good at shaping that burger baby," I say, settling back against Ty's chest.

"There is no way that burger baby looks remotely real," Ty says.

"Don't tell Dean that, but you're right," I say. "It's just a gross ball of meat. Dean has to keep a few of them in the church freezer, ready to go."

"No wonder you got sick," says Ty. "So you really fainted?"

"I really fainted," I say.

"Well, you picked a good moment," he says. "You were in a hospital bed, right?"

"True," I say. "My timing was impeccable."

"So does this early-morning rendezvous mean you're not going to church today?" he asks.

I look at him, surprised.

"Of course not," I say. "We'll go at eleven."

"Okay, okay," he says. "Just checking. I was surprised to see your text on a Sunday morning—I didn't know how much things had changed last night."

I let out a loud sigh.

"What is it?" asks Ty. He bumps his shoulder against me so I have to sit up and face him. He's good at insisting on eye contact when he knows I might otherwise stare at the grass.

I push a strand of stray hair out of my face and tuck it behind my ear.

"I'm quitting Hell House," I say.

"No, you're not," Ty says.

"I am," I say. "I'm going to tell my dad this afternoon so Laura Bergen can do the rest of the rehearsals."

"That's ridiculous," says Ty. "Laura Bergen couldn't act her way out of a paper bag."

"But she believes," I say.

"And you suddenly don't believe anymore, after living your whole life in this church?" he asks. "I don't buy that."

"It's not that I don't believe," I say. "I still do. And I may come back to every belief I had, a hundred percent. Who knows? But I want to think about things. I want to figure out what I believe, in my own time, with my own experiences."

Ty takes my face in his hands then, and he kisses me. It's long and hard, it's letting go. It's a kiss that feels like more than lust. It feels like something real.

"I love you for saying that," Ty says, when our lips finally part.

It's not quite an "I love you," but it's close. I feel my cheeks get red and I bury my head in his chest so he doesn't notice.

"But, Lacey," Ty says, putting an arm around me once again. "You're not dropping out of Hell House."

"I have to," I say. "It isn't fair for me to have these questions in my head."

"You just said you're trying to figure things out," Ty says. "Hell House is part of that. It's been your dream to play this part for so long. And you're brilliant at it! Aunt Vivian says you've raised the stakes for the other actors."

"That's only because they think I'm channeling God," I say. "What I was channeling last night was confusion and repulsion—it's a little different."

"And you can tell them that," he says. "You can tell the truth and they will see what they choose to see."

"My dad still thinks it was God," I say.

"Maybe it was," says Ty. "The Lord does work in mysterious ways."

"Does he work through a burger baby?" I ask, smiling.

"Could be!" says Ty, grinning back at me.

"I don't know," I say. "It seems weird to act out a scene when I'm so confused about it all."

"You just said it yourself—it's *acting*," Ty says. "And the mission is still to bring people to God. Lost people, maybe. People who are searching."

"Ty Davis, you've been anti–Hell House this whole time, and now you're trying to convince me to stay in it?" I ask.

"I do think it's good to bring people into the fold of the church," Ty says. "I was raised in West River, wasn't I?"

"Yes, you were," I say affectionately.

"I may not be down with everything at the House of Enlightenment, but I do believe the church's main mission is sincere," he says. "Besides, you'd regret dropping out. It's *your* role."

And he's right about the acting thing—it *is* a play, after all. And maybe it will help me figure out more about myself. Last night sure was a learning experience.

"Okay," I say. "I'll do it. *If* you promise to walk through Hell House next weekend."

"That's the spirit, Abortion Girl," Ty says. "I wouldn't miss it."

Then he leans in again and kisses me. And there's at least one thing I have no doubts about anymore: he is what I want.

Chapter Thirty-two

Through the whole week of rehearsals, I go to church and nail my part. I don't faint like I did at the first dress rehearsal—I think that was a one-time thing. But I manage to turn up the sobbing and tap into my confusion. I let it feed a deep sadness that comes out in the scene. It feels like real acting. Everyone congratulates me on my performance, and Pastor Tannen continues to hold me up as the star of the show. It feels good in one way and awkward in another. I'm still sorting out my thoughts on everything, but this has been my dream for so long. Ty was right—I couldn't just drop out.

By the time Friday comes, we're ready for our opening night. There are lines around the corner outside the church, and our parking lot has been blocked off for tour buses that come through carrying youth groups from other counties. They know we're the biggest Hell House in this area.

At seven dollars per ticket, we'll make up the production costs and raise some money for the church too. Before we open the doors, I peer out the window at the crowd. Some kids are dressed up in Halloween costumes—most are made up like devils or angels—and some are just in normal jeans and sweatshirts. All of them seem to bounce with nervous energy that has more to do with their mood than the chill in the late October air—they're ready for a good show.

I know Ty will come through and see Hell House for the first time tonight, and that makes me all the more determined to do a great job. But the thing is, although I do believe in leading souls to Christ, I've acknowledged—at least with Ty—that I'm uncomfortable with parts of the show. It's getting harder and harder to hear the Demon Tour Guide's lines, which strike me as harsh now that I can relate them to the girls at Saint Angeles and Tessa.

Still, I lean back in the bed and say the words I've memorized over and over again as crowds of about twenty people come through every five to ten minutes. I scream, "It's my choice!" and then, "I killed my baby! I made a mistake . . . I want my baby back!" After every scene they clean up my legs, but the table stays bloody—we don't have enough sheets to change them out continuously. I hear gasps from the audience each time a new group walks in—it's easy to become immune to the red stains and the burger baby, but they're seeing it for the first time, and hearing their sharp intake of breath helps me remember how shocking this part of the show is.

I hear lots of the girls begin to cry as the abortion plays out—this is always the scene in the show where tears start to flow. Maybe they know someone who's had an abortion or a baby, or maybe they've been in this situation themselves. Maybe they're just moved by the thought of a baby dying—I know I broke down during this scene the year that I turned thirteen, which was the first time I could walk through the full performance. I cried so much I had to wipe my nose on Starla Joy's scarf, and it got so gross that she just gave it to me after the show. Now we're both here, starring in Hell House.

I hear Starla Joy's group coming toward me now. She's in the hall talking about young love, and as she enters the room, I notice that Ty is in this crowd. I start to thrash and scream, wanting to be great in this scene for him. For me too. I feel like I have something to prove.

When the blood flows on my legs, I once again hear the gasps I've heard all evening. And then I hear something else.

"Starla Joy! Starla Joy!" Mrs. Minter's voice echoes down the hall. It sounds like she's running. And screaming.

The door bursts open, and Starla Joy, in full demon costume, turns to see her mother, hair frazzled, eyes wild, burst into the room.

"It's Tessa!" Mrs. Minter says. "She's in labor. We have to go—*now*!"

Starla Joy tears off her mask and looks up at me. I'm already untaping the IV and getting myself off the table. Ty is at Starla Joy's side, and Randy Miller is nervously trying to save the abortion scene.

"You can't get off the table, miss," he says. "The abortion has just started."

"Be quiet, Randy!" I shout. Then I look at the surprised faces in the audience. "I'm sorry. I have to go. Our understudy, Laura Bergen, will take over and do the scene for you."

I throw Laura my hospital gown, and I don't even look back or concern myself with how my exit gets handled from there.

Mrs. Minter, Starla Joy, Ty, and I rush out the door. We have to push past a bunch of kids waiting to get into the next showing, and when we get out into the parking lot I see that Mrs. Minter had to park all the way across the field.

I look back at the church for a moment—should I tell my dad where I'm going? But I don't have to think about that for too long because suddenly there he is, in full devil regalia. His devil is a powdery white figure, not the red horns-and-tail costume that you see in commercial Halloween stores. He's covered in cobwebs with those long nails and that hooked nose. He's wearing ragged clothes that Mom bleached and sewed together for him—they drag on the ground like tattered robes. The only part of him that looks like my dad is his gaze, and it's right on me.

"Lacey Anne Byer!" he shouts, still using the Satan voice because he's been doing it all night. "You will not get in that car."

"Dad, I have to," I say, running back to where he is, wanting to explain and have him understand, maybe even send me off with a hug. "Tessa's having her baby. Starla Joy needs me. I want to be there."

"I forbid it," he says, still using that awful tone.

"You can't do that," I say. "I have to go—let me make my own choice."

"You're covered in the blood of your choice," says my father, pointing at me with his long nail. I look down and remember that my pajamas are smeared in Dean's red dye. Is my dad still playing a role?

And then I see that there's a crowd gathering around me and my father in the parking lot. They want to see the devil and

Abortion Girl fighting. They probably think it's part of the show. I can't believe that my dad is still acting. But I'm not.

"You're not the devil," I say. "And I'm not Abortion Girl. Dad, I'm not a bad person. You can't forbid me to go with the Minters. It's the right thing to do. Please trust me to know that."

"Lacey Anne, you *will not go,*" Dad says, and now his voice is more his own. I even hear it waver a little bit, like maybe I'm scaring him.

Then I see a short, determined figure in a pale pink jacket striding toward us. Mom.

I can't let them team up on me.

"Mom—I have to go," I say as she sidles up next to Dad. "It's Tessa . . ."

"I know, honey," Mom says. She doesn't make any move to stop me, just puts her hand on Dad's arm and starts to turn him around back toward the church. She's on my side.

"Ted, come back inside," she says calmly, softly.

I look at her, surprised, and she nods at me. "You're a good friend, Lacey Anne," she says.

Mom being there seems to snap Dad out of his devil persona. His shoulders sink, deflated, and he listens to her.

"Thank you, Mom," I say.

She looks over her shoulder and gives me a warm smile. "Go," she says.

I turn and run to Mrs. Minter's station wagon, and I see that Dean has piled in, too. He, Ty, and I buckle up in the backseat just as Mrs. Minter pulls out of the lot, narrowly avoiding the gawking stragglers who are about to line up for the show.

I don't know what my dad does when I leave, because I don't look back.

Chapter Thirty-three

We're all quiet in the car on the way to the hospital. We only have to drive for about twenty minutes because Saint Angeles works with a birthing center in a town called Anderson, and it's pretty close.

Mrs. Minter is rambling from the driver's seat, asking Starla Joy to check Tessa's "baby bag," which I guess is the take-to-the-hospital stuff they have ready. Starla Joy is going through each item one by one. Change of clothes: check. New nightgown: check. Newborn snuggies: check. Copies of adoption paperwork: check.

The rest of us stay silent in the back.

When we get to Anderson, there are signs everywhere for the birthing hospital. I guess that's this town's main thing. Inside, a nurse leads our motley crew to a waiting area. She doesn't even blink at my red-stained pajamas. I guess nurses can tell real blood from fake, and it *is* close to Halloween. She just asks, "Who's family?"

Mrs. Minter and Starla Joy speak up, and I reach out to give Starla Joy's hand a squeeze before she and her mom follow a doctor through a door to Tessa's room. The rest of us have to sit down on hard plastic chairs in the hallway and wait.

Dean is playing with the laces on his hood—pulling one really long and letting the other get really short, then reversing it. I'd say he was being weird, but the truth is that I'm just *watching* him doing that, so who's the real weirdo here?

"Do you think she'll really do it?" Ty asks, breaking our silence after about half an hour.

"I think she's on the table and committed to having the baby now," says Dean. "No matter what her pro-choice stance is."

I roll my eyes at him. "Dean," I say impatiently.

"I mean the adoption," Ty says. "Do you think she'll go through with it?"

"Yeah," I say. "I think it's already done, legally."

"So she can't, like, see the baby and change her mind?" asks Dean. "That's harsh."

"Guys—" Ty starts. He nods toward the hallway and when I crane my neck to see past him, I spot Jeremy Jackson and Geoff Parsons striding our way in full demon makeup. Jeremy's mask is off, thank goodness, but he's holding it in one hand like a slain devil.

When I see his face, I feel a flood of sympathy for him. And when he talks, his voice comes out quickly and nervously. "Is Tessa okay? Is she in there? Has it started yet? Is there a—"

The nurse who chased him down the hall catches up and explains that he has to wait outside for a moment. Then she goes into Tessa's room and Jeremy stands in front of us. He looks like he wants to say something.

"Lacey, your parents are just so—" he starts.

"Mad," I interrupt. "I know, I know." I put my head in my hands. I don't want to think about my father right now.

"No," Jeremy says, touching my shoulder. "I was gonna say they're so cool. Your mom came and got me when she saw Mrs. Minter driving off. Then your dad told me to go—that he'd let my parents know, and he'd put in understudies for all of us."

"Really?" I ask.

"Yeah," he says.

"Jeremy?" The nurse pokes her head through the door. "You can come in."

For a second, Jeremy goes pale. But then he finds his leg muscles and moves quickly into Tessa's room. "See you guys on the other side," he says.

"Okay, man," Ty says, running his hand through his curly hair, which looks even more blond under these fluorescent lights.

"This is real stuff," says Dean, voicing what we're all thinking.

And I wonder if maybe, just maybe, my dad sent Jeremy here as a peace offering to me. Acknowledging that it's okay—even right—that I'm here.

I look up and notice Geoff standing awkwardly by the wall. He's staring at Dean. And that's when I notice that Geoff has a fat lip. It's not a makeup thing, it's really there.

"Geoff, what happened to your lip?" I ask.

He looks up at the fluorescent lights, squinting his eyes.

"My father," he says. Then he laughs a little. "He's not really like yours, Lacey."

I look down, feeling embarrassed for Geoff and ashamed of myself, somehow.

Then, a miracle happens. Well, a small one anyway. Dean stands up and walks over to Geoff Parsons, standing toe to toe with him.

Before Dean even says anything, Geoff looks him right in the eye and says, "I'm sorry, man."

And then they hug. They actually hug. Not one of those guy hugs where they're about three feet from each other, but a strong embrace. It's short but meaningful, and we all exhale a little.

Four hours, two sodas, three stale pretzels, and one cup of muddy-looking coffee later, Starla Joy emerges from her sister's room.

"My niece is here," she says, pulling off the paper mask over her mouth. Her eyes are shining with tears.

"Can we go in?" I ask.

"Ten minutes," she says. "They have to clean things up."

"Then I'll be the messiest person in the room," I say. I've gotten more than a few comments on my bloody pajamas by this point, and I'm starting to realize it might be viewed as poor taste that I'm wearing them, but it can't be helped.

Just then, a nurse brings a young couple into our area. The woman sits down, holding a bouquet of flowers in her lap; the man paces nervously.

The rest of us fall silent.

Starla Joy looks away from the couple and peeks back into Tessa's room. "Okay, come in, you guys," she says, a big grin on her face.

When we enter it's like there's a warm glow coming out of the bed where Tessa holds her newborn daughter. I can't really explain it, except to say that they radiate light and goodness.

It's the purest scene of love I've ever witnessed, and I look up for a moment, just to be sure I acknowledge the presence of God here. I can feel it more strongly than ever before in my life. I lean over and give Tessa a kiss on the cheek while I take a peek at the baby girl. For a moment her eyes are open, unseeing but maybe knowing she's here, in our world at last.

I wonder if she feels loved. She should. Before I can stop my thoughts, they move to the couple outside. I know that they're here for her. And I know that's what everyone wants. It's a choice.

I back away from Tessa and let Dean lean in, then Geoff. Ty hovers by the end of the bed, not quite approaching.

Jeremy is standing on Tessa's other side, snapping a zillion photos and probably blinding the poor baby with his bright flash. But he's beaming, just like a father should. He keeps telling Tessa how much he loves her, and I believe him.

I don't get home until four a.m.—Jeremy drops off Geoff, Dean, Ty, and me so Starla Joy and Mrs. Minter can stay with Tessa. She has to hand over the baby to the couple from the hallway. My heart aches for her, and I can see Jeremy biting his lip and fighting back some strong emotions as we drive home. But they made a choice, and I think it's the right one. When we get to my house, Ty kisses me gently on the lips, right in front of everyone, and it feels like the most natural thing in the world. Even Dean doesn't raise an eyebrow.

My parents haven't called—they knew I was safe, even if I wasn't where they wanted me to be. No one is waiting up for me in the living room, and I take a hot shower and change into a clean T-shirt quietly, hoping I'll get a decent amount of rest before Dad starts in on me.

I fall into a blissful sleep. Despite the dramatic events of today, I have a suddenly powerful faith that everything is going to be okay.

In the morning, I hear my parents rustling around downstairs. I can picture Mom in her blue-flowered apron, getting our Saturday breakfast ready while Dad picks up the paper or his Bible and waits patiently at the table. I pull on my bathrobe and head down to meet them with a smile.

"The baby is healthy," I say, as I lean over to kiss my father on the cheek. He rustles his paper a little and I sit in my seat.

"It was good that you were there," Mom says, and again I feel a rush of gratitude that she calmed Dad down last night, that she gave me her blessing to go with the Minters. Then she drops her eyes from mine and says, "Praise be to God that everyone is okay and Tessa's through this nightmare."

"She's beautiful," I say, not letting my mom's comment affect the feeling of peace that I have.

Dad puts down his paper and looks at me quizzically. "Do you have anything else to say to me this morning?" he asks.

"I'm sorry that I had to make the choice to disobey you, Dad," I say. "But I know that being at the hospital was the right thing."

Dad sighs, like he's not quite ready to agree with me. But it's more of a protective sigh than an angry one, I think.

"Thank you for sending Jeremy," I say. "Both times."

"He made those decisions to see Tessa," Dad says. "I just helped him a little bit."

"Thank you," I say again, reaching out and touching my

father's arm, making sure he looks at me and sees how grateful I truly am.

"Do you remember that button you used to have?" I ask him. "The one you handed out at the church one year when a few people lost their jobs and things were kind of grim around here?"

Dad doesn't say anything, so I keep talking.

"It said, 'Love is the answer—'" I start. And then I pause.

"'Now what was the question?'" finishes Dad.

I smile. That button made a huge impression on me, but I didn't understand it fully then. I think I do now.

"Right," I say.

"We've always lived that way, Lacey," Dad says. "Through the church and your mom's charity work and your kindness and honesty . . . at least until recently."

Ouch.

"Dad, I'm sorry that I haven't been completely truthful with you guys lately," I say. "I'm just trying to figure out what truth really is for me."

"What do you mean?" asks Mom, coming to sit at the table with us even though she's not done making breakfast. "Lacey, that's silly. Of course you know what truth is."

"I'm not sure I do. It's not like there's an ultimate truth," I say. "Like when Geoff Parsons went after Dean but he stayed in the show." I look at my father. "What was the truth there?"

"I told you, Lacey," Dad says. "Both boys were at fault."

"I think it was more that Geoff was good for Hell House, and you felt bad for him because you know his father, and you didn't want to remove him," I say.

Dad sighs. "It's complicated," he acknowledges.

"I know," I say, glad he didn't deny it or shut me down. *They're opening up a little,* I think.

I don't want to press them this morning. I'm not even sure what I need from them right now, but I'm going to keep that button slogan in my head when I start to feel myself filling up with questions. Cheesy as it is, "Love is the answer. Now what was the question?"

Nine Months Later

"Take the wheel," says Starla Joy, sticking a cherry lollipop into her mouth as she wiggles out of her rain jacket. I steer smoothly around the turn as the truck barrels ahead through the downpour.

"Damn!" Dean shouts as Starla Joy grabs the wheel back and jerks the truck to the left. "You just made me spill my Coke."

"Here," Ty says, handing him a roll of dusty paper towels that Starla Joy keeps in the tiny backseat.

School let out last week and we're squeezed into Starla Joy's truck, driving to the coast. It's a real road trip—we're staying with my cousins and then Starla Joy's grandmother, so Mom and Dad let me go. Dean and I told our parents we're going to look at colleges, and we are. But really? We all want to see the ocean.

I didn't end up fulfilling my role in Hell House for the remaining two shows. I let Laura Bergen take my spot as Abortion Girl. I know my dad had a hard time with that, and Pastor

Tannen was "deeply disappointed," but I couldn't keep playing the part after seeing Tessa in the hospital. Besides, I wanted to be where I was needed more—with Starla Joy and Tessa.

Still, the outreach was our most successful one ever—three thousand people went through Hell House, and over one thousand of them signed decision cards to accept Jesus as their Lord and Savior. I know we reached way more than that too. Some people just aren't ready to sign their names to something.

"When does Tessa leave?" asks Dean.

"Not till August," Starla Joy says. "But it's not like we'll see her much. She's spending every second with Jeremy."

Tessa's going to State; Jeremy's staying behind to "take a year off." I think that means working for his dad.

After Tessa came back for her second semester, she finished all her credits and graduated on time. It was like nothing had happened at all. She and Jeremy went to prom together, though they lost prom king and queen by a few votes. Tessa doesn't talk about the baby much, but she has a locket with a photo from the hospital inside, and she never takes it off as far as I can tell. She's supposed to get letters from the adoptive family once a year on her daughter's birthday.

"She'll hang out with us some before she goes, though, right?" asks Dean, his voice hopeful.

"Yes, Dean," Starla Joy says. "You should have sufficient time to worship my sister this summer, don't worry."

She reaches back and pats his knee. He rolls his eyes.

"I just like talking to her is all," he says.

Tessa and Dean got into a few heated arguments about her pro-choice stance, but they always ended goodnaturedly, and we'll all miss her next year in the woods. She's been meeting us out there more lately. She opens things up among us all, maybe because she committed sins that a year ago would have been unimaginable to any of us—but she's still here. She's still our Tessa. And though things have changed, they're not awful. There is some heartache, I know, but darkness didn't befall us. We still all feel heavenbound, one way or another.

Dean even talks a little more about what he's been going through. Truthfully, I don't know if he's gay, but it has stopped mattering to me. We'll cross that bridge when he comes to it, if he comes to it. And we'll cross it all together.

When we see the exit for public beach access, Ty tells us to roll down our windows.

"It's raining!" I say.

"Aunt Vivian told me you have to smell the beach," he says.

He didn't have to sell this road trip to Vivian as anything but what it was. When he told her we wanted to see the ocean, she smiled and said, "Go."

Starla Joy and I crank the handles to roll down our windows a little bit.

"All the way," Ty insists.

Starla Joy goes first. As soon as we turn off the highway and onto a smaller road, she opens her window fully. A blast of rain comes into the truck, but with it comes the smell of the sea. Salty, fresh, rejuvenating.

Like a baptism. I roll down my window too.

When we drive into the parking lot for public beach access, there's just one other car there.

"Guess it's not an ideal beach day," Dean says.

But we all know the rain won't stop us. I open my door and pull the seat forward so Ty can step out. Dean and Starla Joy meet us around the back of the truck, and we walk up the wooden plank steps to get our first glimpse of the ocean.

I hear it before I see it, even through all the wind and rain; the waves that break on the shore are roaring with power.

Before I let myself walk onto the beach and look, really look, I tilt my head back to the sky and say a little prayer of thanks. I'm grateful to be here.

The subject of faith is no longer off the table for me and my friends. Not that it ever officially was, but now it feels more like something we can talk about with a question mark rather than with a period. My parents worry about my uncertainty, I know, but I think it'll only make me a stronger person, in thought *and* in faith, as I get older.

When I look over at Ty, I see that he was watching me pray, and he gives me a smile as he takes my hand. "Ready, Lacey Anne?" he asks.

Ty signed me up for all these college mailing lists—schools out of state, small liberal arts colleges, even some Ivy League campuses. As our mailbox gets fuller, I think my parents are realizing that my dreams aren't the same as theirs. We've had a few arguments this year, but since Hell House—even though I dropped out—there's been more trust between us. I know that's because I'm being honest and they're being patient.

It may also be because my dad dug through a drawer and found some old rusted buttons. He put a few up on the church bulletin board, and he keeps one with him at all times. He says it's to remind him that there are elusive answers and differences of opinion on some questions, but there's only one emotional response that works.

I squeeze Ty's hand. Starla Joy and Dean are already at the

top of the stairs, stepping onto the sand. I watch them take off their shoes and look at each other excitedly before heading out toward the water.

"I'm ready," I say to Ty.

My curfew has been moved to eleven p.m. this summer. I often want to break it, but Ty is the perfect gentleman, and he says that since he's my boyfriend now, he needs to stay on my father's good side if he wants to keep hold of my heart. I tell him it's his, now and always.

We walk up to the top of the access stairs together and I look out at the waves. Starla Joy and Dean are already walking into the ocean, and I take my shoes off.

"Let's go," I say to Ty. He's staring out at the water like he's never seen anything so beautiful.

Then he turns to me with that same expression.

I smile back at him, and think about the way movie moments don't always require a spotlight or look-at-me lipstick.

When we talk about next year, Ty says I'll go away to school and meet new people and forget all about the boy I loved in West River.

I tell him I'm sure that will never happen, and I mean it.

He says I can't be certain of anything, that everything changes. Even things we once thought were unquestionably true.

And I know that he's right.

Acknowledgments

Many, many thanks go to . . .

Mom and Dad, always.

Betty Elliott, who (in her Mississippi drawl) was the first person to tell me that Hell Houses exist—even though she laughed at me when my jaw dropped.

My *ELLEgirl* editor, Christina Kelly, who liked the sound of a Hell House story long before I knew that it might inspire a book—such good instincts, CK.

Doug Stewart, my ever-encouraging agent, who heard the idea for this book at a bar in Brooklyn and said, "That sounds awesome!"

Caroline Abbey, my enthusiastic editor, who gave wise and thoughtful notes as I worked through drafts of the story. Her fascination with Hell House quite possibly exceeds my own, and she had the wherewithal to know—even before we'd worked together—that a red velvet cupcake wins me over every time.

Deb Shapiro, Kate Lied, and the whole publicity team at Bloomsbury! Plus cover designers Danielle Delaney and Regina Roff. (I have a thing about book covers, and I think with this one I can safely say: Nailed it!)

Amazing authors Sarah MacLean and Donna Frietas, who both read early drafts of this book and gave invaluable insights (Sarah calling for more kissing and Donna reminding me just how conservative evangelical teens can be).

And a nod to Jessica Ochoa Hendrix, who suggested "more God" in just the right moment.

A conversation with Melissa Walker, author of *Small Town Sinners*

Q: What inspired you to write a novel involving Hell Houses?

A: I pitched and wrote a piece on Hell Houses for *ELLEgirl* when I was features editor there because I had heard about the concept from a friend's mom. I was so intrigued by the small town I traveled to and the warmth of all the teenagers I met, plus their obvious passion for this production, that I had to revisit that world.

ELLEgirl story:
http://www.melissacwalker.com/media/ellegirl-hellhouse.jpg

Q: The concept of a Hell House has the potential to be quite provocative. Instead of dramatizing it, you wrote a novel where a Hell House is symbolic of the circumstances and situations that the characters are grappling with. Was this a conscious choice?

A: Yes. Hell Houses are intense and dramatic—I wanted the story built around the Hell House to have some very quiet, introspective moments. Because when that much commotion is going on externally, there have to be some deep emotions going on for the people involved internally too.

Q: Are any of the characters based on people you know?

A: All of my characters have parts of themselves that are taken from real life, but no one in particular is based on someone real, no. The emotions of some of the teenagers I met while reporting the *ELLEgirl* story are represented a bit though—that was a big inspiration, especially for the church scenes.

Q: *Small Town Sinners* addresses teen pregnancy and underage drinking, two subjects some consider hot-button. What would you say to someone who may take issue with you incorporating them into the novel?

A: I wasn't trying to write a book with "issues" in it, but I did want to present a story that felt true to what these characters—high school students in a small, conservative town—really might be facing. I love books that deal with hard subjects because reading about how characters handle their own situations always makes me wonder, "What would I do if that were me?" When a book makes me care enough to ask that question, I'm happy.

Q: You've written for several teen magazines (*ElleGirl* and *Seventeen*) and launched your own e-newsletter for teens (*I Heart Daily*). What is it about this age that appeals to you?

A: Um, everything. Seriously. I love teenage enthusiasm, how much things matter to you, how engaged you are with the world around you at this stage in your life. Also, I remember my teen years like they were yesterday—the highest highs and the lowest lows happened daily. I think in many ways, your teen years may not always be the best time of life, but they are the truest.

Q: Friendship, family, and faith are three prominent themes of the novel, and Lacey Anne questions the concept, reality, and importance of each throughout. Is that something you remember doing when you were her age? Do you still?

A: Friendship is the part of that trio that doesn't get questioned in the book, at least not by Lacey Anne. She's sure in that, even when everything else feels unstable. Family includes these people whom you're born with, and there are times when it feels like your family doesn't quite fit you—I think we all go through that, myself included, at regular intervals in life (like around the holidays). And faith, well, by nature it's elusive—it requires a leap. And some days you don't feel like jumping, but other days . . . you do.

Q: What were you like when you were Lacey Anne's age?

A: At sixteen I was obsessed with my clunker used car (which I'd saved up to buy since age ten), I was praying I'd find a boyfriend before high school ended so I could have an epic first love story (I did), I was being encouraged to write by my parents (thanks, Mom and Dad), and I spent nearly every moment with my group of friends, whom I laughed with nonstop. Now that I'm older and have met more people, I can confirm that they were and are some of the smartest and funniest people in the world.

Q: What do you hope readers will take away from *Small Town Sinners*?

A: I hope you will take away whatever you need in the moment that you read the book. Maybe that's a sense of kinship with Lacey Anne because your world is changing too. Or maybe it's that there are a lot of ways to have faith in the people around you. Mostly I just hope you like the book, and that something in it stays with you in a positive way.

Q: What were your favorite books when you were Lacey Anne's age?

A: I read and reread Theodore Dreiser's *An American Tragedy* because something in it really struck me as true, but my favorite book was probably *Gone with the Wind* (still is). I was also no stranger to Christopher Pike (who scared me silly) and Judy Blume (who made me feel normal whenever I feared I wasn't).

Q: When did you know you wanted to be a writer?

A: I pounded out a paragraph-long tale called "The Very Vain Cloud" on my parents' typewriter at age six, and I never stopped making up stories. When I joined my high school yearbook staff and got to write articles, I knew I wanted to go into journalism. Fiction came later, after I met some crazy characters out in the world.

Q: What's your favorite dessert?

A: All-time: key lime pie. Lately: blueberries with ricotta cheese and a drizzle of maple syrup—trust me!

Q: If you were directing the film version of *Small Town Sinners*, who would you cast in a few of the main roles?

A: I'm a huge fan of unknowns, and I'd probably like to see fresh faces playing Lacey Anne and her friends, but that's avoiding the question, right? If I had to cast, I'd go with Taylor Swift as Lacey Anne, Ashley Greene as Starla Joy, and maybe David Archuleta as Dean (does he act?). If not him, maybe a Jonas brother—probably Nick, with some weight gain. For Ty, I have a picture in my head that I can't replace with a real actor. Book guys are better. I will say that I'd love to see Kyle Chandler and Connie Britton (Coach and Mrs. Taylor on *Friday Night Lights*) as Lacey Anne's parents. Love them!

Read on for a peek of Melissa Walker's next novel!

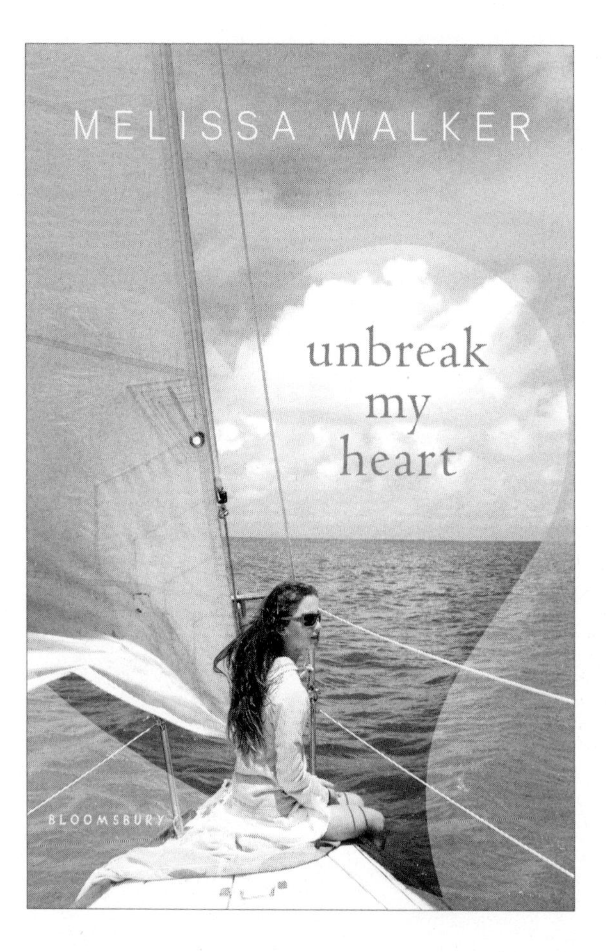

Last year Clem broke one of the cardinal rules of friendship and hurt her own heart in the process. Can a summer sailing with her family—and the new boy she meets along the route—heal it?

chapter one

"Sit on it," I say.

"Excuse me?" asks Olive, with an attitude that makes her seem way older than her ten years. Her tone plus her big angular glasses—green-framed rectangles that look more fancy-architect than fifth-grade—put her somewhere near forty in my book. She's always been our family's little adult.

"The suitcase, Livy," I say sweetly. "Please?"

My sister reluctantly plops down on top of my raggedy plaid bag. It moves just enough so that I can zip it shut.

"Thanks."

"You better get it downstairs right now," says Olive, running ahead of me into the hallway. "The car's almost full."

I sigh and take one more glance around my room. It looks just like it always does—sunny, bright, clean; a bookshelf along the back wall filled with rows and rows of the series I love; a white wicker hamper in the corner with a stray gray sweatshirt on top of it; the flower-covered comforter I've publicly outgrown but that secretly makes me feel safe. I grab my journal off the nightstand

and shove it into the front pocket of my bag. If I'm not going to have Internet or phone service for most of the summer, I need *somewhere* to record my status updates.

I stare in the big mirror across from my bed. My hair hangs down around my face, and my eyes are still a little puffy from crying. I pinch my cheeks to make them pink and try a smile. It looks more like the grimace of someone trying to pretend she's not in pain. I frown again. At least frowns are honest.

I heave the suitcase off my bed. I'm going away for three months, but this is the only bag I'm allowed to bring, because I'll be living on a boat. With my family. All. Summer. Long.

If my sophomore year had gone differently, I probably would have fought harder to spend this summer—the summer I turned sixteen, the summer of making out, the summer of memories that will last forever, the summer I always imagined would be the *very best one*—at home on my own. I'm responsible, after all, and my parents trust me. I could have had an amazing time working days at Razzy's, the Bishop Heights Mall candy shop where I had a job this year, looking for my it's-just-like-in-the-movies perfect guy, and spending nights hanging out with Amanda . . . *Amanda.*

I feel a stone drop in my stomach.

I head downstairs, letting my big bag *plunk, plunk, plunk* on each step.

"There she is," says Mom, smiling brightly. "Little Miss Sunshine."

I don't smile back. She's being sarcastic, and she's wearing a giant floppy straw hat, the kind that only almost-famous girls in LA and very old ladies in Florida can pull off. I guess now that she's less lawyer and more boater she thinks it works. She is wrong.

Dad comes around to the back of the car and slides my bag into the one slot that's left. It fits perfectly, and he sighs with satisfaction. It's a real thrill for him when the sport wagon is well packed.

"How good is your dad?" he asks me.

"You have sunscreen on your nose," I say to him.

He smiles and rubs it in. Nothing is penetrating the parents' Good Mood today, not even me being grumpy. I guess they're getting used to it.

I wasn't always such a downer. Up until, like, two weeks ago, I was Clementine Williams, happy and upbeat and kind of hilarious, if I do say so myself. But that was before everything exploded in my face.

Now I'm Clementine Williams, outcast. And that's on a good day.

"Come on, Clem," says Mom, putting her arm around me and easing me toward the car. She's been gentle with me this week, mostly, and I appreciate that.

I slide into the backseat next to Olive, who's squished against a cooler that's taking up most of our space. Good thing the drive to the marina is only twenty minutes.

"Let the Williams Family Summer of Boating begin!" cheers Dad. Mom gives a quick "Woot-woot," and Olive raises her hands in the air and shouts, "Wahoo!" I add an uninspired "Yay" so they won't get on my case. Then I stare out the window and watch my house, then my neighborhood, then my town, disappear.

As we pull into the marina, I see our boat—*The Possibility.* It's a forty-two-foot Catalina three-cabin Pullman. My parents traded in our twenty-three-foot O'Day—*Night Wind II*—last year, and they've been readying *The Possibility* for this summer trip since then. At first it felt insanely roomy compared to the *Night Wind II,* where Olive and I basically had to sleep on narrow side couches in the main cabin of the boat. My parents' V-berth bedroom didn't even have a door, so my dad's snoring chased me out to the cockpit to sleep under the stars pretty often.

Yeah, the *Night Wind II* seemed small and *The Possibility* plenty big on quick weekend sails. I even brought Amanda up here a few times when Mom didn't come, and Dad let us have the master cabin so we could "stay up late and giggle," as he reductively put it. It was fun.

But now that I'm faced with the prospect of spending three whole months on this thing, it doesn't look very spacious. There are two *heads*—that means bathrooms—and three *staterooms*, which is a fancy word for teeny-tiny bedrooms. My parents have a master berth with their own head, and I have a double berth on the starboard side. Olive's port-side room has bunk beds, but she's still young enough to think that'll be fun. (Wait until she falls out when Dad anchors us too close to a main waterway, and the waves from passing ships knock her right on her butt. It's happened before.)

I lug the plaid bag into my *stateroom* and close the door. I just want to stretch out with my music for a while, so I put in earbuds and hope I won't be able to hear Mom when she starts bugging me to help unpack.

I hit Shuffle just to see what comes up, and when I hear the strains of "Beautiful Girl" by INXS, I feel a tear well in my eye. Like, instantly. I thought they'd all dried up, but no. I swear I deleted this playlist, but I must have had another copy of "Beautiful Girl" stored. I let myself be sad for thirty seconds, and then I angrily wipe away the tear.

My mom gives me exactly six minutes to be antisocial and unhelpful. I know because I get to listen to "Must I Paint You a

Picture?" by Billy Bragg, which is five and a half minutes long, and as it ends, I open my eyes to see Mom's messenger.

"You can't just bust into my room," I say to Olive, who has her hands on her hips and a stern look on her face, which is way too close to mine.

"Yes, I can," she says, pushing her angled glasses up on her nose. "These doors don't lock."

Her serious mouth breaks into a grin, like she knows she's going to get so much time with me this summer because we're in this majorly contained space and she can't help but show her total elation about that fact.

I soften a little.

"Mom needs you," she says.

"Fine." I stand up and make her scramble to get out of my way.

I march into the main cabin—well, I take three steps into the main cabin, anyway, passing my dad in the nav station port side—and there is my mother, organizing the canned foods in the *galley*, which normal people call the kitchen.

"Did you get pickles?" asks Olive, kneeling on the couch in front of the galley and leaning onto the bright yellow counter.

"Yes, I did, Little Miss Dill," says Mom.

"Yippee!" sings Olive. You'd think she won $100 on a scratch-off lotto card. Pickles get this reaction? My little sister is seriously high today.

"And I got the big marshmallows for you, Clem," says Mom, putting up the bag of Jet-Puffeds that I always request for adding to morning hot chocolate.

I nod. I do not *Yippee*.

I watch Mom put about fifty cans up into the top cabinet above the stove. She has a cookbook called *A Man, A Can, and a Plan*. Obviously, this book is for a twenty-two-year-old guy who hasn't learned to make a meal with real food yet, but Mom likes to call it "the Boat Cookbook." Creating a dinner entirely out of canned goods makes her feel really accomplished. "Besides," she told us when we had the "boat grocery list" family meeting last week, "canned goods keep for so long! We'll eat well every night."

I had nodded then—I'd just wanted to be released from the family meeting so I could go back to my room and mope—but now, as I watch the cans of peas, pinto beans, and SpaghettiOs come out of her box, I wonder if I should have stood up for some fresher foods.

"What do you need me to help with?" I ask. I try to keep any sort of "tone" out of my voice. It's not my family's fault I've become a pariah.

"You could make sure everything's out of the car and then drive it over to long-term parking," says Mom. "It'll be your last chance to break in that license for a while."

"Okay," I say. And then, to Olive, "Come on."

My sister smiles widely and I stare back at her and try to look remotely friendly. I owe it to her to let her tag along, especially since I've been nasty all week.

Mom hands me the car keys, and Olive and I climb up the short ladder into the cockpit before carefully stepping off the boat and onto the dock.

I walk briskly toward the parking lot, and she jogs to keep up.

"Do you think Dad will let me unfurl the jib when we get underway?" she asks.

"Probably." My voice has a who-cares tone that I don't try to hide.

When we get to the car, Olive makes a big show of putting on her seat belt, even though we're only driving about a hundred feet to the long-term parking lot.

I give her a look and she says, "What? You've only been driving for, like, two weeks."

Two weeks exactly, actually. I got my license two Saturdays ago. That afternoon, I wanted to see who was around to go for a drive. I ended up texting Amanda and a few other people, but only one person responded right away. Unfortunately.

I pull into a spot in the shade and wrench up the parking brake.

"Nice," says Olive. "I didn't feel unsafe for a moment."

"I'm so glad." I step out of the car. When the sun hits my face, I close my eyes for a second to shake off the memory that's encroaching.

"Clem?"

I open my eyes and look down at my little sister, who's suddenly solemn.

"What?"

"I'm glad you've stopped crying."

I half smile at her. "Me too." I don't tell her that just because the tears have mostly dried up, it doesn't mean I'm better.

As we walk back to *The Possibility*, I see Mom unsnapping the blue canvas mainsail cover. Dad must want to get underway.

Before we go, though, I know we have to do one more thing.

I step back onto the boat and Dad pokes his head out from down below. "Ready?" he asks.

"Do we have a choice?" I ask.

"No!" Dad laughs really loudly. He is *so* happy right now. It's almost contagious. Almost.

Mom folds up the sail cover and sits down on the cockpit seat. Dad settles into his captain's chair, and Olive takes her perch next to him, the ultimate navigator. I sit back on the seat opposite Mom and tuck my legs underneath me.

"Now," starts Dad. "What do you see?"

He smiles and looks around at us. "Livy?"

My sister is still at an age where she's into this family game. Whenever we "embark on a new voyage"—which is my dad's fancy way of saying "go sailing" (you'd think we were heading into outer space)—we have to go around the cockpit and state what we want from the trip, what we see in our future days of sailing.

"I am ready for a really fun summer," says Olive. "I see swimming and fishing and cooking and eating and exploring islands."

Olive likes to jump off the boat when we anchor and swim to the closest land, which is usually some random mud-beach where there's nothing to do and no sand to lie out on. But I get it—I used to like that "explorer" game too.

"Excellent! All of that is very doable," says Dad. "Clem?"

"Mom can go."

"Okay," says Dad. "Julia?"

"I see a warm, wonderful summer filled with family days," says Mom. She's taken off her straw hat and is leaning her head back so her face catches the sun. Her brown hair is styled into that short Mom cut, but she also has these freckles that sometimes make her look really young when she smiles. Like now.

"Family time!" says Dad, clapping his hands together. "I love it! Clem?"

I look at my dad, who's smiling naively in my direction. He's treating us like we're his first-grade class. Suddenly I'm just annoyed. I'm sixteen years old. I don't need to sit here, being forced to do some roundtable "What I See" exercise with my way-younger sister and my dopey parents. This is their dream summer—not mine.

"Clem?" he asks again. "What do you see?"

"I see a summer in exile."

chapter two

We met on the first day of kindergarten, at the Play-Doh station. I was rolling a big blue ball in my hands, and Amanda asked to see it. Then she added a turned-up mouth and two eyes with her pieces of yellow clay.

After that, whenever anything made me sad, Amanda would say, "Do you need me to make you a smile?" She was like my friend–soul mate.

We talked about *everything*—from our first crushes in third grade to our late-arriving periods (Amanda got hers in eighth grade, I got mine in ninth)—while we sat on my bed and faced this big mirror on the opposite wall. We called it mirror-talking. My parents thought we were crazy, but there was something comforting about looking into the mirror at each other, and ourselves, while we talked. It made saying things easier somehow, just looking at reflections instead of the real person.

Maybe that's why, for the past week, I've been trying to write her a letter about what happened. I can't call her, and now that I'm stuck on this boat I certainly can't go see her. So I brought a whole pad of light green paper with my initials, CSW, in dark blue script at the top.

> *Dear Amanda,*
> *How can you just forget the entire history of our friendship? Doesn't being best friends for over half our lives mean anything?*

I crumple up the paper before I can write any more.

"Kidnap Picnic!" Amanda had yelled as I opened the door after she'd rung the bell three boisterous times in a row.

Last summer she had a tendency to show up unexpectedly with a plan for the day. Usually, I went with it.

She stood on our front porch in cutoffs, a striped T-shirt, and oversized sunglasses, and she carried a beach bag that was almost twice the size of her entire body.

"My mom dropped me off. I've got sandwiches, chips, two sodas, and four magazines," she said, walking past me through the door into the house. "But I forgot sunblock, so grab some when you go upstairs to get changed—forty-five or higher, please." She patted a rosy cheek. "I'm fair."

Amanda smiled and raised her sunglasses to the top of her head as she plopped down on the couch in the living room.

"I have to ask my—"

"Mr. and Mrs. Williams, Clem and I are going to the park!" she shouted, cupping her hands together like a megaphone. Then she grinned at me. "Done."

Ten minutes later, with a nod from my mom and just one round of "Why can't I go too?" whining from Olive—which was shut down by Dad telling her he'd take her to the pool instead—Amanda and I were heading for the park at the center of my neighborhood. We each took a handle of her giant bag of picnic supplies and walked straight to our usual spot—a central patch of grass in the sun where lots of people pass by as they cross from the soccer field to the ice cream truck.

"This way we can watch everyone, but people can also see *us*," she told me the first time we'd staked out this area two years earlier. Because this park was in walking distance of my house, our parents had been letting us "picnic" there since the summer we were thirteen.

I had traded my pajamas for a pair of bright red shorts and a white tank top, but as soon as we spread out the orange-and-blue-patterned blanket Amanda had brought for us to sit on, she peeled off her striped shirt to reveal a white triangle bikini top with multicolored butterflies on it.

My eyes must have gotten big, because she said, "This is why I really needed that sunblock."

It wasn't that people in the park didn't sometimes wear bikini tops, it was just that *we* never had. And my stiff beige bra under a boring plain white tank suddenly seemed really homely in comparison to what my best friend was wearing.

Amanda read all of these thoughts on my face. We were connected that way.

"Ooh, I should have told you I had on a bikini top!"

"Uh, yeah," I said. "I mean, not that we have to wear the same thing, but . . ." I stopped, not sure how to phrase *I want to look cute too!* without sounding whiny.

"I have an idea," said Amanda, reaching over to pull up the bottom of my tank top.

I stiffened.

"Clemmy, *trust me*," she said, her eyes sparkling.

So I lifted my hands and she looped the bottom of my tank through the neckline, creating a makeshift bikini in one fell swoop. She adjusted it over my bra straps expertly.

I looked down at my chest. *Not bad.*

"Thanks!" I said.

"One more thing." Amanda reached into her bag and brought out a bottle of bright red nail polish called *That Girl*. "I'll do yours first."

With our glossy ruby nails, we sat up on the blanket, peering from behind dark sunglasses and lazing around like we owned the park, giggling at our horoscopes and reading guy advice from *Seventeen* out loud.

And by the end of the afternoon, I felt as cherry-red hot as Amanda did, because she rubbed off on me like that.

Marcie Hume

MELISSA WALKER

has worked as *ELLEgirl* features editor and *Seventeen* prom editor. She is also the author of *Unbreak My Heart*, the Violet on the Runway series, and *Lovestruck Summer.* Melissa manages a daily online newsletter, *I Heart Daily*, and handles blogging for readergirlz.com, an online book community that won a National Book Award for Innovations in Reading. She grew up in Chapel Hill, North Carolina, and now lives in Brooklyn, New York, where she drinks iced coffee that tastes like ice cream and still listens to high school mixtapes for inspiration.

www.melissacwalker.com

CATHLEEN DAVITT BELL
Little Blog on the Prairie

LINDSEY LEAVITT
Would you recognize love if it was right in front of you?
sean griswold's head

Two sisters. One secret. And the summer that brings them together.
the sweetness of salt
CECILIA GALANTE

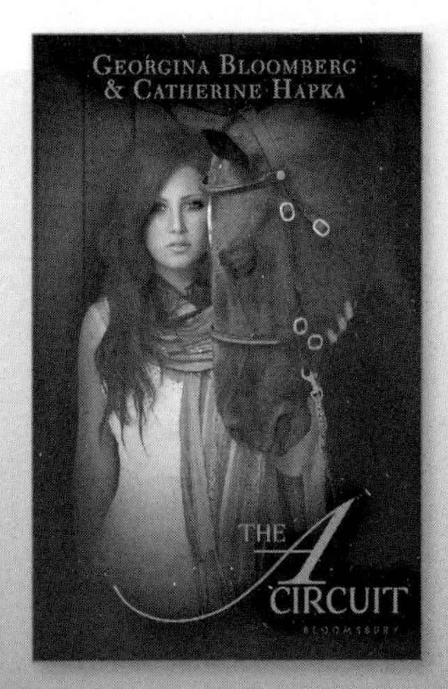
GEORGINA BLOOMBERG
& CATHERINE HAPKA
THE A CIRCUIT
BLOOMSBURY